He awoke by the stream, clothed in the tiger skin the demon Garuda had given him, the magic pelt that gave him the strength and cunning of the great beast. The fur was streaked with blood, but he did not remember the hunt last night or the crazed feast afterward.

And each time, it became harder and harder to remove the pelt. Although he was repulsed by the blood and gore, he was thrilled by the power he felt while in tiger form.

He *was* the tiger...

wendy wees

OU LU KHEN
AND THE
BEAUTIFUL MADWOMAN

Jessica Amanda Salmonson

Illustrated by Wendy Wees

ACE FANTASY BOOKS
NEW YORK

Ace Fantasy Books by Jessica Amanda Salmonson

HEROIC VISIONS
OU LU KHEN AND THE BEAUTIFUL MADWOMAN

The Tomoe Gozen Saga

TOMOE GOZEN
THE GOLDEN NAGINATA
THOUSAND SHRINE WARRIOR

OU LU KHEN AND THE BEAUTIFUL MADWOMAN

An Ace Fantasy Book/published by arrangement with
the author

PRINTING HISTORY
Ace Original/July 1985

ISBN: 0-441-63500-8

Ace Fantasy Books are published by The Berkley Publishing Group,
200 Madison Avenue, New York, New York 10016.
PRINTED IN THE UNITED STATES OF AMERICA

*"From my wings are shaken the dews that waken
The sweet buds every one."*
—Shelley

"Illusions beating with their baffled wings."
—Amy Lowell

to Wendy Wees

❧ CONTENTS ❧

❧ ILLUSTRATIONS ❧
by Wendy Wees

৪ ONE ৮

The Flame
Dove

YEUNG MAI SU was the name of the madwoman who lived in the smallhouse in the forest. It was there her family kept her, apart from her kin, for they knew themselves too impure to keep the company of one so touched and holy. It was no cruel exile, for it was apparent that she enjoyed solitude more than she did not; and it was not as though no one ever came to call.

There were the curious and awe-inspirable who came to see if the beauty of mad Mai Su were so vast as tales implied. These pilgrims were never disappointed in the madwoman's loveliness and stately manner. Her hair was dark and silky as the nighted sky, replete with starry glisten. Her eyes were wide with gorgeous madness; and these eyes seemed to be smiling in order to disguise some sad, wry, secret knowledge that none but she might bear. Her lips were full but small. Her hands were long and graceful, her feet tiny and narrow. She was extremely tall and slender, and subtly curved. Those who were witness to the beauty of Yeung Mai Su returned to their homes or lands to try in vain to remember her through brush and verse.

Then there were the singers and musicians who came by night to hear Mai Su sing. They never interrupted her music with their own, for her sound was hypnotic. Thus she never learned any melodies but those of her personal device, which were a challenge to all tradition. If not for the melancholy songs of Mai Su, people would have presumed her mute, for she never spoke at all. Only those who came to the small-house by dark, and who were quiet enough never to disturb her into silence, could hear the sweetness of her voice. Yet no singer or musician ever came away able to recreate the lyrics or the strains, and no one could recall the words. Morning would always find the listeners' memories fading, as though the music of the madwoman had been part of a dream.

Also there were the nuns and monks, priests and priest-esses, who came upon quests of enlightenment or simply to care for the holy grounds and keep the smallhouse in repair. It was a thing to be honored, this madness, a state upon which to gaze in reverence and admiration. Many were the holy women and men who went from the presence of Mai Su having glimpsed the wholeness and perfection of this singular universe. They knew best of all that Yeung Mai Su was not *simply* mad, but lost in divine meditation. They knew that she was wiser by far than they would ever be until many of their lives had passed.

But these people did not come all at once like a crowd to a festival. They came one by one, weeks apart. There were many lonely days for Mai Su, though only in her songs was there any hint of sorrow. During these long periods, there were only two persons whom she would see with any reliability. One of these was her grandmother.

Grandmother Yeung limped on her bad leg, bringing rice and fruit to the smallhouse. She set the food on a tiny table woven from liana vines. Mai Su's stool, and the chair the old woman rested upon, were also the works of weaver artisans. The old woman fed her granddaughter from fingers and sticks, for otherwise Mai Su would leave the bowl unemptied, so unconcerned was she for worldly needs.

Grandmother fed Mai Su fingerfuls of rice, and pieces of tangerine, lichees, and persimmon. Mai Su would never touch meat, though in the past grandmother had tried to tempt her with the finest pickled fish and dried water buffalo or, to Mai Su's greatest dissatisfaction, freshly cooked and basted fowl.

As grandmother fed her, Mai Su stared out glassless windows at things no one else could see. She stared beyond the flowering grounds; beyond the small, highly arched bridge over the spring; beyond the very forest.

Afterward, Grandmother Yeung gave Yeung Mai Su drink, then took the carved rosewood bowl and left the smallhouse. From the top of the bridge she turned to wave good-bye. Mai Su watched grandmother go, but did not wave in return, or reveal any emotion.

There was another person who came with certain regularity, unbeknownst to Grandmother Yeung or anyone else in Mai Su's family. He had this day been hiding in the forest waiting until the old woman had hobbled out of sight. Then Lu Khen of the house of Ou hurried over the bridge and stepped into the gardens surrounding the smallhouse.

The garden was aflower with hibiscus and camellias. Birds were everywhere, singing, splashing, playing. A fisherbird of iridescent blue perched on a smooth rock by the pond, eyeing carp of brilliant orange. The air smelled of the perfume of the gardens, and of camphor and cinnamon from the surrounding forest. This was a magic place to the mind of Ou Lu Khen, with one especially magical inhabitant.

Mai Su sat behind the glassless, round-topped window of the little stone pagoda which was her home. Her head turned slowly and, seeing the young man, emotion registered on her face for the first time that day. She gazed upon Ou Lu Khen with happiness.

Pheasants, peahens and cocks, mandarin ducks, wrens and other birds lived in the gardens around the smallhouse. Swallows lived in the tiered roofs of the pagoda. Birds seemed to enjoy being in the vicinity of Yeung Mai Su; it was said flocks and coveys attended her birth.

A peahen sat in a dwarfed tree, watching the young cock

strut and quaver his big-eyed fan. The hen looked away,
unimpressed by her dandy suitor. Elsewhere in the garden's
gentle wilds, a lyre-tailed pheasant ruffled his gaudy plum-
age and puffed up his chest, also to impress a plain lady.
She was kinder than the peahen, and flew away with her
suitor to a nest hidden among flowering shrubs. Mating
dances and songs made the garden lively and indiscreet; the
birds provided a grand addition to the color of flowers.

A few early hatchlings peeped. Pheasant chicks ran across
Lu Khen's path.

Like the pretty suitor birds, Ou Lu Khen wore his finery
for his visit. Elaborate hairpins held his topknot in place.
He wore brocaded cloth slippers instead of his usual straw
sandals, and a red, buttonless jacket over the more standard
wear of a long tunic fashioned from plain, bleached hemp
fabric. On his belt jangled a row of porcelain coins, strung
through square holes at their centers. For a poor farm boy,
this was dress more suitable for a temple holiday.

Ou Lu Khen smiled broadly, and bowed, his hands cast
up his sleeves. He walked a little ways up the path, almost
hopping with excitement. Nearby, the peacock made a drum-
like musical sound to the disinterested hen. Seeing the cock
rebuffed embarrassed Lu Khen so much that he began to
step more formally.

All the birds and their industry fell silent when, walking
with rigid posture, Lu Khen stumbled over a root. The
fisherbird shot away, a turquoise streak across the sky. Yeung
Mai Su laughed; her rarely heard laughter was like tinkling
bells. Lu Khen brushed himself off and, for all his bruised
dignity, he laughed too, and hurried on to her door.

Ou Lu Khen entered the smallhouse of the madwoman.
He held his hands up his sleeves and made a deep bow
of greeting. When he removed his hands from his sleeves
once more, in one he held a porcelain sparrow. This gift Lu
Khen carefully placed into Mai Su's hand. She sang briefly
to it in a whisper. She turned around and hid it somewhere
in the intricate folds of her floor-length gown. Then she
hurried to her woven table and felt around underneath it.
There, she found a hidden prize.

It was the gemlike feather of a flame dove. Lu Khen had

never seen its like before, but he did not think that anything less than that rarest of all birds could have shed a feather which shone like fire. Mai Su held the feather to him, and Lu Khen accepted the present, his heart filled with tender emotion. He did not question the magic of it, for in his heart he believed even more than others that Yeung Mai Su was herself as mystic and magical as the immortal dove.

Outside the smallhouse, song birds had become enamored of their own sweet music. Even the coarse-voiced peacock crooned. Yellow and white mynahs fluttered back and forth by the windows, as if hoping to see something worth telling. It was spring and the birds approved of this time for lovers. But what could birds know of Buddha's law regarding madwomen and ordinary men? They might not sing so loudly or so well, if they knew what difficulties need be surmounted for the young couple to find more contented happiness than these furtive meetings.

Ou Lu Khen's duties were sorely neglected because of the secret excursions, which often kept him away from the farm a whole day at a time. But Lu Khen, being eldest son whose father had died, was the family head. Thus none dared ask where he spent so much of his time, for none were allowed to question the rights and authority of the head of any given house. For this reason even drunkards and fools were highly regarded in their own homes, if they were family head.

Only Lu Khen's tiny sister knew where his visits led, and she, in her great love for him, told no one how once she had followed her brother to the smallhouse of Yeung Mai Su. Even Lu Khen did not know of his sister's knowledge. One evening she saw him returning to their house, dressed in his best clothing with nice pins in his hair. He stopped short of the rice paddy where Ou Koy was working. She hoped he could see what his neglect had wrought.

The paddy had at least been plowed with a borrowed water buffalo, but irrigation was insufficient, and little rice had been sown. Ou Koy worked in one of the few areas kept sufficiently muddy by an irrigation ditch from a nearby canal. Koy worked in the mud with expansive vigor, lest her brother be too dumb to notice how hard she worked alone. It was obvious that she was tired and, as it was late, clearly she should have long retired to dinner. But she diligently planted the young rice plants one beside the next, the seedlings carried in a dripping wicker basket hung from her neck. Her white teeth shone from a weary grimace. Her narrow eyes squinted into slits on her gold, sun-colored face. Her knees were bent, her ankles hidden in muddy water.

As Lu Khen watched his sister, she perceived his feelings of guilt. If he were reprimanding himself inwardly for his negligence and for the burden left upon a girl too young for such labor, Ou Koy thought it was only deserved that he should feel so bad. Certainly whatever pain his guilt caused him was not greater than the soreness of Ou Koy's muscles.

Lu Khen kicked off his fine cloth shoes and set them aside with his red jacket. He hitched his tunic up behind his legs and tied the hem through his belt. He took up a woven basket of seedlings and waded out into the muck.

Tiny wormfish wiggled blindly through the silt and muck and nibbled harmlessly at his feet. As Lu Khen approached little Koy, he said, "Go into the house."

"There is much work to be done," she said, carefully placing another seedling into the mud. She stood much, much shorter than her brother, too frail to work so hard.

"It is not work for a little girl," he said.

"Still," she told him evenly, her large narrow eyes not meeting his, "it is work to be done."

"My word is law in this family," he reminded her. Koy looked up into his face, her bright black hair sticky with mud and sweat. She said nothing more, but obediently turned and started for the irrigation ditch to clean herself. Then, dutifully, she picked up her brother's folded jacket and his good shoes and marched to the house without once looking back to see what her brother might be doing.

When a pale moon hung in the sky, sprinkling the silver of a broken reflection between the sad, drooping fronds of rice, Ou Koy peered from the window of the house. She saw her brother still working in the cold, nighttime mire. The sound of his splashing footsteps and the occasional sigh of exhaustion filtered out from among the songs of frogs, crickets, and bellowfish. He was presently using an empty basket to scoop mud from the irrigation channels, for tender rice seedlings would die quickly if water could not reach them. He poured the mud on the narrow pathways to keep them raised between sections of the flooded field. There was much yet to do, his duty having been long neglected.

Her anger dispelled, Koy took pity on her belatedly industrious brother. While mother, old uncle, three grandparents, and a great-grandparent slept, Koy slipped out into the dark and sat like a toad at the corner of the moonlit paddy.

She had crept there quietly and Lu Khen did not immediately notice her presence. He wove between young rice plants, a wraith among slender stalks, dumping load after load of mud upon the pathway. When the irrigation ditch was clear and water flowed smoothly, Ou Lu Khen breathed a sigh and ran a slick, dirty arm over his forehead. Then he saw his sister crouched not far away.

Legs that clearly pained him carried Lu Khen to Koy's side. He sat down. She pretended to ignore her brother's excessive attempts at apologies for various things, such as sounding angry at her when he was displeased with himself, for being an ill provider and overly preoccupied these past weeks, for spending little time with her, for leaving her and their mother to care for five old ones, even for trivial things that had occurred days or weeks before.

She squatted there without a word, attempting to look as though she were not listening. He rambled on and on, sounding nervous and sad, occasionally on the verge of incoherence. He was tired. When he was down to apologizing for common events she had long forgotten, which had for no good reason worn at the back of his consciousness a long while, she interrupted:

"I followed you once."

He did not ask what she meant, but looked out to where a frog had hopped in the water. Ou Lu Khen nodded his head.

"Small one," he said, "I am in love with Yeung Mai Su. How am I to confess such a thing in the house of Ou?"

"It is a thing that must be confessed," she said. "Either

you must forget her, or bring her to be our family. But you
do her and yourself, as well as our whole family, vast in-
justice with this secrecy."

"You are wise for such a little one," said Lu Khen. "I
would proudly make her your sister, but that Buddha forbids
the union of someone as ordinary as myself to someone as
profound as a madwoman."

"I am too young to counsel you," she said. "Perhaps
great-grandfather, who is wiser than all, can tell you where
to turn. Or perhaps you could bring offerings to the monastery and ask the monks if Buddha grants exceptions. I
cannot say what is right. I can only see that what you do
presently is wrong."

Lu Khen sat there a long while after Koy had stood and
gone back to the house. She looked back from the covered
porch and saw his motionless silhouette in the moonlight.
Her heart went out to him.

Alone, Ou Lu Khen went out at dawn, and sat down near
the canal. He placed his head upon his knees and made a
solemn prayer. His old prayer had gone unanswered, so now
he devised a new one. Rather than asking that Yeung Mai
Su be made sane, he asked instead that he be made mad.
Then they could be joined as one, under the law of Buddha,
for this life and all lives to come.

Later, he sought Po Lee for counsel.

Great-grandfather Ou Po Lee was the oldest man in or
around the town of Ki along the Mak-lai Canal, and therefore recognized as the wisest. But his wisdom was not easily
tapped since senility bound his tongue. Often as not, he
would forget what he was saying in the middle of saying
it. Too, he was forever falling into the dialect of far Uk-
ma, a province in the northern country of Ho where Po Lee
was born more than a century before. When he spoke in
that dialect, no one could understand him at all. He spoke
slowly and brokenly at best. Any question put to him needed
to be repeated over and over, and asked very loudly since
he could not hear well. Sometimes he would merely smile
toothlessly, shake his head, and say, "That's a good idea,"

which would not be at all a proper reply. It was all very frustrating for Lu Khen.

At last Po Lee seemed to understand. His toothless grin was gone and he took on a solemn appearance appropriate to the occasion. He seemed to be concentrating in a manner more fitting for a man supposedly wise and assuredly ancient.

"When I was a little boy like you," Po Lee began, although Lu Khen was not little anymore, "there was my friend Won Se'en who loved a madwoman. He took her madness and sealed it in an urn, and they were wed."

Lu Khen closed his eyes a moment and sighed, for this sounded like one of great-grandfather's tall tales, such as Lu Khen and Koy had listened to upon the old man's knees. Ou Lu Khen was too old for them now. He thought: *I must be respectful to great-grandfather, but sometimes he forgets what was a story he once heard or invented, and what was an experience which actually occurred.* Lu Khen opened his eyes and asked carefully,

"Is that a true story, great-grandfather?"

"It is! It is!" he assured, his voice crackly like a fire. "And when Won Se'en allowed that urn to be stolen by his greedy enemy Shan Be Kwing, a surprising thing happened. Shan Be Kwing believed something valuable must be concealed so carefully in the urn, and burst it open. Thus did Won Se'en's foe go mad and was kept in a dry well for the rest of his years."

His tale finished, great-grandfather smiled once again, seeming to have forgotten utterly the seriousness of Lu Khen's plight. Lu Khen stood, bowed respectfully, and said, "Thank you, Great-grandfather Ou Po Lee. You have been most helpful." Then Ou Lu Khen left Po Lee's side. As he went away, he was shaking his head and muttering words either sorrowful or disrespectful, which Po Lee's ears were too worn out to understand.

The rest of that morning Lu Khen worked in the paddy with Koy. Their two grandmothers and one grandfather and Old Uncle tried to be helpful, but they grew tired easily and rested often. Great-grandfather trundled to and fro with his short, thick bamboo staff, occasionally telling the others how it should be done, until Lu Khen's mother came and took the feeble soul into the house.

All but Koy and Lu Khen wore straw hats to keep the fierce sun from burning their faces as they worked in the paddies. The old ones were hot and panting by noon and, without a word to the young ones, stopped working and returned to the house. They were stronger than they pretended, but habitually expected the youngsters to do the greatest portion of work. That it should be this way was a matter of tradition and it did not matter to them if the elderly outnumbered the young. Some or all might return to work later, or none might come, as suited their whims. Lu Khen began to think his purpose in life was to coddle those who doddered. He would love them better when they became his ancestors and not his relatives! Such thinking gave him severe pangs of guilt, but the thoughts would not part from his mind.

It seemed to him that the only reason people bore children was so that parents would have someone to care for them in old age. Indeed, this was the way of things; but was there no other use for children aside from the assurance of a comfortable winterlife, and descendants to venerate one's ashes? Was happiness in one's strong years forever to be denied? These were blasphemous thoughts, he knew, and he knew himself a villain to have such ideas.

He had brothers in other villages along the canal. They were not the eldest, so were not as heavily bound to the farm. They had fled this gaggle of a decrepit family, and Lu Khen was left, feeling more the slave than the master of house and farm. It was no honor being eldest son.

It occurred to Lu Khen that he might flee, take Mai Su, and steal a houseboat, then drift far from this place and find a natural river, a river too shallow and winding for junks or fishermen. In a wild place, he could live with her—in a secret place far from cultivated land.

If it were an emperor's law he fled, Lu Khen would be more brave. But it was Buddha's law that made him sorrowful, and who could hide from Buddha?

After the noon meal of rice and fish, Koy went off to

work in another section of the farm where it was dry. She had planted a crop of yams by herself. She hoed among the tiny hills. Ou Lu Khen continued to work in the difficult paddy, alone with his thoughts—alone but for the wormfish between his toes. One section of the paddy had been planted early and would soon need the water drained away so that the rice could dry and ripen. He worked hard to block the irrigation ditch to that part of the sectioned field of rice. Then he used a mattock to cut a drainage ditch to a lower paddy.

As he worked, he recollected his promise to himself, to take care of the farm, to be a useful fellow. But the old ones did not come out that afternoon to offer the least help, and Lu Khen struggled with his promise. It was cruel not to visit Mai Su, for she would expect him! He thought such things as this, and his constitution weakened. Then he told himself it was wrong to feel resentment for his family, who would suffer if he did not repent his desires and stay at home instead of traipsing through the woods. Thinking this, his resolve grew strong again, and he worked hard. But soon enough, he would be considering the way in which his family expected so much but appreciated so little. And he pictured Mai Su standing in her flowery garden, looking down the path, waiting for someone who failed to visit her.

When he saw the two mandarin ducks paddling along the irrigation ditch, Ou Lu Khen lost the argument with himself, for surely the ducks were emissaries from his beloved, and he must not disappoint her. He left the work behind and ran along the dusty road toward the cool forest, envisioning the paradisiacal gardens so unlike the grudging yellow earth of the farm. He ran past Koy, hardly noticing how she looked up from her hoeing. He did not want to see her anger; but if he had turned to her for a spare moment, he might have seen less anger than sorrow in her expression. Ou Koy began hoeing more vigorously, disguising her emotions.

Once beyond sight of the farm, Lu Khen became a bolt of iron caught between two magnets. He could not continue forward. He could not turn back. He knew he should return to his duties, but also he must see Mai Su. He was barely at the forest's edge when the guilt and desire struck him front and rear, holding him in opposing grips. "How can I make a decision?" he asked himself. "I cannot move at all!" There were only uncertainties about his loyalties—to family, or to love. He realized it was not possible to choose. If he returned to the farm, he could never forget Mai Su, yet he was equally incapable of seeing her in this dreadful, sneaking fashion.

He could neither return nor go forward. Instead, he turned another way, toward the hills where lay a Buddhist monastery. Perhaps where an old man failed to help him, a priest would succeed.

The hills were neither near nor small. It took the day to reach the foot of the particular hill on which the monastery was built. It would take him hours more to attain the heights where stood the gray stone walls. The paths were not steep, but wound back and forth, well-marked by the passing of multitudes of pilgrims through the multitudes of years.

Lu Khen had not ventured idly through woodlands and foothills. He had inspected many of the nests of yellow mynahs and stolen several eggs, carrying them in a giant leaf folded in a way to form a bag. He had not carelessly filched the eggs, but was careful not to rob the mothers poor. He had held each egg to the sunlight, too, carefully choosing only the properly aged embryos which were a delicacy not often had by the monks of the highlands where mynahs rarely nested.

The blue-speckled, fragile eggs were to be his offering to Buddha and his pious followers, for only the most wretched of poor would think to call on the austere habitat above without the least tribute. Even though it was said the monks would grant anything within their power without reward, it did not seem right to take undue advantage.

It was dark when Lu Khen finally passed under the outer gate of the time-worn wall surrounding the monastery's grounds. The thin air made the sky seem inky blue, the stars jewel bright. Lu Khen felt light-headed and tired from the height and the climb.

There was no sound beyond that of the crisp wind. No

light but that of moon and stars touched the gray, monolithic temple. It was as a place deserted, maybe haunted, but the occupants merely slept, or meditated in darkness. It seemed a mild discourtesy to interrupt the quietude, but as holy men kept no special hours, and would avail themselves to all who came at any hour, Ou Lu Khen took up the cloth-wrapped mallet and struck the gong outside the door. It made a deep, hollow sound that went on and on. He waited some while. A moment before he was about to strike the gong a second time, the weathered teakwood door (brought from some distant place) began to creak open.

A head-shaven monk, sleepy eyed and cloaked in saffron, peered at Ou Lu Khen. "I have brought unhatched birds," said Lu Khen somewhat nervously, holding his leaf bag open for the monk to see. "Carefully chosen," he added. Without expression, the holy man opened the door wider and bowed as Lu Khen entered.

"Is your errand urgent?" asked the monk. His voice was high-pitched and casual. "Or might it wait for dawn? Do not hesitate to say so if your mission requires immediate audience! But if there is no cause for haste, then I will show you to a place to rest from your journey."

"I can wait," said Lu Khen, not wishing to have anyone else awakened. He went after the monk down unlit halls, following largely by sound since he could barely see. The monk seemed adjusted to the dark, or else so familiar with the halls that he required no sight to find the way. At various corners, Lu Khen heard distant-seeming chanting, muffled behind thick stone walls. Once he was led past what must have been a door, through which he smelled sweet incense and heard a tiny bell ringing incessantly.

The monk stopped suddenly and said, "Here is where pilgrims stay. There is no one else but you tonight." Then the monk took Lu Khen's leaf bag and left the visitor to find his own way through the black room to some resting place. In the hall beyond the closed door, Lu Khen heard the sound of the monk cracking an egg and greedily sucking out the contents, then pad on down the hall. Lu Khen lay upon his back on a pallet in the cool darkness, gravely doubting that it was proper for a monk to have eaten of an offering before it was shown to Buddha at the altar. The too-human act of the monk caused Ou Lu Khen to think that he had ventured into the hills not to find solutions, but to sleep on a hard board in a cold, dark monastery of stone, and discover he had fed men who were, after all, only men.

Often she had spent days upon days without any visitor aside from her lame caretaker, but Lu Khen had spoiled her of late, and Mai Su was in despair that he had not come that day. She sat looking from the pagoda's window, down the forest path beyond the gardens. Her grandmother had come and gone. The boy she expected to see come forth from hiding had failed to appear.

With welling loneliness, Yeung Mai Su explored her gardens that day. Peachicks, hatched that morning, followed her about as though she were their mother. They tried to hide beneath her skirt when she stood in one place. The hours passed slowly and when at last darkness fell, Yeung Mai Su began to sing.

She sang a verse of a heartbroken, deserted lover. Yet she knew Lu Khen had not deserted her, and that he would come if not tomorrow, then the next tomorrow; it was not really for him and herself that she sang the sad, sweet song. It was for the multitudes who never knew the feeling of love so that neither the loneliness nor the glorious reunion could be theirs. She sang for those who hated so easily, who only with immeasurable difficulty revealed affection. And, more terrible than all these others whose lives were lacking, she sang with heavy heart for the many who had never known the oneness of insanity.

Sunset became night. The birds of day climbed into trees to roost, or vanished into shrubbery to nest until dawn. Nightingales and starsparrows moved half invisibly against the night, joining Mai Su in song, providing counter melodies and choruses. Chirping insects and piping amphibians added a final touch of accompaniment that never could be matched with hand drums, flutes, or harps. Her song blended with nature. Nature blended with her song.

The song of lovers had changed into a song of all kinds of unhappy people, people disconnected from the reality of

wendy
wees

the whole universe, living in their narrow parts instead. This
song, too, changed, to one that was almost happy but too
ironic to convey absolute joy: It was a song about a world
gone mad. It was difficult to say, by the tone of this song,
if the madness it attributed to all people was the peaceful,
pleasant madness of Yeung Mai Su, a madness from whence
all joys are great and all sadnesses humble, or if it were
about raving, fearful, dangerous insanity. The language of
the song was mostly ambiguous, alien, and vaguely sar-
castic. But to see the beautiful face from which the beautiful
voice originated, one could not imagine that the music was
about danger. It was a song about the beauty of the forest,
unmarred by frightening shadows; it was about the beauty
of a hawk's graceful descent, untainted by the death sought
by those taloned claws.

This did not mean that Yeung Mai Su wished upon all
people a kind of blind madness, for she herself was aware
that the hawk slew and the shadows were inhabited. But in
madness even fear and death and sorrow were beautiful.
They are part of the circularity that does not divide darkness
from light, but is whole. People who suffer from sanity
believe there is no beauty in pain. But those same people
would discover, by passing near the smallhouse on this
moonlit night, that there was only beauty in the heartsinking
pain and sorrow of Mai Su's song and voice.

Yeung Mai Su did not appear to notice the falling star
approaching. A glowing streak of fiery red shot from heaven,
straight for the smallhouse. Even diurnal birds had seen it,
for they had been stirred awake by the beauty of Mai Su's
singing. Their small, alert eyes observed the crimson fire
in the sky. Only Mai Su failed to see.

It became evident that this was no star at all, but the
brightly shining flame dove herself, come to hear the music
of the madwoman. It perched on a windowsill and cooed
for her to come in from the garden. She obeyed, knowing
that, like grandmother, the flame dove was sent to care for
her; it did not want her standing in the cold night.

Mai Su had few memories, living each day for itself, but
the flame dove she recalled without fail. Months before she
had found it injured; it had fallen at the edge of the gardens.

Perhaps an autumn wind had snatched and dashed it down; perhaps an eagle or a black-eyed forest cat had injured the small thing. Whatever had happened to it, the flame dove had lost flight feathers and could only fumble about the ground with its heart racing and its eyes startled. Yeung Mai Su had nursed the bird, and hid it under her tea table so that none would see it with their greed and desire. It was, after all, the rarest of birds. Mai Su had instinctive knowledge of what sane people were like. They would want to cage the flame dove or, worse, cook the meat of it hoping to be made immortal. They would place the feathers on a hat, or turn them into fans, gifts for an emperor's courtesan or the princess of some realm. Knights would slay the tiny bird as readily as a sacred dragon, to bring marvelous tribute to a lord and gain favor. Thus did Yeung Mai Su hide the bird beneath her table of woven liana. When it regained its feathers, she had set it free, without the least regret. But it often returned, whenever she was saddest, whenever she had need.

On the day it was completely healed and she had set it free, she found two of its feathers left behind, beneath the table. The feathers were bright as embers in a firepot. Later, when she realized she loved the boy who came to see her, she gave one of the feathers to him so that they would be united by the flame dove's light. The second feather she kept secreted in her gown, along with the porcelain bird Ou Lu Khen had given her.

Tonight the wondrous bird came to perch upon her window, its brilliance lighting Mai Su's delicate features. She put her face against its feathers and the flame dove cooed to her lovingly. Mai Su sang her songs for this bird alone, while it ruffled and preened and listened. Mai Su felt that no creature more than the flame dove could completely understand all aspects of the lyrics, the melodies, the meters . . .

The song carried over the roof of the forest. It was the perfect composition, requiring no additions or subtractions, so the night creatures listened without offering their own notations. All life around was silent and rapt. The song went even beyond the outer boundaries of the forest. It enfolded

every leaf and every beast whether sleeping or awake. It
carried to the villages and beyond the hills. It went on up
to heaven.

Song engulfed the universe.

In the darkness of the chamber, Lu Khen suddenly awakened. A dream had awakened him, or, perhaps, it was the
dim light. On that thought, he realized there were no windows in the cell. Also, he did not feel as though he had
slept long enough for it to be dawn. The vague light was a
mystery. Slowly, he realized the radiance came from himself. The feather Mai Su had given him had nearly fallen
from the place inside his tunic, its tip poking out of a fold
and casting a bit of ruddy light throughout the chamber.

By day he had not been able to fully appreciate the
intensity of the feather's unusual quality. He had never looked
at it in such a dark place as the windowless cell of a monastery. Presently he removed it from his tunic; its crimson
glow was bloodlike against the gray walls. There on the
palm of his hand sat the miniature quill, like a coldly burning
coal. As his eyes remained transfixed—mesmerized by the
unhot blaze—he thought he heard again the sound of distant, sad, beckoning song.

There he sat, unmoving for a long spell, until the brilliance of the feather faded before his tired eyes. The sound
of the singing faded as well, and he was not certain he had
ever heard it. Then he lay back on the hard pallet, sleepy
but wide-eyed and unable to rest, wondering if even at this
moment he was actually dreaming.

In the morning, a saffron-robed monk, different from the
one who had led him to the room the night before, awakened
Ou Lu Khen and took him to an audience before the priest.
Before speaking to the head-shaven man, Lu Khen approached a green, tarnished bronze bowl of yellow coals.
He took up a pinch of incense and tossed it into the bowl.
The fire flared momentarily. The room filled with the scent
of sandalwood. Then Lu Khen bowed three times to the
gold and jade statue of wise Buddha, and whispered a respectful address.

Only after these pious observances did Lu Khen turn to

face the ageless holy man, repeating to him the same address he had made to the Buddha. Then he commenced explaining the nature of his problem.

Having told all, a long silence fell between Lu Khen and the priest. Lu Khen stood the whole while with head held low. The priest sat cross-legged upon a raised dais, appearing to be concentrating deeply.

"Buddha's law," the priest began at last, "is irrevocable."

Lu Khen had expected to hear precisely this information. All the same, his heart sank to be told what he already knew. The priest continued,

"Yeung Mai Su is special to Buddha. She is more than mortals are. Think, young master Ou: Are you worthy of such a woman? He who was worthy of a most beautiful princess of a noble house might well find this one beyond his reach. She is above us all. You have asked Buddha to make her sane, that you may both be wed. Is this not a grave selfishness, to wish Yeung Mai Su deprived of her gift of heaven?"

"I love her as she is," Lu Khen whispered, certain it was an improper confession, though it at least meant he did not truly intend that she be robbed of madness. "If the sane cannot be joined with the mad, then pray to Buddha in my behalf, that I be made mad as well."

The priest looked at Lu Khen severely. He may have felt immeasurable compassion, but it was not shown. His voice was cold when he said, "You are most presumptuous to ask this gift of Buddha for yourself. Madness, as enlightenment, must be sought, not begged."

"Where do I seek madness?" asked Lu Khen. "Where do I go to earn this special gift?"

The priest made no pretense of limitless wisdom, only of pure belief. He was a studied seeker, but could never be all knowing until the moment of nirvana, a moment that could not be shared. All the same, he gave Ou Lu Khen a scholarly opinion in regards to madness and where it might be sought:

"There are many places where madness is said to reign. Some places are feared, others worshiped. There are many who believe madness guards the tombs of the Lost Dynasties, and that those who seek to discover the identities of emperors ages dead shall flee those distant tombs wild-eyed and mindless."

"You speak of a far and dreadful land!" exclaimed Lu Khen.

"You are wise to fear such a journey," said the priest.

"It is not only that I'm afraid," said Ou Lu Khen. "As oldest son and heir, I am bound to a farm. I care for many old ones, a young sister, and my mother. My recent tribulations have made me negligent, yet I am aware of my responsibility. How can I venture so far, and be gone so long, to risk so much, when so many are reliant on me here?"

"On such things as these you must meditate," said the priest, his tone more caring than before. "Those answers you must find alone."

"Then I will meditate."

Lu Khen approached the green and gold statue of Buddha and sat cross-legged on a mat before it. His hands were held in prayer near his throat, steepled toward heaven. He sat with eyes closed, breathing gently. The priest descended the dais and left Lu Khen alone. Although monks came and went many times for various reasons, Lu Khen did not notice them, and they did not disturb his meditation. When he opened his eyes at last, he did not realize that three days had passed.

When his meditating was complete, he called for aid. His legs were too stiff and he could not move them. Two monks answered his call. They lifted him from the mat and forced his legs to straighten. As they walked him and exercised him, the priest arrived to ask what Ou Lu Khen had learned in his three days of meditating. "Young master Ou," said the priest. "Have you found your answers?"

Lu Khen sighed and answered, "I have realized that it is my duty to care for my family; that it would be a selfish quest to abandon them in search for madness. Not only would Buddha be unable to smile upon me, but I would be less worthy of Yeung Mai Su's love, and unworthy of madness."

There was no joy in Lu Khen's revelation. His legs gained

strength while he spoke and now he stood unaided. He bowed to the priest and to the monks in turn. Some of them followed him to the farthest walls of the monastery, wishing him well on his way back home. They were all proud of him for his decision, yet Lu Khen could not help but walk with head slung low. He trudged down the zigzagging paths alone, down the slope toward the farmlands in the valleys. He could find neither pride nor joy in his sacrifice.

And as Lu Khen walked, he began to hum a sad melody. He did not know where he might have heard it before, unless it was in a dream.

Old Uncle had died that first night of Lu Khen's absence, of causes unknown and painful. One grandmother, whose brother he was, still wailed with grief at the side of the grave. Great-grandfather Po Lee, patriarch of the house of Ou by dint of years, whose sixth and final living son Old Uncle was, stomped about on the far end of the rice paddy, stabbing his wooden cane into the ground where he walked. It was great-grandfather's habit to seem angry when he grieved.

Upon returning, Lu Khen saw the older of two grand-mothers weeping aloud over the fresh grave. He approached his sister Koy, asking, "Which one has died?" Ou Koy jumped, startled by her brother speaking behind her. Her lips were set fast together. Her eyes gazed coldly. She was much like Po Lee in the manner by which she confused her emotions, and in her terrible sorrow she was only able to be angry at whomever was nearest and most vulnerable. She parted the line of her lips and said, "It is our great-uncle." Her tone was abrupt. "He dies in pain while you proclaim your own holidays."

This was unfair of Koy, and certainly undutiful inasmuch as Lu Khen was the young master of Ou, meriting respect because of his position if not his deeds. But there was guilt in Lu Khen's heart, for once he had thought he'd love his elderly relatives more when they were ancestors. He felt too dejected to reprimand Koy for her failure to respect the family's head. Instead, he turned and shuffled toward Great-grandfather Po Lee, who at least had never accused Lu Khen of anything nor preyed upon his easy sense of blame.

Nearing the paddy, Lu Khen saw that the irrigation ditch was clogged with silt from the canal. The paddy was dry. The young rice was withered and bent; none could be salvaged.

This sight angered the young master deeply, for even old men and women in mourning should have known to keep the ditch flowing. He stopped, stared at the ruined crop, and the crop beyond it which had been planted earlier but was too spare to feed the whole family. He reflected on the laziness and spitefulness of the old, who expected constantly to be cared for, and of the obstinance of little Koy; she had doubtlessly allowed this harm to be done because of her stubbornness and temper.

He looked up when he heard the northern dialect that Po Lee used when befuddled or angry. The old man, standing on the narrow, raised path between sections of the paddy, shook his cane and screamed blasphemies that were best left untranslated. This was the hardest thing for Lu Khen to bear, that even great-grandfather found the young master blameworthy.

Again, Lu Khen hid his own anger and turned without response from the rage of the incredibly old man. He passed the house and came again to the new grave, around which the other grandparents had regathered, two standing, one perpetually kneeling and in tears. The body of Old Uncle would remain in the ground one year, until his flesh had returned to the earth; only then would his bones be cremated and placed in an urn; only then would Old Uncle become one with all ancestors. It would not be until that time, Lu Khen realized, that the three grandparents, and especially Old Uncle's sister, would cease to blame Lu Khen for an inevitable death.

Tearful grandmother stopped her wailing for the first time since her brother's death. She looked up at Lu Khen. She was silent, eyes accusing.

Once more Lu Khen was angered, yet kept his feeling contained. He accepted the blunt end of abuse despite the fact that his five days away were not the cause of Old Uncle's death.

There was only one person left to cast blame on him, and that was his mother. But she never judged people good or bad. She merely sought pity from heaven and from everyone around her. So when Lu Khen entered the house, his mother burst into tearful disparagements, shouting with woebegone intonations about how horrible Buddha had treated her, robbing her of beauty, of her husband, leaving her with more old relatives to care for than children to help, submitting her to misery after misery as her family died around her or went away, and cursing her with a useless son who would not even listen attentively to his mother's countless sufferings.

This self-pity, this solicitous ranting was the stone of excess atop Lu Khen's burden. He went and stood upon the porch and did not face anyone as he shouted for all the family to hear:

"I proclaim myself without family! I vow never to speak your miserable names and to never worry you with my bothersome company! Think of me as dead. Forget you ever had a grandson, great-grandson, brother, son, ill provider, bringer of grief, lover of a madwoman, scum upon a rice paddy! Tell my brother he is now eldest son and has no brother older! Speak my name no more, as I pay you like courtesy! I am no longer master of the house of Ou, but only Lu Khen who lacks a family name. Do not look at me as I go. I am smoke. I am nothing. I am dust beneath your feet. I am irretrievable. I have no ancestors. I have no kin. In the name of Buddha and the Law of Heaven, this is my vow!"

He took immediately to his heels, swift along the road, running, running, running . . . running for fear they would see his lips shaking and his face contorting with unhidden anguish. Already he regretted his vow. But it was spoken. It would bind him.

The three grandparents surrounding the grave did not watch Lu Khen flee. It was thus he bade them, and tradition was strong in this terrible matter. They may have been secretly disheartened, but could easily bury sad feelings beneath superficial feelings of relief to be rid of a useless grandson.

For the next younger son, who had set out on his own to become a scholar in another village, would now become eldest, and perforce return to the house of Ou as heir and master. He would be a better provider than Lu Khen had been, for Lu Khen always left more tasks than were the interest of old people. Since the farm would fall upon a better man, the three grandparents were not so much concerned about Lu Khen's oath.

Lu Khen's disowned mother stood at the doorway, looking bewildered. She said nothing to anyone, for she, too, was bound by Buddha's law in this situation. Yet her most terrible grief was not that a son had gone from her, but that she must obey Lu Khen's invocation of the laws of disinheritance: She could never speak his name. How, then, could she complain to her friends of this most recent and ferocious woe?

Great-grandfather Po Lee was hurrying like a hobbled rabbit, spry for his age, but clumsy. He had been across the paddy and too deaf to have heard more than the barest meaning of his great-grandson's proclamations. He stopped between porch and grave site, panting, heart fluttering. He asked Koy excitedly, "What did he say? Where does he go? Tell him I was not angry! I was not angry! Run tell him I was not angry!"

Koy did not run. She could scarcely see through the blur of tears. She took the old one's bony hand and went with him toward the house. He kept looking back over his shoulder, though Lu Khen was long beyond sight. For a moment he pulled loose of Koy and shook his cane while exclaiming:

"I will say his name if I please! Lu Khen! Lu Khen! Lu Khen!"

Although the less elderly relatives surrounding the grave thought Po Lee merely feeble-minded, Ou Koy knew her century old great-grandfather was the only wise man left in her pitiable family.

Feverish from exhaustion, Lu Khen broke out of the woods and into the garden. Birds squawked and scattered at his sudden intrusion. The lame grandmother came out of the tiny pagoda and stood at the top step.

"Who are you?" she asked. "Why are you here?"

Mai Su ran past her, ecstatic in a manner the old woman had never before seen from her usually placid granddaughter.

Lu Khen addressed Mai Su: "We are leaving here today. Maybe you will never see your gardens again." Mai Su nodded her head once, trusting to his abrupt decision, though he knew it would confuse her to leave the smallhouse.

"Leave!" the old woman demanded. She limped down the steps, came at Lu Khen with her rosewood bowl raised as a weapon. Lu Khen caught her gray, thin arm and the bowl fell from her grasp. Calmed by necessity, the grandmother rubbed her wrist where Lu Khen had grabbed it. She said evenly,

"I knew someone was visiting her. I could tell. Very well! If you want to keep her, she is yours. None in our family but me desires to care for her, and I will not be able to get around on this leg much longer. So you take her. But never dare despoil her! She is Buddha's. And do the courtesy of telling a lame old woman who cares where you will live."

"I do not know where we will live," confessed Lu Khen. "I have disowned my family. I am free to care only for Mai Su. We could live in the deepwood, far from civilized towns. I might steal a houseboat and venture from the canal up a winding, natural river. We would never be seen again."

The old woman scowled. "You would live as gibbons? In a tree? So be it! It is your business. But remember Buddha's laws. You cannot hide from him. He will see you in your stolen houseboat, or in your tree, or lurking in the wood. He will not be pleased if a common boy has taken for himself a madwoman to wife."

Lu Khen tugged Yeung Mai Su away from the smallhouse, deeper into the surrounding woods, along a tiny trail made by hares rather than by people. But he had not ignored the old woman's lecture. She was right. He could not hide from Buddha. He could not hide from himself. Mai Su and Lu Khen could never be truly joined until he, too, were mad.

But he had a plan. He would have told the old woman at closer range, speaking face to face, but that he did not

wish to hear her screaming near his ears when she heard
what he intended. He waited until many trees stood between
himself and the gardens around the pagoda. Then he yelled
back his reply:

"Then we shall not live in the deepwood. We shall live
in a tomb of the Lost Dynasty, where we shall both be mad!"

He was glad indeed not to be near the old woman, for
her screeching was even louder than he had imagined it
would be, and more sustained. He heard her thrashing in
the undergrowth, too befuddled to find her path back home,
too scared to stand in one place. As she thrashed about, she
yelled in a high-pitched voice how doom would fall upon
the whole of the world if he ventured there; that he and Mai
Su would die; that demons would be unleashed; that he did
not have to go beyond the mountains to become mad, he
was already mad to consider it.

Her hysterical raving faded far behind. Lu Khen eventually came with Mai Su upon a deep, narrow spring. They
followed it to the canal. There, true to his word, he stole a
boat with a cover, and poled up the canal until they came
to a natural river which flowed from the distant mountains.
He set himself to fighting the current, for it was beyond the
snow-tipped peaks that the lands of the unrecorded dynasties
had once been. There a crumbling capital and the tombs of
unknown emperors would be found.

⚄ TWO ⚄

Tomb Gold

IF EVERY SCROLL of recorded time were unwound, the lands
beneath Heaven—from the Three Kingdoms of Ho in the
north, to the wet jungle states at the southern tip of the
Great Peninsula; from the island empire of Naipon where
the sun is daily reborn, to the land of Buddha's birth west
beyond a sea—would all be clothed in layer upon layer of
scribed silk, crisp papyrus, and soft rice paper. If the clay
tablets of the ancient universities and temples were brought
together from these many lands, a drab city of gargantuan
expanse with towers probing Heaven itself could be built
from them. Yet in this wealth of records, nowhere is there
to be found a chronicle of the particular thousand years
known to tradition as the Lost Dynasty, believed to have
extended its dark power the full length and breadth of the
Great Peninsula, where now a hundred countries exist.

That malignant power may well have touched mighty Ho
itself, and reached west across the sea to Buddha's first
domain. In all these places, as throughout the peninsula,

there were scattered the remains of terrifying architecture with a unified mien and ghostly disposition—shunned places mostly, or else the homes of ghouls.

Scholars did not speculate on the particulars and the full import of history's missing millennium, framed as the period is in the easily fascinating documents of the ages before and the ages which came after. Regarding the Lost Dynasty, superstition ran deep even among the literati, and no useful discourses could be found about this topic. Yet folktales made sly allusions to the mysterious, crumbled capital located at the center of the peninsula (at the hub of ancient trade routes, ages in disuse). Many a parable held a moral predicated upon unspoken but widespread knowledge of a once-tremendous empire's utter erasure from the annals of time.

By one such tale, the deities of antiquity smote the Lost Dynasty for the sins and iniquities of its unknown emperors and vile peasantry. Only a few immortal monsters, who once were men, survived in hidden places. Those emperors had been violently pernicious, the only earthly lords who ever feasted among demons upon the flesh of humanity.

In a variant of the story, the antique deities met in combat at the capital of the Lost Dynasty, to fight for opposed factions. In those days, gods replied wholeheartedly when called upon for the sake of vengeance, pride, or power, so that the gods were as bitter as the peasants and as cruel as the lords. In the end of that inconceivably titanic battle, only the gods remained standing. Having lost all of their worshipers, they turned to stone, or dust, or ashes.

In another legend, the once-enduring line of tyrannical aristocrats found a changeling in their midst, a shining golden boy who grew to be the first and only man of conscience to rule from the capital. This emperor looked back upon his family's ill deeds and met with so overwhelming a shame that he spent his lifetime and his resources seeking out and destroying all records of the dynasty, undoing the work which had unified the world through terror. When his work was done, he looked about at the peasants who were free of restraint, and discerned that they were irrevocably tainted by their millennium of proximity to the capital. Fiendish men and women and children took advantage of newfound liberties to emulate and rival the perfidy of vanished power; the last dynastic ruler could not stay the infamy and horror with his kindness or his tears.

At last he released the Uncreator from beneath the Eastern Pillar of Heaven, so that the end was quick and absolute. This story has two popular endings. In one, the last emperor, alone in his country, leaped from a high place so that there would not even be himself as a reminder of the cruel millennium. By the other account, the Uncreator spared him to live forever, to wander through the nations of the world, smiting infamy wherever he might find it, to this very day.

Thoughts such as these passed through Lu Khen's mind as he poled the little boat up winding, narrow, forking streams. He considered his folly and the dangers which might await beyond any bend. His imagination worked most greatly when the sun was setting and the liana vines impinged upon streams like the fingers of unholy monsters or the legs of gigantic spiders. The forest had become a veritable jungle; the shadows were alive with watchful, glowing eyes. Lu Khen recollected those tales which had frightened him as a child, and frightened him now. How much more fearful would the world become when he was actually near his destination?

Little was known about the Lost Dynasty, yet did themes of it recur in supernatural yarns. It was a place in time easily cited as the source of any and all misfortune or inexplicable phenomena. It was fearful merely to consider what evil could have been so intense that even Time could not bear to be the witness. What events could be more terrible than some of those attested to by the *Li Shu* or *Record of Things Past*, which Lu Khen had read in a temple library? He could not imagine deeds more hideous than the single example of General Wei Chow: his torture and murder of a gentle emperor in public view, his despoiling of the royal concubines and forced wedding with the empress, the living burial of three hundred thousand who dared mourn the martyred emperor, the leveling of the Holy City of Li which was not rebuilt until three centuries later, the interim being an age of consistent pestilence and famine. What greater villain than Wei Chow could have ruled and walked the lands of the Lost Dynasty? The *Li Shu* did not offer any clues about that thousand years.

Perhaps Lu Khen would have found more information on this topic had he been allowed to pursue his studies. But when his father died, Lu Khen was forced to give up his dream of becoming a scholar, and tend to the house of Ou. Yet he had read selections of *Shu Chi Ching,* the *Book of Ancient Rites,* while helping his younger brother to obtain a degree. *Shu Chi Ching* was the largest historical work ever compiled, running to several thousand volumes, and in it was contained the only official reference to the Lost Dynasty. The reference was little more than a shuddering condemnation of the black arts practiced at that time, and the alien deities honored by wicked monarchs.

Lu Khen feared that indeed the only villainy which could have surpassed the crimes of General Wei Chow would be ill-used sorceries in connection with devilish deities who never belonged between the Four Pillars of Heaven.

Lu Khen tried hard to put further thoughts of this kind from his mind, lest his resolve be shattered. He reflected upon the words of Grandmother Yeung: that he was mad to travel west toward the ruins of a sorcerous land. Yet for love of Mai Su, he would hold to this seeming madness until it was made complete.

In the stolen boat, he poled onward day by day, the stream twisting here and forking there, so that the route was jagged and complex. His legs ached from standing and pushing. His progress was slow, for the current ran against him. Mai Su lounged beneath the boat's tattered canopy, appearing to be content. If Lu Khen ever resented her uselessness, he hid it beneath his sense of being solely responsible for the madwoman, bound to protecting her from turmoil and from labor.

Along the banks there were many wild fruits. Though they were sometimes green and sour, they were plentiful and filling. However, for a long while, Mai Su did not eat anything at all. Lu Khen worried that it was because he took her from the smallhouse, or that she was somehow incapable of eating from any hand but that of her grandmother. He scarcely had time to eat, between his fitful nights of slumber and the constant daily poling. He was greatly relieved when on the third day Mai Su ended her fast, and thenceforth ate, without aid, anything that Lu Khen plucked from the overhanging trees or from the bushes that encroached along the sides of the streams. She even revealed her concern that Lu Khen also eat more often.

Whenever the mountains were visible through the thick forest, they seemed always the same distant, misty lumps forever far away. The currents constantly fought his progress. But slowly, very slowly, day by day, the lumps grew higher on the horizon.

On a certain day, when eerie mists had risen and the mountains should have been visible, Lu Khen could not discern their presence. He climbed a tree, leaving the little boat anchored to the pole he had stuck deep into the mud. From the tree, he could see to all horizons. There were no mountains.

For two days prior, the weather had been wet and misty. Yet as Lu Khen reflected on the terrain previously covered, he could find no logical way that he could have gotten them so utterly lost that the very mountains should cease to provide recognizable monuments. The only thing he could think was how, on the night before, the boat had come loose from a branch he had tied it to, and drifted on its own while he and Mai Su slept innocently in one another's arms.

He came down the tree with a sinking feeling in his stomach. "I am a farmer," he said to himself, "not an adventurer."

Then he said to Mai Su, "I have gotten us lost." She smiled at him without concern, trusting to Lu Khen. Though her faith warmed his heart, it added guilt to his fears and burden.

Throughout that long day, he poled westward. By all that was logical, the mountain range should eventually return to sight. Whenever there was a view of the horizon, however, there were still no mountains. Toward evening, he felt his panic so intensely that it was like a stone inside his chest. The stream led to a larger one which went in another direction, and in a frantic state of mind, Lu Khen decided to follow this new tributary northward. When the sun was completely down, he turned west again, going along a spring so shallow that at times he was forced to get out and push the boat upstream. He was very tired but refused to rest. His judgment was impaired by fright and despair, so that he continued in his attempts to find the proper route even though it was too dark to succeed. The tiny spring finally joined a deep, narrow stream. Lu Khen decided to go with the current for a while and let this new stream carry them south.

In the blackness of night, he could not see ahead. He stood at the prow of the boat with his pole guiding the course when an overhanging branch struck him on the head. It was an unexpected and very sound whack. He turned around and faced Mai Su, who slept calmly, unconcerned. Then, dizzily, he fell forward into unconsciousness.

Yesterday Harada owned a boat. Today he did not. Harada was a foreign settler in the village by the canal, not much liked by anyone. He had come from the island empire of Naipon, more or less in exile for petty crimes and debts incurred in his homeland. As it happened, even the most generous and good-hearted of islanders were little loved by mainlanders from northern Ho to the southern jungle states. Although nobody was old enough to recall firsthand the raids of far-ranging navies and buccaneers of far Naipon, it was nonetheless well-remembered in oral histories. Harada's obnoxious nature only reinforced this prejudice. He was aware that it would be hard for him to obtain justice because the local citizens, whom he held in equal contempt, treated him as an outcast. In his own country he had been poor but of high caste, so that his treatment by people of the Great Peninsula made him bitter and short-tempered. Though he had few illusions about his chances of redress, he yet intended to stir up a troubling stink about the matter of his boat.

At first he ran up and down the canal's bank tearing at his hair and crying sneak thief, fiend, and more foul imprecations, accusing everyone in sight of one criminal act and several others. He was convinced every fisherman was in collusion with every trader, and indeed their collective response to his outrage suggested, to him, some sort of conspiracy against him. He was in so vast an hysterical state of mind that a witness to the theft had to hit Harada atop the head with a bamboo fishing rod to make him shut up long enough to listen. While Harada rubbed his whacked head, he was informed that it was the first son of the house of Ou who, along with the madwoman of the smallhouse in the woods, stole the boat in the middle of the night and fled against the canal's current.

No one had pity for Harada's loss. He was considered an unwisely greedy man who wanted much but had little, besides which he was from that warlike archipelago, in addition to which he had a mean personality, and basically nobody cared who had done what to him. It was widely circulated that Harada was himself a thief, though none had ever proven it; those whom he had cheated in the past were quick to jeer vindictively when he claimed to be the victim.

"The boat of Harada," said a gleeful villager, "was an ill-patched worthless log. He will surely swindle another boat just like it from some equally vile and stupid fellow, preferably an inland tribesman or someone from his own island country."

"Why should the magistrate trouble the Ou family over a trifle?" a trader added quickly. "They are an honorable if small clan who have done only good work in the region."

Discovering this to be the attitude of everyone he approached, Harada became angrier and angrier. He stormed to the house of Ou and rapped hard upon the door. Receiving no response, he rapped again, and harder. He did not stop rapping until old Po Lee came up behind him and knocked him on the head with a cane, considerably harder than the fisherman had done with a rod, and in the same painful spot. Po Lee demanded querulously,

"Do you seek to beat down our house, dishonorable Harada? The family works in the fields and the paddy. What brings you smashing down the door while nobody is home?"

The ancient, withered Ou Po Lee was rumored to be a man of kindly disposition, although not entirely in command of his senses. Harada felt, with much justification, that only an islander like himself would be so soundly insulted by this old man. Once more Harada's anger welled, until he felt he could barely contain his wish to lash out with his fists.

It was not only angering to be insulted by a purportedly kind old man, but surprising to hear the feeble codger's nasty eloquence. The only other time Harada had tried to speak with the old man, there was nothing but babbled nonsense for reply. With the initial shock of Po Lee's fluency passing, Harada spoke heatedly and to the point: "Your great-grandson has stolen my boat and I demand recompense! Otherwise, how am I, an honest fisher, to make my decent living?"

Harada watched the old man's venomous glare vanish from his wrinkled visage. Perhaps the old man had never thought Lu Khen capable of robbery and was tempted to call the islander a fisher of lies. But it was a serious matter. Unloved though the victim might be, family honor would not survive mere denial of a charge of thievery.

After a period of silence, it became obvious to Harada that old Po Lee had no more eloquence left in him, but had expended his moment of lucidity. The news that his great-grandson was a thief had apparently muddled his mind. Po Lee stood there saying nothing, possibly deep in thought, more likely too confounded to think at all.

In the interval, Lu Khen's mother—dusty and sweaty— approached from the direction of the yam garden to see what was going on. Thinking to acquire a more reasonable response from the woman, Harada repeated his complaint. He thought she would cry out, "Woe upon me! My son has become a criminal!" But she was apparently too weary from the morning's labor even to solicit pity, as she was famous for doing. She said sharply,

"I have no son such as you speak of."

Today the insults were too prolific! Harada spluttered and

spat. He shook his fist before the woman's face, loudly demanding payment for the boat, telling her it would do no good to deny kinship with the culprit.

"I know nobody by that name!" the mother persisted, uncowed by the fist. By this time, Ou Koy had been attracted to the shouting of oaths. She approached, dragging a wooden hoe behind her.

"It is true," she said, more compassionately than any other person with whom he had spoken that day. "I had a brother by that name, but he has disowned his family in Buddha's name. So he is ours no longer, and we are therefore not responsible for his debts or crimes. In any case, we are incapable of paying for your boat. We are forced to work doubly throughout the season to make up for spoiled first crops, and if we manage to grow enough to see us through the next winter, it will be the first true miracle I have ever witnessed."

Harada did not wish to argue with a child, even if she did seem smarter than most of the Ou family put together. He did not much care about the likely starvation of the thief's clan, either, but if in Buddha's name the thief had disavowed any kin, then Harada knew he would have to seek elsewhere for retribution. Without one more word, curse, or farewell, Harada pushed the old man aside, snarled at the girl and the woman, and stomped off in fury.

Mother Ou returned to the gardens, for once keeping her complaints to herself. Po Lee remained in the shade of the porch, thinking more clearly than anyone realized, but keeping silent. He thought: *If I had money, I would give it to filthy Harada as payment for the boat.* But he had no money. Though he had come to this land wealthy from successful adventures, one emergency and then another had caused him bit by bit to give his horded cache over to one part of the family and then another. The last of it had gone for the education of Lu Khen's younger brother, after Lu Khen gave up his own studies in order to rule the house of Ou. Now Grandfather Po Lee could think of no way to right Lu Khen's wrong, to restore honor to the Ou family. To the folk of the islands, honor was an even more grave matter than to people of the peninsula. It struck at Po Lee's pride to think vile Harada could so righteously and justifiably gloat over an old man's disgrace.

Po Lee was glad that Koy had stayed near the porch for a while. She interrupted his self-condemning thoughts to ask, "We can speak Lu Khen's name if we want, can't we, great-grandfather?"

"We can do more than speak it," he answered. "We can go and find him."

"How is that so? And why should we do it?"

"Little one," the old man began, bending close to her ear and whispering so softly that not even the cricket on the doorstep could overhear: "You know there will be too little food for this family to survive the summer monsoons and the chill winter, for nothing has grown well. Ours will be a hungry, impoverished family of beggars because of the state of our first crops. But this could be avoided with two less mouths to feed."

"Then we will follow after my brother?"

"For the honor of the house of Ou, and so that none might starve or beg, yes. It has been long since I have adventured, but once I was good at it. I was the first to settle here, with a wife I met in my travels. You look like her, precious Koy! It will be good to travel once again. Already I feel renewed vigor!"

"The forests are wicked," said Koy, shuddering with doubts.

"I still know the ways of survival in the deepwood and the mounts," said Po Lee. "And you will learn quickly, I think."

"Yes I will," she agreed, more eager.

"And if Lu Khen will not return and take back his vow, we will settle with him in whatever country he runs to, and begin a new clan, all of us together." He lowered his voice again to tell her, "I have told few, little Koy, but this clan would not have been founded but that I, too, was forced to leave my village in distant Ho. But never mind that. We must seek clues as to Lu Khen's whereabouts. We will go

to the madwoman's kinfolk and see what they know. Rush
now. Tell no one."

Excited, Koy dropped her hoe and ran into the house to
prepare for travel. Po Lee stood on the porch, not smiling,
but not sad either. This was no hasty plan, but one nurtured
since the moment Lu Khen departed. The decision had re-
juvenated him, though to others it might not show. He felt
purpose in his life again, blood pulsing through veins. Old
muscles flexed with new anticipation. He could even see
clearer, hear better. It was a sad thing what Lu Khen had
done; but to a part of Great-grandfather Ou Po Lee, it was
more a thrill than a tragedy.

While Koy was busy slyly gathering the things great-
grandfather said were the bare necessities of foot travelers,
and hiding them for later retrieval, Po Lee ventured to the
house of Yeung, setting his staff far before each step. It
was his intent to ask the Yeungs for information regarding
Lu Khen; for in light of what Koy had told him, it appeared
unlikely the lad would go far away without the madwoman.

He discovered that the Yeung family was in a tumult.
The arrival of Po Lee, elder patriarch of the house of Ou,
only intensified the turmoil the Yeungs were experiencing.
They answered his innocent queries with rocks and abusive
language. Po Lee held his arms up to protect his head from
the projectiles, and cursed better than they, though in a
dialect they could not understand. He stumbled and fell
down twice in trying to get away.

But their cursing and shouting had not been wholly unen-
lightening. Each embellished epithet gave not only bad
wishes, but reasons for each curse. Po Lee gathered that
his grandson had kidnapped the madwoman. Worse than
that, Lu Khen had confessed his intention to take Mai Su
to the tombs of the Lost Dynasty.

This was shocking news. When Po Lee was beyond sight
of the angry Yeungs, he brushed the dust from himself and
sat down on a roadside bench of stone. He pondered the
situation.

As it happened, in all the province of Lin, Po Lee was

very likely the only person who would consider the challenge now before him. Long years before, when Po Lee was a stout young man, he had stood on a mountain overlooking the capital of an empire forgotten by all but the most shaded of myths. In those days, Po Lee was daring, having been cast from his northern homeland and as yet having established no clan of his own. He had nothing to lose, and could not settle down until his adventuring had yielded the capital required to start life anew. All the same, he did not go down the mountain in the direction of the ruins. He only gazed at that distant place, awed by the gruesome majesty of weed-choked monuments, then went elsewhere to discover his fortune.

Years later, when life was more comfortable, curiosity began to tickle at his fear, but the obligations of a settled life never let him go. Year by year he regretted more and more that he had been afraid to pursue the greatest adventure. He had many secrets from his family. The reason for his exile when a young fellow, and the cowardly fear he had felt which caused his road to veer away from the mystery of the forgotten empire, were chief among his secrets.

No one but himself knew of his lack of courage. In actuality no one would have blamed him for turning away from that haunted country; rather, they would have praised his boldness in getting as close as he did, close enough to see the faces carved upon fat towers. Yet Po Lee had kept secret from everyone but himself a sense of his own cowardice, whether or not his shame had any justification. He had lived to see a hundred years, and for more than seventy-five of those years, he had been haunted by this feeling.

Now, his great-grandson had provided the excuse needed to rectify a past moment of fear and weakness. The adventure had been put off long enough! What had gone undone in his youth would become the crowning experience of winterlife. Yet . . . how was it that he dared involve Ou Koy? There would be danger, after all. Though Po Lee had already exceeded a common share of life, little Koy's life had scarcely gotten started. If an old man died, it would be a smaller tragedy than if a tiny girl did so.

Po Lee could not face his motivations very easily. Somewhere beneath consciousness was the belief that Koy was the incarnation of a woman dead more than forty years, who had shared Po Lee's adventures for a while, then settled with him on the farm at a time before the province had a name. Each year, Ou Koy looked more and more like Fa Ling. Sensing as he did that Fa Ling had returned to him as a great-granddaughter, how could he be so cruel as to abandon her for the sake of a selfish, last adventure? Surely Fa Ling's ghost had worked hard to be reborn into the family, to see Po Lee again! He must share his last adventure with her, just as he had shared everything from the day they met until the day she died—and longer.

These thoughts only rarely tried to surface where Po Lee could understand himself better. When he was close to realizing his subconscious way of thinking, suddenly his mind would become fogged and seemingly senile, until the memories of the loss of Fa Ling and his aching sorrow were muted once again.

Instead of understanding this, Po Lee justified involving Koy with the thought that she was a born adventurer like himself, which may well have been the truth. He said to himself that only Ou Koy loved Ou Lu Khen with as much sincerity as Great-grandfather Po Lee, and this was also a true observation. It was, therefore, really Koy's decision to become a vagabond child. Po Lee's wishes had nothing to do with it—or so he told himself—and possibly his method of rationale was not so incorrect.

Having rested feet and mind, Po Lee rose from his seat along the roadside and set off toward the farm, feeling proud and confident about his decision, regardless of the incredible destination. It was a good decision to follow Ou Lu Khen.

The direction his great-grandson had taken would be impossible to deduce accurately, Po Lee realized. There were hundreds of tributaries, gorges, and rivers, especially in the valley regions halfway to the mountains, and Lu Khen's stolen boat would navigate a confusing route. There was no chance, then, of overtaking him. "Boats leave no tracks," thought Po Lee, but in the long run this would not matter, for Po Lee knew where Lu Khen would end up.

It could be supposed that Lu Khen would not abandon the boat, for it would be required for the comfort of Mai Su. The waterways provided the most indirect route, and it might well be possible to arrive on foot in the region of the tombs ahead of Ou Lu Khen. What a happy reunion it would be when Lu Khen found familiar faces waiting!

As Po Lee went along, he heard something in the grass to the left side of the road. He stopped to look that way. Out from the grass came the islander Harada. For a moment the old man and the foreigner stood on the dusty road staring at one another with mutual dislike. Then Po Lee averted his eyes and went on in a huff, pretending he was not uncomfortable about Harada standing motionless in the middle of the road, watching an old man hurry home.

Late that afternoon, Koy helped her mother prepare a repast, serving the three old ones outside as they rested in the shade of a lone willow. They fanned themselves expansively, being tired from their long day of trying, with an insufficient number of seedlings, to replace the paddy's spoiled crop. Their feast of steamed rice, lemon grass, and pickled eels eased their spirits some. But for the most part, they remained full of anger for the boy who had abandoned them to this work, the boy whose name they dared not speak.

Koy felt sorry for them. They were crotchety and stubborn, but in a few more days it would occur to them that they had lost someone they loved. Also, they did not know that after today it might be a very long time before they would see her and great-grandfather again. This would make them lonelier still, all of this so close on the heels of losing Old Uncle. For these varied reasons, Ou Koy pampered them and did not snap back at them when they were rude or indifferent to her attention.

They were served a nice meal today, but by the time winter came, good meals might well be scarce. A messenger had already been sent to a village two districts away, so that the next-younger brother would be informed of the difficult

situation and so that he would know of his new status as
oldest brother and master of the house of Ou. It would not
be possible for him to come immediately for he would have
affairs to put in order. But it was his responsibility to come
as soon as he could.

This brother, whose name was Ou Ki Vim, had become
a low-level civil servant in the place where he had moved
to, scholars not being allowed to hold office in their own
village. A low-level government commission was not exceedingly impressive, truth be told, having no attendant
salary beyond that of legal bribery from those hoping to be
served. All the same, he was the family's pride.

It could well be that Ou Ki Vim would not welcome
mastery of the old farm any more than had Ou Lu Khen.
Still, it would be unreasonable if Ki Vim resented what Lu
Khen had done; for there would be no scholar in the family
at all except for Lu Khen's insistence. Lu Khen's own desire
to pursue a degree had been fulfilled vicariously through
helping Ki Vim. When it had looked as though there would
be no funds for Ki Vim to take his examination, Great-
grandfather Po Lee revealed the last of his horded silver
and allowed Lu Khen to use it for a brother's sake. As a
result of these sacrifices, Ki Vim had become a little more
successful than he would otherwise have been. Koy felt it
was only proper that Ki Vim now wish Lu Khen success
in his first and only selfish pursuit—his pursuit of love.

Though Ki Vim would now be asked to sacrifice a minor
post, he could yet be successful at home, being adviser and
calligrapher for the local farmers who lacked education.
Therefore Koy suspected her scholar brother would not feel
so badly about the circumstance. Once everyone had made
it through this troubled year, there was no reason to assume
the farm would not prosper once again.

It would be disastrous, though, if he were unable to put
his affairs in good enough order to return before winter. It
was also to be hoped that he had been able to put aside
some savings, or at least would arrive home with a supply
of beans and rice. Otherwise there was only more misfortune
waiting for the house of Ou, though threat of winter star-

vation would certainly be eased with Koy and great-grandfather living somewhere else. Koy had to admit Lu Khen's neglect contributed to the mess of things, but others by the by would be confessing their errors, too.

When the meal beneath the willow was finished, Koy insisted that her mother relax a little longer while her good daughter took care of the pots and bowls. Since Great-grandfather Po Lee had not as yet returned from his secret errands, Koy put aside some eels and rice for him, and took the empty pots and bowls around back of the house where there was a well-curb to wash them by. As she was cleaning everything, great-grandfather slipped up unnoticed by anyone. He whispered, "I saw everybody eat a lot. They are lying underneath the willow now, bellies too full to move."

Koy gathered up the clean pots and bowls as she said, "They are sure to sleep, except for mother, but I made her promise not to move until I had cleaned these pots. If we don't go around in front of the house, she won't know I'm finished."

The conspiring pair climbed into the house through the back window. When great-grandfather stumbled and dropped one of the pots he was helping take inside, Koy said, "Shhh! If they hear us, we won't be able to slip away unnoticed!"

Po Lee hurried to the kitchen table. He took paper and brush from his pocket so that, between bites of the meal Koy had saved for him, he could write a letter.

"We must leave a note of farewell," he said, with his mouth full of rice.

"What will you say to them?" asked Koy.

"Read with me as I write it and you will see," said Po Lee. He enunciated each character in a hushed voice while Koy tried to read along: "I, Ou Po Lee, and I, Ou Koy, go upon a quest. Now there will be food enough to last through winter. Do not worry! We will return wealthy."

Po Lee looked at Koy and said, "That will keep them from fretting too much about us."

"Is it true, great-grandfather? Will we return wealthy?"

"If we return with Lu Khen, little Koy, we will return wealthy."

Wise as Ou Koy was for her few years, yet did she have naive responses to many things. She saw the quest as an easy adventure. She trusted her great-grandfather implicitly. Everything was like a game. If she knew how much danger existed in the wild world, she might well have been afraid. If she understood what a month or a season or a year really meant, she might think twice about being away from her mother. If she thought about what it must be like to live in a lean-to structure on a long, cold winter, eating nothing but swamp roots while huddling near a few small coals, she might actually have doubted it was possible to survive their journey. But all she knew was that she was going to find her brother and would have great-grandfather for protection. It had been a while since life had seemed so full of hope and joy.

She showed her great-grandfather where she had hidden four medium-sized baskets in a closet. Po Lee sorted through what Koy had packed, taking out what he thought was frivolous and putting in what she had forgotten or he had forgotten to tell her. Everything together did not add up to much, for the family could not spare much, and an old man and tiny girl could not carry a lot.

They put the baskets out the back window then climbed out after them. They thrust bamboo poles through the handles of the baskets and walked off toward the woods, each of them with baskets balanced one in front and one in back, the pole upon left shoulders. They wore straw hats and straw sandals, and Po Lee held his cane firmly in his right hand. Their clothes were already dusty by the time they were in the woods. They appeared to be poor vagabonds, which indeed they had become the instant they climbed out that back window.

They would not go far the first day, starting late as they did, and their first camp would only reinforce Koy's feeling that the trip was a veritable holiday. Pilgrimages were common in all families, so none of this as yet was very odd. After an uneventful first night in the woods, which was not so different from sleeping outside the house by the well curb for one night, Koy still had no realistic idea of what they had set out to accomplish, how hard it might prove to be.

On the second day away, Po Lee remarked, "As I told no one the precise nature of our journey, nobody is apt to worry. If I had told them we followed dear Lu Khen and his beloved madwoman to the tombs of the Lost Dynasty, surely should they die of shock!"

Great-grandfather had said this with a sort of careless gleefulness, and did not look behind to see Ou Koy's reaction. She was silent, but if he had looked at her, he would have seen by her expression that she was not happy to be informed that their destination was a place she knew about only from the scariest story anybody had ever told her. It was like a slap across her face. In light of this surprise, it was very curious that Koy did not slow her pace or waver in her determination. From one moment to the next her perception of their journey had changed entirely: from thinking of it as a holiday, to thinking of it as terrifying and dangerous. Yet, brave girl that she truly was, to the center of her soul, her new perception merely reinforced her resolve.

By the second night they still had not come very far, for her legs were short and great-grandfather's were slow. Yet in terms of emotional distance, that second night was as far as any human being had ever traveled. She had to weigh her fears against her excitement, her doubts against her trust, her love for her brother against her love for her home and the limitations of her tiny body; she even had to weigh what was logical (turning back) against what was moral (adhering to determination). She awoke often throughout that second night, picking up threads of thoughts which followed her in and out of dreams.

For a while, she became uncertain that great-grandfather was really any better at living in the woods than she—and she was no good at it at all. Her faith in the old man was a little less blind for pondering this, but in the long run she decided his wisdom in such matters was all but boundless. He had, after all, survived (and even profited by) his journey from the kingdoms of Ho, the original home of most village

clans if they traced their ancestry more than two or three
generations back. To Koy, there was nowhere on earth farther away than the motherland, where all sages except Buddha himself were born, the land which was the fount of
civilization. Great-grandfather's journey from that distant
place surely must have taught him a lot, the least of which
being how to survive in the woods of the Great Peninsula.

The morning after their second night, Koy began to miss
her mother, her two grandmothers, and her grandfather. But
great-grandfather was with her, and a brother would be
found at the far end of their road. She folded up their thin
blankets and packed them in one of the baskets. They started
on their way, great-grandfather never realizing the intense
thinking and great changes that had occurred during Koy's
long night. The changes were for the better if one most
valued courage; they were for the worse if one most valued
innocence.

Near evening, Po Lee killed a jet-black squirrel, so fast
Koy had barely seen how it had happened. The creature had
darted across the path and, quicker than a blink, great-
grandfather's staff came down on the animal's skull. It did
not even have time to feel the pain.

Great-grandfather dropped his pole and two baskets and
snatched up the dead squirrel. "We eat!" he said. And they
camped on the spot of the slaying.

Po Lee made a fire by striking two stones together, and
the two unlikely adventurers feasted on squirrel roasted on
a stick. Afterward, they cremated the bones, and blessed
the squirrel into the dens of its ancestors and thence to its
future life. When all this was done, Koy fell asleep in her
great-grandfather's arms. They leaned together against a
tree, covered with a hemp blanket. As she drifted into slumber, her final doubts were fading. Great-grandfather had
made fire with stones. He had gotten them meat with his
staff. Koy knew it would not be a bad journey, with so wise
a guardian to teach her lore and survival in the woods.

On the day when Ou Po Lee went to the house of Yeung
in search of information regarding his wayward grandson,
there was a foreigner following him. Po Lee did not detect

this shadow, nor grow suspicious later on, even though encountering the fellow on the road back home.

Harada had seen and heard everything. When the old man fled the wrath of the stone-throwing Yeungs, Harada had enjoyed the spectacle very much, feeling Po Lee merited punishment for being rude earlier that day, when visited with a complaint about a stolen boat. Harada listened to the lame granny's list of curses, and each ill wish was happily endorsed by the secret observer. He also heard, along with Po Lee, that Lu Khen was a kidnapper (in addition to being a boat thief), which crime was the source of the Yeungs' particular grudge against the house of Ou. Most important of all, Harada overheard where the thief was planning to go with the kidnap victim, Yeung Mai Su.

Due to the fact that Harada Fumiaka was from another land, the beliefs of the local population did not impress him very much; he did not perceive the overwhelming implications of Ou Lu Khen's intended quest. In fact, Harada had so little understanding or respect for local customs and points of faith that he found it inconceivable that even the villagers, fishers, and farmers took their outlandish notions seriously. Tales to scare children, that's all they were! Surely no adult believed in such things as bamboo bushes turning into snakes, flute-playing toads, talking persimmons, or a thousand years of demonic rule on earth.

From the point of view of the native populace, Harada had stupid beliefs, too; but this did not cause him to consider the possibility that whatever he believed was no less wise and no more foolish than whatever the people of the Great Peninsula took for granted. As a matter of fact, Harada did not consider himself a superstitious man. He was not very religious, and he didn't think any of his perceptions of the world were based on anything but observable fact. He sometimes felt that his ability to see through the falsehoods in people's faith and lives was what made people hate him, what caused him to be forced into exile. Although, when he was feeling less pompous, he had to admit it was actually his own criminal activities which made it expedient that he leave his homeland.

Harada considered himself smarter than other people, but

he was not smart enough to notice the similarity in his prejudices against the villagers and their prejudices against him. This mutual dislike was only reinforced by the differences in their beliefs. Once Harada had been caught throwing beans around his shanty by the canal, and the fisher thought it was a wasteful practice. He had been performing this activity due to a terrifying nightmare of the night before. The fishers made a big joke of it when he explained that beans were a weapon against evil spirits. Their laughter merely proved to Harada that the villagers were very stupid indeed, having no knowledge of things as fundamental as the power invested in beans. It was not proof that he was as superstitious as anyone else, but proof that he had settled among morons after fleeing from the archipelago.

Due to his different upbringing and a generally unperceptive nature, Harada did not even realize the two words *lost* and *dynasty* combined in such a fashion as to equal a considerable amount of dread for anyone raised in the provinces and countries of the Great Peninsula. His lack of comprehension may have been in part forgivable, as those two words were more often insinuated than spoken, and Harada could not be expected to absorb every nuance and subtlety of a language he had only learned in recent years. Tales of the Tombs of the Lost Dynasty were completely puzzling to Harada, as those tales were predicated upon a body of common knowledge, perceptions, and automatic responses which were alien to a foreigner like himself. When villagers shuddered upon hearing the conclusion of some storyteller's supernatural yarn, Harada was often left to scratch his head and wonder, "What was that about?"

Finally, even had Harada been a religious man, the form of Buddhism taught in his native land was quite different from that taught in mainland nations, this being the result of the archipelago's relative isolation. Therefore, the religious motivation for Ou Lu Khen's quest for madness struck Harada as supreme balderdash. He felt it was an absurd lie invented by the thief to hide the true purpose of the journey.

In light of all this, it is easy to see that Harada would

try to justify Lu Khen's actions in a manner more closely aligned with Harada's personal views. He tried to look at it in terms of what his own motivations and intentions would be if he were in a similar situation. Kidnapping the girl made perfect sense to Harada when he thought of it in his own terms. He had once visited the gardens around the smallhouse so that he could see the famous madwoman. He might have kidnapped the beauty himself, but for fear of reprisals!

Ou Lu Khen must have feared reprisal, too, which would explain his stealing a boat to escape from the province of Lin. But why escape in the direction of the usually shunned Tombs? Perhaps he went in that direction because it was the place where he was least likely to be hunted and brought back for punishment! On second thought, this choice of direction could be more troublesome than helpful. It would be difficult to live in an area inhabited only by backward tribes or not inhabited at all. The wiser course would have been to flee to some northern or southern district along the Great Peninsula, there to settle down with a new name. It was not likely that he would ever be discovered if he went far enough. He might even have caught a trader's ship and worked his way to Ho, a trip many people of Lin dreamed about.

Instead of any of these logical actions, Ou Lu Khen had decided to take his stolen wife inland to the ruins and tombs of an ancient capital. Harada struggled hard to think of a good reason. "If it was me, why would I go there?" It was a puzzle.

In a flash of enlightenment, Harada became certain of the answer! He was so startled by the realization that he jumped up, forgetting that he had been hiding all this while in some high grass. Po Lee was on the dusty road and saw Harada jump, so it was no good to duck back down. Harada strode boldly onto the road and stared at the old man. Pretty soon Ou Po Lee hurried away without figuring out that he had been followed to the house of Yeung. Harada took a fork in the road, going along a path in the direction of the main canal. As he walked, he looked a little less miserable

than he had looked that morning when he found his boat
was missing.

He had come to the private conclusion that the youth—
already a proven thief of boats and women—was off on a
mission of even more audacious robbery. No doubt his intentions were to open those ancient Tombs in order to remove gold and whatever else was placed with the dead
emperors of old.

A search for madness had made no sense at all, but a
search for riches was sensible to Harada. It made him feel
less helpless to have understood the boy's actions so completely. But Harada still had a few feelings of self-pity over
the matter, and thought to himself, "How unfair is life! I
live in exile, all but incapable of making a suitable living
because people in this land do not treat me with the favor
deserved by someone of my blood. I tried to make an honest,
humble living among fishers, but others take the best fishing
spots before I have a chance to get out of bed, and my
meager catches tend to spoil before I get around to selling
them. How am I to blame for this? It is the unfairness of
the situation which has forced me betimes (much against
my true nature) to participate in shady enterprises just so I
can eat. Not only have I been the repeated victim of cir-
cumstances, but I have been robbed of my boat as well,
then deprived of justice, restitution, or simple compassion
for my plight. At the same time, the thief dares to use *my*
boat to go collecting gold and such, benefiting while I suffer.
Alas! Life is indeed unkind to Harada Fumiaka!"

This wretched lecture did not really cause Harada to feel
sorrier for himself, but provided instead a foundation for
further rationale. He went on to reason that since the boat
was his, so should be the riches fetched from the Tombs
using his boat. This conclusion caused him to walk with a
bouncy gait as he went along the path.

For a moment he stopped in his tracks and looked serious.
It occurred to him that Lu Khen might settle elsewhere, due
to the fact of his illegal bride. If he never returned to the
province of Lin, how would Harada collect his boat and
everything in it?

Harada proceeded more slowly, pulling at his small beard in a pensive way. "Hmmm," he thought to himself. "Suppose the Tombs *are* guarded by some fabulous beasts. It might be unlikely, but unlikely things do happen in this world. Suppose the thief fills up my boat with riches but is overtaken by ghosts who suck all the blood out of him and his stolen bride." Harada shivered at the thought; vampirish ghosts were something that islanders believed in as much as anybody else! "Suppose this happens and my boat is just floating down the river with nobody to claim the riches!" Harada shook his head. "Well, that's not very likely to happen, is it? There are no fabulous monsters to pick him up and smash him, and no ghosts to drink his blood. He is just going to get all the gold from the Tombs and go off somewhere and live with the girl he kidnapped, and what can I do about that?"

Once more his mood was gloomy. He trudged along with head held low. But before the canal was in view, his head was held up again, for he was thinking, "People in these parts believe in fabulous monsters even though such things aren't likely to exist. If something happened to Lu Khen and his stolen bride, no one would suspect foul play, for after all he did go someplace dangerous, didn't he? Oh, what a terrible plan I have! What a wonderful, terrible plan!"

It struck Harada as tremendously clever to let Lu Khen take the risk and do the work of loading up the boat, only to be overtaken by the true owner of the boat and killed right along with the madwoman. No one would ever suspect him. And he could reclaim his boat and everything in it, which to Harada's way of thinking was only proper justice.

The problem with his plan was that there was more than one route which Lu Khen might use after leaving the Tombs with the riches, depending on whether he wanted to settle down in the north or in the south. Harada would have to get more clues before he could follow through with the plan. He would need to go snooping around the house of Ou in order to find out whatever nosy old Po Lee had uncovered about the boy.

This was just the sort of thinking and plotting which had

gotten Harada in trouble in his own country a few years
before. Even exile was not enough to teach him a lesson.
Though he thought highly of himself (due in part to his
lineage, which meant nothing to anyone outside of the
archipelago), in reality Harada Fumiaka wasn't nearly as
smart as he thought he was. He had clever aspects all right,
but basically he was shortsighted, narrow-minded, and
greedy. Maybe he was stupid, too, but people who act mostly
out of narrow-mindedness and greed often look stupid
whether or not they are.

In his mind's eye, he pictured the contents of the Tombs:
surrounding a sarcophagus were teakwood chests of jade
and silver; statues stood all about, cast in solid gold; the lid
of the sarcophagus was itself encrusted with rare jewels.
Harada imagined this and more, all waiting to be claimed
by whomever was smart enough to overlook silly superstitions. Harada's mouth watered. He drooled. He stood outside his shanty on the canal's bank and rubbed his hands
together, getting more excited as he thought about how
things were bound to go for him.

With wealth, the people of Lin, or another province,
would certainly begin to admire him. People always liked
whoever was successful. They would envy him, too, and
bow down in the dirt when he walked along the streets. He
would have his choice of many wives as well. Maybe he
would take his wealth and move to the kingdoms of Ho,
where civilization was oldest and there were many sophisticated splendors to amuse the rich. Or he might be able to
return to his own country, since it was always possible to
buy one's way back into favor, crimes being instantly forgotten at a price.

He scurried into his little lean-to shanty. The place was
a mess. He threw open a battered chest made of lacquered
pigskin. Inside were mostly tattered raiments, but at the
very bottom was something of value kept in a secret com-
partment. He took out a long bag and removed from it a
sheathed sword.

Many times Harada had considered pawning the sword,
but mainlanders had no concept of either the intrinsic or

spiritual value of such a weapon. He could never get as much money as it would require to balance out the loss. In his own land, the longsword was evidence of class standing. A man might be impoverished and criminally minded, but if he owned a sword such as this, it proved that somewhere in his family tree there was blood of worth. People moved aside for anyone with such family ties. During his years in exile, the sword had often reassured him that he was an important fellow, however badly he was treated.

He couldn't use the weapon very well, but on the other hand, he wasn't totally inept with it. Against farmers or fishers who had probably never held a sword in their lives, he could be most formidable if he wanted to make an issue of it.

He unsheathed the weapon and gazed along its curve, imagining the contents of the Tombs reflected in the polished metal. "A lord must protect his holdings!" he said aloud, for he had decided on being a lord, one way or another, when he was rich enough to buy important friends.

Later that evening, he was hiding in a copse of trees behind the house of Ou. He saw Ou Koy washing pots by the well curb. Pretty soon, Ou Po Lee came sauntering out of the woods, not far from where Harada had been hiding, which gave the foreigner a start. If Po Lee's hearing and vision had been perfect, he might well have noticed where Harada was crouching.

Po Lee and Koy crawled through the back window, which naturally caused Harada to think something was afoot. He slipped out of the copse and slunk along until he came to the window. He hid beneath the sill and listened to what they were saying inside. In this way he uncovered their secret plan to follow after Ou Lu Khen.

Harada slipped away to the copse once more, thinking how well everything was working. He wouldn't have to find Lu Khen on his own, but need only follow the old man and the child. There would be no difficulty killing feeble Po Lee and tiny Koy, once they had found Lu Khen for him.

Pretty soon the oldest and youngest members of the house of Ou were putting baskets filled with travel needs out the back window. Directly, they were merrily on their way, not suspecting that Harada Fumiaka and his sword were never far behind.

A shimmering black cloud moved against the darkness of the starry sky, descending from the mountain heights into the lowlands and the river valleys. The size of the cloud appeared to vary from smaller than a house to larger than a village full of houses. The stars could not shine through it, although the cloud's icy glimmer was in itself quite star-like. It came lower and lower until it brushed the tops of the trees. Its touch did not cause leaves to move, so the cloud must have lacked true substance. But when it had flowed onward through high branches, the motionless leaves it left behind were iced and brittle despite the warmth of the late spring night.

A lone monkey sleeping in the crook of a tree chanced to wake and, seeing the approach of the expanding/contracting blackness, made ready to dash away. But the cloud grazed the monkey in passing and froze it to a branch. Much later, when the monkey's blood began to thaw, its frozen grip came loose and the poor thing fell to the ground where its corpse was found by insects and worms.

The cloud moved swiftly, without regard for the direction of any breeze, seeming to have a mind of its own, and a destination. Its dimensions had contracted to their minimum and elongated somewhat to slip between the heights of trees. It continued eastward, having come from the direction of the Lost Dynasty's final stronghold west of the mountains.

The cloud slowed its speed when it came to a certain stream and sent a narrow finger of black mist downward as though to sniff the surface of the water. The finger pulled back into the main body of the cloud. Then it changed its direction for the first time since appearing in the west.

It followed above the spring as though the water were a highway. Soon it had come upon a boat with two occupants, one of them unconscious. The cloud began to pulsate with malevolence. It began its slow descent toward the boat, intent upon enveloping the small vessel with murderous frigidity.

* * *

Yeung Mai Su had been roused from slumber by the sound of Ou Lu Khen's head connecting with the overhanging branch, and his collapse onto the floor of the boat. She sat up and gazed around until her eyes settled upon Lu Khen's sad repose. It took her a moment to understand what had happened to him. The leaves of the thick branch above the boat were still shaking from Lu Khen's impact. When she realized how he must have knocked himself unconscious while poling through the darkness, she felt immediate empathy, for he was bound to awaken with a large, sore knot upon his forehead.

It took the tiniest fragment of time for a number of impressions to pass through the madwoman's mind. She had come along on the journey in order to be near Lu Khen, whose company pleased her always, but there was nothing beyond this togetherness which struck her as having much importance. Thus she had not done much more than ride along in a disinterested posture, letting Lu Khen handle things as he decided. Lu Khen by contrast was of a much less fortunate disposition; he took the quest so seriously that he was unable to enjoy the passing moments of his life. He tried hard to succeed. Yet he was so unclear about his chosen path that he probably would not recognize success should he achieve it. He would probably struggle right on past it, missing his only chance. How much better it would be if he could cease to consider yesterday with regret and tomorrow with trepidation, to begin instead to feel the passing moments to the utmost—be they moments of pain or happiness.

Although Mai Su did not share in Lu Khen's emotional investment with the journey, she did at least wish that Lu Khen's mind could be more at ease. She felt compassion for his terrible fixation on the irrevocable past and the unknowable future; she wished to do something or another to relax his constantly nervous state.

She noticed that the boat was drifting away from the overhanging branch and from the pole which Lu Khen had left stuck in the mud when he was whacked on the head. Mai Su thought, almost abstractly, that Lu Khen would be awfully upset to lose the pole. She stood up, walked to the edge of the boat, and made a grab for the upright pole. She caught it just in time, nearly losing her balance but not quite going headfirst into the water.

It was rare for Mai Su to take such an active part in things, even such a simple part as saving the boat's pole from being lost. She did not hesitate, however, for it would keep Lu Khen from having one more reason to consider his existence too much trouble.

Standing in the boat beneath the night, one hand holding the pole which trailed behind the drifting boat, Yeung Mai Su suddenly became aware of a sable, shimmering presence. When she saw this fragment of night-darker-than-the-night, she was reminded of satin silk softer than kitten's fur. She smiled at the descending cloud and somehow her lack of fear stayed its progress. It lowered itself onto the surface of the stream. Water turned to ice beneath the glistening blackness. White crystalline fingers shot out across the surface. The crystals snapped and tinkled, reminding Mai Su of gentle music.

The cloud kept pace with the drifting boat, but so long as Mai Su's smiling face was watching, the cloud seemed incapable of getting closer. Mai Su never suspected danger. There was an inexplicable sameness about the shimmering blackness of the cloud and Mai Su's moist, dark eyes. She and the cloud were, perhaps, polar extremes, twins but opposites. As she found beauty in the terrible cloud, so must it have found something terrifying in Mai Su's beauty. Poles can never touch one another; thus the boat and its occupants were safe.

In a while she became disinterested in the cloud, but even when her dark eyes turned away from it, it could not get close. Mai Su's attention was drawn to Lu Khen, whose expression looked tortured as he lay motionless. She began to sing one of her strange melodies, intent upon soothing Lu Khen, turning his unconsciousness into a normal slumber. As she sang, Lu Khen's tight expression began to relax.

The melody was weirdly beautiful, conveying the ache and overwhelming pity she felt for all beings, most especially the boy she loved. Her ache and pity was not born of any sense that the world's unhappiness was inherently pitiful. The pitiable part was that most people, including Ou Lu Khen, could not comprehend the joy of sad emotions. Mai Su rejoiced in sorrow, considered it as meaningful a friend as happiness. The deepest agony could be a boon, but only to the mad. Poor Lu Khen was an excruciatingly rational fellow; and rational people rarely made sensible order of their lives. Sanity and logic were illusions. Madness was the means by which to escape the falsehood of reasoning. That most of humanity could not comprehend this was the source of Mai Su's pity.

Mai Su spied a phosphorescence far down the narrow river, coming toward her from the west. As it came nearer, she saw that there were actually two glows: The one that flew above the water, and the one that was its reflection. It was a blood-colored light and a familiar sight to Mai Su. She continued her song, attracting the glow, and the cold black cloud behind her began to withdraw into the forest. Whether it wished to avoid the magic of her song or the approaching ruddy light was hard to say.

As the cloud withdrew along the underbrush, leaves of ferns and young trees became white with frost. Small mammals luckily slept beneath the ground, but nonetheless felt the sudden chill above. Little furry families huddled closer in their burrows and among the roots, sleeping less easily than they had done a few moments before.

The flame dove lighted on the tip of the pole Mai Su had been holding all this while. She was glad to see her favorite bird friend, and curious about the object it was holding in its beak. The flame dove dropped its gift directly into Mai Su's free hand.

It was paper thin, hammered from pure gold. It was oval, large as her palm, and engraved with ancient symbols. It was heavy considering its flimsiness, and flawless, which was a miracle considering it was so fragile that Mai Su might easily have crinkled it into a foil ball.

Mai Su had never happened to see gold in her life, for it was not a thing the daughter of a peasant ever acquired.

All the same, she was excited by the object, for there was an odd familiarity about the embossed symbols, which she felt instinctively were somehow related to the words she used when singing. She had ceased to sing while examining the oval of gold foil, and her expression became somewhat puzzled while she suspected some affinity between curious symbols and curious songs.

As she gazed upon the thin object, the tiny symbols seemed more and more obviously to be arranged in a way to form a larger pattern. It was a map. The symbols had been inscribed in such a way as to form a picture of the major features of the Great Peninsula's central lands. She recognized the range of mountains, dividing the oval down the middle. On the east side were the forests, rivers, streams, valleys and such, through which Ou Lu Khen had attempted blindly to lead them. On the east side was the mysterious country which was their intended destination.

Judging by the map, Lu Khen had gotten them as far as a deep, wide, forested basin, crisscrossed with hundreds of streams and tributaries. From within the basin, it would not be possible to see the mountains, though the horizon would still look far away. She could also see that it would be possible for a boat to travel about the intricate maze of waterways, never finding a route out of the basin. Only a few small rivers would take them away from the labyrinth.

She looked again at the sleeping youth, whose face was now utterly peaceful. He stirred and for a moment Mai Su thought he might awaken. His movement startled her enough so that she dropped the gold map. It floated on the surface of the water for a moment, then sank slowly, slowly, like a feather on a breeze, or a fishing lure tugged gently on a line. It vanished into the silt and mud and darkness.

The flame dove cooed softly from its perch at pole's tip. It flew off, then hovered near Mai Su. It cooed again and started to fly away, but came back. Mai Su was still considering the characters on the gold foil she had dropped overboard. The flame dove wanted her to follow.

Yeung Mai Su began to pole the boat up the river, keeping near the bank. The flame dove lit the way, a meteoric marker in the dark ahead. The madwoman became quite confused but not the least upset as she tried to think why she was doing this, why the flame dove wished for her to do it. It was not entirely due to her wish to help Ou Lu Khen be a happier man, though certainly he would be pleased to awaken and see the mountains had returned. Her vague recognition of the symbols on the foil brought to her by the flame dove were part of Mai Su's newfound motivations. They had awakened something inside her, whether vague remembrances of dreams or past lives she was uncertain. Although she had never formed any clear understanding of the reasons why Lu Khen wished so much to visit the nameless, ancient capital across the mountains, she did know that for the first time she, too, must find it, if for altogether different reasons.

The quest was now hers as well.

Ou Lu Khen never knew what changed Yeung Mai Su. He had awakened with a sore head, and saw her sleeping at the front of the boat, looking like an angel or heavenly fairy. He could also see the distant mountains, and was much relieved to find them less illusive than the day before, when they had seemed to vanish altogether. He did not suspect that Mai Su had brought about their fortunate circumstance and rendered absurd Lu Khen's fear that a whole mountain range was missing. To Lu Khen, it seemed merely that the boat had drifted back on course of its own accord while he had been unconscious.

He did, however, by the end of the day, realize that Mai Su was no longer a burden which he had taken upon his shoulders by his own desire, someone incapable of helping things along. Rather, she was taking equal responsibility for their journey and survival. She stood in the boat and gathered small, sour, but nourishing fruit from the briars they passed along the riverbanks. She fed these to Lu Khen, as once her grandmother had fed her, so that he could continue to pole toward the mountains in pursuit of their shared quest.

She even indicated from time to time the direction she preferred the boat to try. Despite the fact that Lu Khen had no reason to believe she knew the way any better than he did, there was at the same time no reason to believe he knew the direction better than Mai Su. Therefore it did not trouble him that she desired to play navigator. Her choice of route might well be divinely inspired, whereas his own choices could only be the chance and random guesses of an ordinary man.

Neither did Lu Khen ever know the flame dove had visited the partly covered boat in the night, for he had not once awakened from an odd and pleasant dream. Pleasant dreams had been rare of late, so he cherished what he remembered of this one, rethinking and rethinking the experience as he poled toward the mountains. His thinking kept him company, too, for Mai Su still had never spoken save in song.

He recalled how, in the dream, he had been a pheasant. Perhaps a subconscious longing for the peace of Mai Su's garden had brought about a nostalgic dream for a flowery place of birds; or the dream may have been a remembrance of a former life, supposing he could have been a pheasant before he was a man. In any event, in the dream, he was definitely a pheasant, bold and colorful, self-assured, long plumed, with no cares in the world, and with a covey of admiring hens.

This was not Mai Su's garden that he dreamt himself within. It was far larger. Even allowing that a pheasant's perspective makes things quite a bit more vast, still this was not Mai Su's place. And that was no small pagoda, either, even allowing for his lower perspective. It was a gigantic temple, larger than the entire monastery in the hills near Lu Khen's home village. As a pheasant, he had no recollection of the village or the monastery in the hills, yet some detached part of himself was making such comparisons anyway. This place of his dream would have been awe inspiring even without the extra dash of wonder a pheasant's view provided.

Out of curiosity, the pheasant which was Lu Khen strutted about, inspecting his boundless, flowery territory. He half flew, half hopped up one wide, gray stone step. Then he took another step, and then another. Finally he came to the top-most stair.

He investigated the perimeters of the terrace, glancing

here and there, nonchalantly approaching the temple. Soon he came upon an entrance and peered inside. There was a long, long corridor leading into darkness. The bird entered, less cocksure, but wondering.

He turned his small head one way and then the other, so that his two fields of vision could scan the considerable heights of the stone walls. There was a strange, narrative tableau engraved on the high walls, but Lu Khen's bird thoughts could not pick out a story. On the pillars there were written characters which, to a bird, looked like the marks left by industrious hens, though how they could have been scratching for seed on a vertical surface, he could not figure out.

Walking around a corner, the pheasant was confronted by an engraving of a huge, winged monster! The pheasant ruffled up his feathers and threatened the engraving, but it did not move. Lu Khen the pheasant considered his opponent's immobility to be evidence of victory, and was no longer frightened.

Far along the dark corridor, a tiny light appeared. It was a candle in the hand of a black-robed, bald-headed old man. The man came scuttling down the hall yelling, "Shoo! Get out!" The pheasant took to flight, a flurry of feathers heading back toward the sunlight.

In the huge gardens, beneath a flowering plum, with only his bruised ego, the pheasant preened his feathers and made indignant clucking sounds.

❧ THREE ☙

The Killer

KOY BROKE HERSELF a stout limb from a fallen tree and walked along behind the old man, casting her stick before her feet in imitation of Po Lee with his staff. Like him, she balanced two baskets across her shoulders and stooped a bit, and hobbled. Po Lee was a kind of hero to her, for what reason she could not say, never having witnessed him performing heroic deeds. But hero he was, and being so, she felt as though she were emulating someone wonderful, not mocking the gait of some doddering codger.

She listened closely when he pointed out which plants were edible and which were not; how to find birds' nests and ducks' eggs; set traps to capture small mammals; and recognize animals by their spoor. He told her which herbs were medicinal, which were deadly, and which helped preserve food or improve taste. She remembered everything.

She helped him dig certain kinds of roots which they would later cook and eat, using an excellent recipe Po Lee remembered from the old days of his youth and travels, when roots were often the only things he could find to eat. It seemed to Koy that their meals were more variegated than when they lived on the farm; and certainly the meals were more fun.

Mostly they walked along, their baskets balanced on their poles across their left shoulders, their staffs held forth in their right hands. They stopped to rest fairly often, since neither was used to the endless pace.

"In the week we've been traveling, great-grandfather, we haven't seen another human being!"

"That's not so unusual," said Po Lee. "Our race has lived up and down the coast of the Great Peninsula for only a few hundred years; our own particular village has been settled for barely two generations. In fact, when I brought my wife there, there was nobody else at all, except in that old monastery which was founded by some wandering saint a long time ago. None of our race has penetrated inland very far because there is no reason to do so; it would only make it harder to trade lumber and native spices with northern countries. Our own village is about as far inland as any of our own race ever goes. Even so, we are liable to meet some kind of people or another pretty soon!

"It was none of our race made the canals. We didn't make all the roads, either. Some of the people came down the peninsula because of northern famines which people have almost forgotten now. They came through thick forests and their bodies were sliced by bamboo leaves. They were surprised to find a good place to live already started up by me and your great-grandmother, whom you never knew! And I was surprised to have them coming from all over! When they asked who made the canals, and who made the grown-over roads, there wasn't anybody had an answer, least of all me. But the monks speculated that it was connected somehow to the older race that still lives here in the forest under primitive conditions.

"It seems unlikely they could do it, but it's possible they were a mightier people at one time or another. Maybe they are all that remains of the Lost Dynasty. Or they might have had nothing whatsoever to do with the road building and canal digging. How can we know? If we run into members of some tribe or another, we can ask them about it!" Po Lee spread his gums and laughed, but Koy did not see the joke.

Children were sometimes told about the aborigines in a way to make the forests seem fearful, thereby to keep children from wandering off too far. When Great-grandfather Po Lee mentioned there might be some people of that sort around, it made her shiver. "Do they eat children and chop off heads?" she asked, trying to sound complacent about it, as though it were merely a point of idle curiosity.

"I never heard of them eating children," said Po Lee, who had just put down his load and was sitting on a log. He pulled a large leaf from a tree and used it to fan himself. "It's true they're known to chop off heads, though. They do it to enemies. This is a common practice in the kingdoms of Ho, too, so it isn't necessarily an uncivilized trait! I don't think we have anything to worry about, as long as we don't do anything to make enemies out of them."

"You're sure of that?" asked Koy, looking relieved but wanting a double check.

"I haven't passed this way in more than fifty years!" said her great-grandfather. "Who can be sure of anything?"

"I guess things could change a lot after so long," said Koy, not feeling so relieved after all.

"I guess they can," agreed Po Lee, never once realizing Koy had been hoping for more specific and encouraging replies. Sometimes he just didn't realize she was a little girl. It was nice to be treated with the respect of an adult, but sometimes she frankly felt confused about things though she was compelled to put up a good front, trying to seem a more mature sort.

Some people said the primitive condition of the inland tribal people was due to their being descended from the Lost Dynasty's slaves or peasantry, that once they were a sophisticated people but were toppled by the infamy of that dim age. If they were really somehow related to the frightful Lost Dynasty, then surely there was cause to worry about meeting them. Koy imagined them as a race of bogies! She didn't like to think about it, and changed the subject.

"Remember when we stayed at the monastery that one night?"

Po Lee made a face. "The forest floor is more comfortable than that cold place!"

"I keep thinking," said Koy, "about what that one monk said, about what Lu Khen had in mind."

"What about it?" said Po Lee.

"Well, do you think he can succeed? That monk thinks Lu Khen decided on a quest for madness, so that he could be more like Yeung Mai Su and therefore a proper husband for her. What if he succeeds? He might not be the same brother at all if he were crazy!"

"It's no good to worry about such things before we have to," said Po Lee. He took some wild fruit out of one of his baskets and passed one to Koy. "But there's no call to be afraid about it. We are going a shorter route than Lu Khen, so we will get to the Tombs first. We can keep him from opening them up. He is bound to listen to reason. No sense playing with old bones!"

"If he's committed to doing it in order to go crazy," said Koy, "we might not be strong enough to hold him back."

"I've been thinking about that, too," said Po Lee, "and I believe I know exactly what to say to make Lu Khen feel better about everything. It's too bad I didn't think of it before, because he came to me asking my opinion previously, but I wasn't thinking straight just then. I didn't quite understand what he needed. Now that I have begun to feel like a useful man again, and started to feel stronger and think more clearly, it may be possible for me to act like the wise old man everybody wanted me to be! Yes, I know just what to tell Lu Khen; he won't be disappointed in me again."

"I don't think anyone ever doubted your wisdom, great-grandfather," Koy said with a note of indignation, for she at least had never doubted him. Po Lee was glad of her opinion. Then she asked, "What exactly can you tell him that will make him decide against his quest for madness?"

"As I see it," said Po Lee, "it's really a point of religion, and religion is a malleable thing. Although the Wheel-Turning Buddha says the sane cannot wed the mad because the mad are special, the Stick-Swishing Buddha doesn't say the same thing. Not very many people follow the Stick-Swishing Buddha these days, but once he was very popular. I don't see any reason why Lu Khen couldn't change religions."

"Lu Khen is a pious fellow," said Koy. "Maybe he won't change religions just to suit his end."

Po Lee sighed. "If my first argument doesn't work," he said, "I have another. I will make him come with me to a district in Ho, the place where I was born. I'm not supposed to go back there, but I'm sure I've outlived everybody who might remember me! I've no personal desire to return, of course, but for Lu Khen's sake I would do it. As it happens, there is a temple there where a beautiful bodhisattva named Kwa-Hin blesses anyone who wants to get married, without regard for the laws of other Buddhas or of mortal governors. In this temple, people of opposing faiths may wed, people of the same sex can marry one another, and people of upper and lower classes can be united. The ceremony is the same for everyone. All other sects admit that in such matters, Kwa-Hin is the final authority and voice of Buddha. I'm sure the nuns who speak for the bodhisattva will be able to bless Lu Khen's desire to marry a madwoman and hers to marry him. There's no question about it."

"I'm impressed to hear it!" exclaimed Koy. "But Ho is a long way off, isn't it? Isn't it at the far end of the world?"

"Not so far as that," said Po Lee. He smiled and, for a moment, felt philosophic as he added, "Really it is closer to the *center* of the world!" Probably it was not true that Po Lee had no desire to return to Ho.

"Well, we cannot take advantage of any of your good ideas if Lu Khen beats us to the Tombs and opens them up before we can stop him."

"We're slow, it's true. But I know the direct route, whereas Lu Khen will have to try several tributaries and streams before he will find one that goes safely between the mountains. Even if he gets lucky about it, the rivers are very winding and indirect. If he leaves his boat behind and decides to climb over a mountain rather than find a pass between them, in that case we would be in trouble. But I think he will keep the comfort of the boat for Mai Su's sake. She has lived a protected life and wouldn't like to hurry."

Po Lee took up his load and they started walking again. He checked the position of the sun periodically to make sure they were going in the right direction. As the day progressed, their legs were aching more than usual, for the lay of the land was tilted slightly upward. Though not steep, it was wearing.

Ou Koy spun around at one point and said softly, "Did you hear that?" Po Lee was glad of any excuse to stop and mop his brow. He looked back the way they had come and said,

"What did you hear?"

"Tribal people maybe."

"Oh, they are still a little ways ahead of us, Koy. You shouldn't start worrying about them any sooner than is necessary."

She took a few steps down the mild slope, looking intently. It was not possible to see far through the dense woods.

"I heard something, though."

"A fox?"

"Bigger than a fox, I'm sure."

"Anyway, foxes don't make noise," Po Lee remembered. "My hearing isn't good, so I have to take your word for it. Do you hear anything again?"

"No."

"Then maybe it was nothing after all."

Koy nodded her head and said, "I guess it wasn't anything." She rejoined her great-grandfather and they trudged up the path, seeming awfully slow. Po Lee wanted to stop and rest again, but Koy pointed out that they had already rested several times. "If we're to get to the ruins of the Lost Dynasty's capital before Lu Khen does, we really shouldn't stop so many times." Po Lee agreed to that.

They came to a rise, and things leveled off. The forest opened into a breezy meadow, grasses swaying and looking like the sea. They had a perfect view of distant mountains. They were faded and looked as though someone had painted them with watercolors on blue parchment.

"It's far away," said Po Lee. "Doesn't look any closer than the last time we had a view."

"We do travel pretty slowly," Koy reminded him.

"I wonder if we're slow because we're afraid of where we're going?" Po Lee speculated, never having considered this before.

"If that's the only reason," said Koy, "then we should forget our fears and hurry up."

"I guess you must be right."

Throwing away her toy walking stick, Koy clutched the hem of her great-grandfather's robe and urged him onward with herself. The path was easier now that there was no more uphill slope. She looked into Po Lee's wrinkled face, and he looked into her flat features, and they smiled at one another, as though they shared a secret. The secret was that they were indeed very much afraid.

An unexpectedly heavy rain sent Harada running for the insufficient cover of a half-hollowed tree. The tree was still alive, but only barely. An old wound—originally the loss of a single limb—had given a foothold to some wood-eating bugs. The bugs had enlarged the tree's injury until there was a place big enough for a man to sit inside, if he hunched himself together enough. Harada squatted in the hollow with his sword across his lap, teeth chattering. The bugs still infested the interior of the tree. They dropped down his shirt and crawled up his ankles, making the dry place as uncomfortable as the deluge.

Harada had been having a hard time. In the week of trailing Po Lee and Koy, he had lost a lot of weight. He had been a bit overweight previously, but if things continued to be difficult for him, his new trim figure would eventually become rawboned. He hadn't thought it would be so difficult to survive in the forests. Had he been tracking some hail and hearty fellow instead of an old man and a little girl, surely Harada would have been unable to keep up at all.

It wasn't that he wasn't a strong enough individual; strength had nothing to do with surviving in the wilderness. He simply didn't know what was good to eat and what was deadly; didn't know how to set traps or where to look for nests and burrows; lacked the most basic skills which were required if one's route were to be made easy.

More than once he had spied upon the campsite of Po Lee and Koy, envying old Po Lee's knowledge of living in the wilds. Harada had smelled their stews of wild grains, roots, and sometimes squirrel and rabbit, laced with sweet wild herbs, and he was barely able to control the urge to run into their camp and steal what they were cooking.

By observing them he had at least figured out how and where to dig certain roots, and he had sometimes spent nights at the abandoned campsites of Po Lee and Koy (Po Lee was expert at making hasty tents from leaves and branches). But it was necessary that Harada keep his distance and thus it was impossible to learn much from his poor vantage points.

Since Harada had investigated the workings of several of Po Lee's traps and snares, there had been, for a while, the hope of catching meat. Unfortunately, Harada lacked Po Lee's knowledge of where to *set* the traps to catch something fairly quickly. Basically all he had been able to figure out was which sorts of roots were edible. After a week, this diet was becoming most unpalatable, especially considering that Harada lacked cooking expertise. It looked as though he would continue losing weight.

Huddled in the bug-infested hollow, Harada sneezed. A stream of water found a new route down the bark of the tree. The runnel came to an end at the top of the hollow and arched into Harada's dry place, wetting his face. He thought of the old man and child in one of their fine, leafy lean-to tents, a fire at the entrance, eating something nice while they waited for the rain to stop.

He envied them so much, and felt so miserable, that hatred began to form in a more and more tangible desire to punish them for what he imagined to be insults and injuries to himself. As soon as they had led him either to Lu Khen or the tombs of gold (or both), he vowed to kill them on the spot. Thinking this, and caressing the wooden scabbard of his sword, he felt a little better.

When the rain abated, he waddled out of the hollow and slowly straightened himself out. He soon realized he was bitten all over his back and legs. There were so many bug bites on him that he looked as though he had a terrible rash. It itched something awful. "Nothing's going quite as well as I had thought," Harada said to himself. But hardship only heightened his stubbornness. The imagined riches would make all the present indignity and trouble worthwhile; he would not give up.

He slapped his own face, leaving a smear of bug upon his cheek. Then, cursing, he went slinking through the forest to see what sort of progress the old man and the child were making.

The moon had grown from new to full by the time Lu Khen and Mai Su found they could go no further in the small, covered boat. A tremendous waterfall stood in their way, a gorgeous thing but a nuisance, so tall they could not see what was on the plateau above. The waters shot downward and bounced and frothed along the way, parting in several places, turning into a deluge by the time it struck into large pools. Clouds obscured the falls and misty spray obscured the bottom. The full moon lit those mists; moonbows made a road of colorful arches, zigzagging upward. Mai Su craned her neck to look up and up, her face serene as though she saw only the paradisiacal lay of the land, rather than the troublesome barrier.

It no longer seemed to Lu Khen (at that moment at least) that Mai Su's choice of route had been divinely inspired. He thought it might have been better if he had been less influenced by her variously subtle and overt indications of the way she preferred them to go. Often when a stream or river had forked, she would point emphatically at the tributary she liked best, as though she knew where they were going. It hadn't been possible for her to know, Lu Khen reflected, and this dead end was what the gamble had led them to.

Had they happened on a better route, they should have been able to take the boat between the high mountains without having to dare the heights. There were numbers of deep gorges, and one or another certainly ought to prove a handy pass. But they had found no such pass and, as it stood now, the choices were to abandon the comfort of the boat and bold the high trails, carry the boat across land in search of another stream, or retrace their route and try to find some passable gorge somewhere else.

Realizing he had been thinking Yeung Mai Su had led them to this place, Lu Khen slapped his head guiltily. "It shouldn't have occurred to me to place the blame on you," he said, not certain serene Mai Su was listening. "Our route has been random all along, our success a matter of luck. If it hadn't been this huge waterfall standing in our way, sooner or later it would have been something else. Really this is my fault for lacking a better plan."

A plan was necessary now, that was for sure. Lu Khen didn't think he and Mai Su were strong enough to carry the boat up the steep paths to the top of the waterfall, nor could he be certain there was a safe river up there if they made it. Retracing their route would be a waste of a lot of time, but perhaps it could not be helped. On the other hand, if they went afoot, forgetting about the boat completely, they might well find a straighter route than the winding tributaries provided. It would be a harder trip but a shorter one.

Now that he had thought of all these options, Lu Khen felt less helpless about things. He was able to enjoy the beauty of the place they had come upon. Really it was easier to take in all the beauty and cease to think about everything else, than to make a final decision on which option he would choose for them. Imperturbable Mai Su at least did not worry about a thing.

"Really we should retrace our route for a while," Lu Khen said to the madwoman. She was gazing into the moon-lit mists of the great falls, not seeming to listen. Suddenly she was on her feet, rocking the boat in her haste. Taking off her shoes and clutching them in her hands, she leapt into the shallow waters before Lu Khen could stop her. She hurried to the shore of the wide pond and dropped down on the wet moss as though ready for a midnight picnic lunch.

Lu Khen called to her from the end of the boat, reiterating his feeling that, "Really we should go back down the river and find another way through the mountains!" Maybe she could not hear him because of the roar of the falls. Certainly she did not budge.

Somewhat annoyed, Lu Khen stuck the pole into the sand and silt, then tied the boat to this anchor. He took off his sandals and waded ashore, joining Mai Su in silent reverie. After a while, he leaned near her ear and said gently, "It's a lovely place, I know. But really we must find a way to continue our journey."

Still she would not listen and Lu Khen was afraid he might be forced to pick her up and carry her back to the boat. It would be the first time he had used force of any kind to get Mai Su to do his bidding. He did not like the idea of doing it. "Well, maybe we can camp here until morning," he relented.

Yeung Mai Su raised a slender arm and pointed with a long finger. A chill ran through Ou Lu Khen, for he had imagined the roar of the waterfall was the voice of a giantess. He looked where Mai Su was pointing and his eyes grew round.

The mists at the base of the falls were swelling toward the top while the clouds and spray at the top moved down to meet those from the bottom. It was difficult to be sure if the waters of the great falls were coming down or falling up! The swelling mists began to coalesce into a monstrous shape. It was a tenuous shape at first, still so much cloud and mist and spray that Lu Khen was uncertain what he was seeing. Surely the darkness and moonshadows were conspiring to fool his vision!

The shape was that of a crocodile raised up on its back legs, its tail wrapping around itself, its head near the top of the falls. The moonbows had become a colorful sheen of scales.

Lu Khen felt as though he and Mai Su were insects near the heel of a goddess; and goddess the lizard seemed, rather than a god, because of the sensuous and stately curve of its stance. The snout of the mist monster was long and spindly

wendy wees

thin and had a knob at its end; the full length of the thin, rigid snout was lined with white teeth.

Mai Su was still pointing at it, her expression as placid as ever. For the first time in her life, she spoke without it having to be a song. She said a single word:

"Makara."

Lu Khen did not know which thing to be more shocked about, the monster, or Mai Su speaking. It felt miraculous that she should speak at all, but that she should speak the name of a creature she could not possibly have seen before was all the more surprising.

Lu Khen went immediately to his knees and held his folded hands above his head, shouting a prayer to the Makara, the spirit of the falls. He praised Earth and Water for the beauty they had made together in this part of the world. He praised the sharp teeth and sleek body of the Makara. He praised and thanked the Makara for inducing Yeung Mai Su to speak for the first time in her life. In response to all this, the crocodilelike being flexed its small talons. Its long, toothy jaws seemed to smile. The creature swelled larger and higher.

The prayer of Lu Khen became more fervent as he begged safe passage, never quite saying that he was afraid the Makara might bend down and gobble up the two small humans. The pool churned white and frothy around the haunches of the creature. It turned its long, thin face in the direction of the madwoman and the praying man. He closed his eyes, gritted his teeth, and alternately chanted sutras of Buddha and begged the Makara to overlook their obnoxious presence in her wild domain.

When Lu Khen dared to open his eyes, he saw that Mai Su had gone to the edge of the pool and had lifted her arms to the misty being as though she were the priestess of Makara. Moonlight bathed her and she seemed to glow. The slender, upright Makara bowed toward Mai Su, causing Lu Khen to lose his breath, until he realized the monster was only bowing as in obeisance to Yeung Mai Su!

When the Makara stood tall again, its tenuous form began to dissolve back into spray and cloud. Its fading, vaporous

image enfolded the little boat and drew it toward the center
of the falls. The boat began to spin around and around,
caught in the crashing waters. Soon it was sucked beneath
the surface just as the Makara, too, completely vanished.
A cold breeze carried the last remnants of the Makara away,
like common mist.

Lu Khen joined Mai Su at the water's edge. He tried to
match her calm, but it was difficult. He said, "The Makara
seems to have taken our boat as a tribute. I suppose that is
better than taking *us* to the bottom of the pool! But it means
a hard time for you and me. We will have to take that steep
trail to the top of the falls and see if we can find a path
through mountain forests. Can you do it, Mai Su?"

Offering her his hand, he pulled her toward the cliff wall.
Neither he nor she had ever climbed mountains before; but
goats or some other animal had already marked a trail which,
though tiring, was not dangerous.

The stars were bright, the moon the largest Lu Khen had
ever seen, seemingly made of molten gold. It was easy to
see the steep path. By the time they reached the top, the
moon had set, and he and Mai Su had worn themselves out.
He found some large ferns and broke off enough of the long
leaves to make a mattress, and broke some more to use as
covers. He and Mai Su cuddled chastely in the pile of ferns
until awakened by the birds of dawn.

Lu Khen could not solve the matter of Mai Su having been
able to name the Makara. Probably it was a water spirit
better known in other lands or ages; there were no natural
means by which Mai Su could have learned of it, protected
as she had been in her gardens in Lin province. But it was
no stranger than other puzzling things about Mai Su, such
as the nature of her songs, their incomprehensible yet beautiful lyrics. If Mai Su had grown up able to speak normally,
possibly her every word would have revealed knowledge of
wonderful sorts, telling of beasts as remarkable as the Makara. Perhaps her mind was so filled with details of previous
lives, or of Heaven, or who knew what, that there had simply
never been a way for her to communicate her tremendous

experience with other people. Hence her vigilant silence.

She didn't speak another word, although Lu Khen had hoped she might communicate regularly after having spoken that single word. It was hoping too much, he realized. Even if she had poured forth a stream of words, they might well have been of the same unknown tongue she used in songs.

If Mai Su had ever been able to meet another human being with knowledge of that secret tongue, it might have turned out that she could converse with ease. As it was, no one understood her, not even Lu Khen who loved her. So she and he proceeded through the forest communicating only with their expressions, which often was enough.

It was a rugged path. Mai Su was stronger than Lu Khen had suspected. He did not have to help her along. She was, as usual, in better spirits than himself. Once he got a thorn in his heel and Mai Su was gentle about removing it. He limped for a while, feeling sorry for himself. Mai Su didn't seem to be having nearly as hard a time as he. The ease or difficulty of any given task is in great measure a state of mind; his tendency to gloominess made his path a series of obstacles, whereas Mai Su's placid nature made the same path relatively devoid of hindrance.

Sometimes Lu Khen led the way, giving Mai Su a hand over fallen logs, or helping her up a steep grade, out of politeness and concern if not because she required such attention. Other times she became the leader, encouraging Lu Khen to be less impatient with the path and its detours. They descended the far side of the first mountain in a few days, only to find another mountain in front of them. This made Lu Khen gloomier still, for he had counted on the going being easier after the first mountain.

To make matters worse, the weather was colder between the mountains and food was harder to find. It was unthinkable to trap small animals to eat in front of Mai Su, or to catch fish in the gemlike lakes twixt mountain peaks; she would not eat flesh of any sort and would be appalled to see Lu Khen do so. It looked as though they might soon be very hungry; but it turned out he was wrong in this prediction.

Mai Su began to gather large mushrooms while following the well-worn deer trails. Lu Khen had never seen their like before and was reluctant to eat them, or to let Mai Su do so. But she would not countenance his interference. In her passive manner, she could be stubborn. So, as he had trusted her in other matters, he finally trusted her in this. He made a fire with the aid of flint and iron, wrapped mushrooms in leaves, then baked the little packages in the coals. Come nightfall, they were both full and happy, and slept as they had done on previous nights in one another's arms.

Lu Khen awoke in the middle of the night with a sick stomach. Mai Su was nowhere to be found. He tried to call her name, but was too sick and light-headed to make a sound, except for groaning. The campfire had burned down to a few coals which looked like malevolent eyes watching him from the ground. Lu Khen was freezing. He staggered to his feet, thinking he would vomit. Instead, he belched a tremendous, rude sound which helped his queasy stomach but at the same time stuffed his ears and implanted weird sensations in his brain.

He was not quite dizzy. In fact, considering the darkness of the forest, his vision was shockingly clear. He could see everything quite sharply, even though the sky was overcast and the campfire was no help either. It was a slightly skewed vision, it was true, as though the world had swung up on one end. "Those mushrooms made me sick after all," he thought. "Mai Su must be sick also. I must find her right away."

The urgency of his search was intense, in the way things are when one is dreaming. Lu Khen vaguely felt he might not have awakened at all. Also as in dreams, the realization that everything could be a dream did not lessen the urgency. He could not be certain if he was in a half-doze and sleep-walking, or still sound asleep in Mai Su's arms with a nightmare about getting up and finding Mai Su missing.

There is often an inevitability which haunts dreams, a sense of something having to happen, and it does happen, whether or not it makes much sense on waking. Lu Khen hurried through the forest, not bumping into anything because of his heightened vision, having no idea which way he was going, but convinced he would eventually find where Mai Su had gone, because dreams are usually like that. Things in waking life may well have a sense of inevitability, too; but in dreams, it is much more extreme.

"Those mushrooms are making me dream this," Lu Khen decided. "They're making me dream that I am having this dream, or they are making me think that I am dreaming when really I am running through the forest imagining it's a dream." The dream, if dream it was, was unnervingly like being awake, living one's life as though one had no control over where things were going, drawn inexorably onward, toward something which seems like Fate but which turns out, in the end, to be nothing at all.

As little control as any living being has over his life, as manipulated and trapped as one may feel under the thumb of gods and society, still there is no climax except old age and death. Isn't it so? Lu Khen thought so. If there was such a thing as destiny, if gods indeed directed paths, then the point of everything must have been this: a dirty trick on everybody concerned. "Sometimes life seems very dear and important," thought Lu Khen. "But what is the point of it in the end? It has no point at all!"

Having dreamed these thoughts, Lu Khen stopped in his tracks, deciding not to be manipulated any longer. "Since there is no reason to go anywhere, I won't go!" Then he thought, "But there is no reason to stay here either." He got very confused. "Even so, whatever else happens, I must be with Mai Su." Despite this realization, his feet were somehow stuck to the ground. He managed to get going again, but his legs were extremely heavy and he could not go as fast as he had been going before. "This is the part of dreams I hate the most," he said aloud, finding his voice for the first time so that he could hear his own thoughts. "This is no fun at all."

His feet were getting stickier and stickier. "At least nothing is chasing me," he said. "It's worse to be stuck like this with something terrible coming after you through the dark."

As though his words conjured the demon, Lu Khen felt

a cold, cold breeze at his neck and knew it for the breath of a malevolent force. He looked back over his shoulder and saw a shimmering black cloud. "This won't do," he said, feeling the bottom fall out of his stomach. It was no longer possible for him to move. "I don't like this."

At that moment Mai Su stepped out from nowhere in particular and stood between Lu Khen and the cold black cloud. "Watch out for that thing!" he shouted, but she didn't listen. She was protecting him from the demon. How she could do it, he didn't know. "It's only a dream, but you just never know!" he warned her. The cloud began to dissipate as Mai Su faced it off; when it was gone, Mai Su turned around to look at Lu Khen, causing him to draw back from what he saw.

For the slenderest moment, her eyes were like the glistening cloud. In the next second, they were completely changed; they were aglow like the campfire's final coals. Darkness and light collided within the eyes of Yeung Mai Su, and to see those warring forces took Lu Khen by surprise. When he looked again, her eyes were only the smiling eyes he had always known. It made him feel ashamed to have felt something akin to fear where Mai Su was concerned.

It had never before occurred to him to be afraid of Mai Su's madness. He had felt only love for her from the beginning. Even now, he wasn't sure that what he had felt was exactly fear; but for the first time he realized there was more within her than love for birds and flowers and Ou Lu Khen.

She approached him in the darkness and took both his hands in hers, warming him to the center. They gazed at one another with the mutual good feelings they had always shared. But Lu Khen was pressed for the first time to have intellectualized feelings regarding the madwoman, in addition to the usual pure emotions that washed over him when they touched.

There was no vulgarity in her face. There was unique purity radiating from within those dark, dark eyes. Her brows were wonderful, her cheekbones high; these features enhanced the most remarkable eyes and lent them their smiling quality. This smiling quality sometimes carried over to the lips. When her lips and eyes smiled together, the whole world seemed, to Lu Khen, to take on aspects of Mai Su's beauty, everything in her proximity shining as did she. At other times, the smile was in her eyes only, and not upon her lips. This changed the effect of the look within her eyes; it became a sadder thing, the way love is sometimes gleeful and sometimes a terrible pain but still it is only love. In all, her face revealed a fineness of spirit, a more important consideration than the fineness of her flesh.

They found their way back to the campsite and blew the coals so that a fire could be started up again. They squatted on opposite sides of the flames, looking across at one another's lit expressions. It seemed as though each were learning something new about the other. For once Lu Khen was able to appreciate the language of silence, far as they were from civilization, and from the need to speak. He felt as though he were having revelations about Mai Su, and wondered if she were having revelations about him.

It could be construed as self-centered, this madness of hers, this helpless pose, this manner of being disconnected from everything. But really she was bound to the greater portion of the universe, as the hub of a wheel contains the least momentum and yet is the center of the hurried spokes and rim. Had Mai Su been in any manner selfish, she would drift from this selfless center, and her face could no longer reflect a spirit so refined, for rare is the face that conceals the soul. Awareness of her own beauty, were it to creep forth from those eyes, would spoil her perfection. In Mai Su's perfect beauty, there was no ego, no self-awareness.

If there were any exception, if she were in any manner aware of her own exceeding comeliness, it was only by way of seeing beauty in all things, herself and others. She did not distinguish between what was fine and what was not. This being the case, perhaps she saw homeliness in all things, too, even things which to everybody else appeared flawless. She felt the world's ugliness as her own ugliness, the world's pain as her own pain . . . as much as she felt the world's joy and beauty to be her own.

The hub of the wheel, after all, has the finest vantage

point for seeing all that radiates outward. Lu Khen was like the spoke of a wheel, capable of seeing only a small wedge of reality, but Mai Su could see everything. That which is passive sees the most; that which is weightless reposes at the center. Because the center is hollow, it seems to contain nothing when viewed from the outside; few can understand that absolute knowledge is absolute emptiness.

They gazed at one another for a long time, but as Lu Khen lacked perfect emptiness, he could not help but break the silence after a while. He remembered a fragment of poetry composed by an ancient sage, and he could not hold back from sharing it with Mai Su:

> *"On the right, infamy beckons*
> *To the left, mercy calls.*
> *That which is held in the middle*
> *cannot be moved."*

Maybe there *was* something fearful in this, in the clash of light and dark revealed for one fleeting moment in Mai Su's eyes. For the mind which knows that beauty is both fine and evil, and which knows homeliness is both vile and refined, must then be capable of witnessing the most horrendous events without flinching, without moving to halt such actions. Infamy is beauty of a sort, as in a dance of blades, and that is why Mai Su's eyes always laughed, without regard for her lips' agreement or contradiction.

Had those eyes beheld some evil in another life, something which was the source of Mai Su's madness? What cruelty witnessed in another incarnation struck her mute in this one? Did she laugh at what she saw, or did she weep? Mai Su had never wept, not that Lu Khen had ever noticed. Occasionally she laughed, however. Lu Khen wished he could stay these thoughts, but he could not. It occurred to him that she might well laugh at the greatest iniquity, seeing the part of it which was beautiful; at least her eyes would laugh, even if her mouth outlined a deepest sorrow. He whispered once again, "That which is held in the middle cannot be moved."

When he awoke with Mai Su in his arms, the fire was completely cold, the dawn was fresh and damp, and their camp beneath a dense conifer was surrounded by singing birds. He did not recall having gone back to sleep and wondered all the more how much of the night before had actually occurred. His mind reeled in an effort to hold onto its revelations, and he succeeded to a degree.

Mai Su opened her eyes, too. Eyes and lips alike were smiling, erasing anything of doubt which lingered from the previous night's actions and experiences, dreamt or real. For a moment their faces were very close indeed. Then Lu Khen rolled away and got to his feet.

Despite the vow he had made on leaving home—never to think or speak the names of the House of Ou for as long as he lived—it was not possible to stay the memories of Great-grandfather Po Lee, sister Koy, Mother Ou, or even the worrisome elders who had always denied him the respect due a house's heir. Guilt plagued him afresh. It seemed as though he spent half his life exposing his own selfishness to himself, and the other half regretting what he found true about himself.

He had left the family with poor crops. He had delivered a burden to his brother, who had made a good life in another village and would have to leave there. He had failed his duty. Others besides Old Uncle might die before the troubles caused by Lu Khen's laxity were corrected.

It might not be true that he was as much to blame as he sometimes felt, but presently he was so reproachful toward himself that it seemed true, that he was solely the source of misfortune in the House of Ou.

"Do you think I've done wrong?" he asked Mai Su as they walked through the thick forest. He held a low limb aside and let Mai Su walk by. As usual she did not respond to his query. He began to vocalize and bemoan his fate, his station, his unworthy life, his terrible lot. He went on and on about sad things from his past, his childhood, his loneliness before he met Mai Su. He found ways to relate past tragedies and private woes to his present outlook on life, which was negative and self-effacing; he rambled on about the difficulty of making it through one day at a time.

Mai Su may or may not have been listening to him. Certainly he was listening to himself and after a while he'd gotten enough of it. He stopped along the trail, stopped speaking and walking, and recognized that he was turning his guilt into self-pity, which was a trait of his mother. Finding himself a bit like her, he began to understand her, as well as himself, a little better.

They never attained the snowy level because the trail wrapped around the mountain's midriff. All the same, they shivered. Finding an area of dry grass—not enough to constitute a meadow—Lu Khen dallied. He cut grass and began to weave two capes, one for himself and one for Mai Su. The one he made her was better looking, but both did an equally fine job of protecting the wearers from the elements.

It had taken an hour or so to make the grass capes, but Lu Khen no longer felt their quest was of such immediate urgency that they hardly dared rest. He had begun to calm down a bit. They had shaved time off their journey by abandoning the winding riverways, so there was no call to push themselves hard.

It rained. The capes kept their shoulders dry, but they had lost their straw hats when the Makara took their boat and everything on it. It was easy to find a dense conifer, beneath which it was dry. Fallen needles made it uncomfortable to sit until Lu Khen brushed the ground free of debris.

They sat under the tree for a long time. They used their capes as shared blankets and Mai Su fell asleep with her head on Lu Khen's shoulder. Though it was not night, and only a little dark because of the storm, Lu Khen also fell asleep, though he hardly realized it. When the rain stopped and Lu Khen woke up, it was deep night. The sky had become extraordinarily clear, the stars were bright, and the mountainside was a maze of blue shadows.

Since Mai Su was not awake, Lu Khen did not move, for it would unsettle her position. He lay quietly and saw beyond the fringe of branches how beautiful the sky appeared. Rested, and holding Yeung Mai Su, he was at a loss to figure out why he had been so miserable earlier that day.

He heard the sound of thick drops of water falling from trees. It made a sound like the pattering of many naked feet. The more he listened to the sound approach, then fall away, the more convinced he became that he was not hearing water drops but, rather, a group of animals of some kind passing unseen through the night.

As he watched the sky, a white streak appeared, then vanished just as quickly. Pretty soon there was another, less bright; it came and went so quickly he hardly had time to notice it. Lu Khen thought how lives were like those shooting stars, bright and fleeting, noticed by hardly anyone, and always a new one coming after.

As he lay against the tree's trunk, cuddling the sleeping madwoman beneath the cloak of two grass capes, feeling for once that his life was in its humble way a grand one, he saw one more meteoric streak. This one was different. It came out of the south and was bright red. It moved more slowly than seemed possible, then gained speed, and its light was constant rather than fleeting. Then, miraculously, it changed direction, heading west. Without flickering once, it disappeared beyond his view.

When he looked at Mai Su in his arms, he saw that her eyes were opened, and she had seen the strange ruddy light, too. He took it for an omen, and decided that he and Mai Su would go in the direction of the magic star.

"The stars are like candles tonight," said Lu Khen as he climbed out from under the protecting limbs of the conifer. "They're very bright. The mountainside is blue beneath the silver light. It's cold, but a nice night for walking." He wrapped Mai Su's cape around her and tied it at the neck, then did likewise with his own.

Before they got going, he noticed by the starlight that there was an impression on the ground and he bent to look at it. It was a footprint, not slippered like his and Mai Su's, but unshod. He crouched and saw that there were several other prints in the moist loam, and they were made by feet of varying sizes. It was as though a whole tribe of people had run past them earlier in the night, the sound of their passing disguised by the rain.

Mai Su did not look at these many prints and Lu Khen did not draw her attention to them. As the footprints were all headed east, it seemed unlikely they would meet any of the people who made them.

Though it was several hours until dawn, they started on their way, Lu Khen feeling confident of the path because of the omen of the red star, and because of the brightness of the stars shining through the thin mountain air. Somehow Mai Su ended up leading, perhaps because her large dark eyes were like those of a nocturnal animal and she could better choose the route. It was curious that she led them exactly in the direction Lu Khen had considered. Perhaps it was less strange than he first imagined, as she had seen the path of the red star, too.

The path descended easily, leading them toward the warm, almost tropical forests below. It was still chilly on the mountainside and they kept their capes tied close, but already Lu Khen felt improving temperatures as they approached lower altitudes.

About a half-hour before dawn, they came to a brief mesa, and thereon discovered a village made of thatched walls and roofs. For a moment they stood at the edge of this village. Lu Khen was leery. He had seen a few aboriginal people in his life, but never in their own environment. Some of them were quite wild, or that's what people claimed. They didn't like Lu Khen's race, perhaps with good reason, since the northern clans had displaced many tribal peoples, forcing them further inland, closer to the ruins of the ancient capital which all would rather shun.

There was no movement in the village, no firelight, no sound. It seemed deserted, although a village built of grass would not look to be in such good condition if it had been abandoned long. This one had been lived in until recently. Lu Khen remembered the footprints he had seen, the prints of people fleeing eastward. What had frightened them away?

Lu Khen led the way into the heart of the small village, stepping tentatively, looking left and right lest some wildman or wildwoman leap from the dark doorway of some hut, brandishing a bronze knife of the sort aborigines fashioned.

Birds began to sing in anticipation of dawn. This eased Lu Khen's feeling of apprehension. From the vantage point of the village on the mesa's edge, it was possible to see the jungles far below. The western sky was still pitch black. The sun was hidden behind the mountain they had skirted. Looking back the way they had come, Lu Khen saw the mountain's crown beginning to shine, as though it were the abode of some Buddha.

Then Lu Khen caught sight of some small creature lurking between two huts. He gasped and grabbed Mai Su, making her stand still. He looked closer and thought it must be a monkey crouching down, black eyes shining. Unafraid of monkeys, he stepped toward it, still cautious, expecting it to leap away. On closer inspection it turned out to be a naked, dark-skinned child with a wild mop of hair—someone overlooked in the exodus, or left behind for some reason.

Lu Khen knew a handful of aboriginal words, not enough to make a sentence. He said, "Hello." The crouching child stayed there in the deeper darkness between huts, apparently eating something raw, something still living or at least with muscles contracting. The chewing sounded horrid. The child's fingers were slick and darkly gleaming with blood.

The child was eating a rat.

As Lu Khen came closer, the child hissed. The unexpected sound surprised him and made him jump back. He could see the child was a girl. She seemed to be afraid Lu Khen would steal her food, which he absolutely would never do.

He'd never heard that aborigines were like this! What he saw crouched in the abandoned village was madness, madness of a sort starkly contrasting to Mai Su's gentle disregard for the material world. This was small, greedy, ugly madness. Such a child as this would be left behind without regret!

"Have you seen the ancient Tombs?" Lu Khen wondered aloud. "Have you touched the bones of forgotten tyrants and been driven mad by lingering antique sorcery? Is yours the kind of madness I will find, or would I be like Yeung Mai Su if I entered the Tombs?"

Gray and then blue light began to move across the heavens from east to west. The light of the mountain's crown became the color of blood. The wild child looked up as though she were loath to see morning. She jumped up from her crouch and started down the narrow paths leading to the jungle, quicker than a rabbit.

Some creature of the jungle below greeted the bloody dawn with a tremendous, guttural roar. It sounded like a gigantic cat. Lu Khen hurried back to Mai Su's side. She did not seem afraid of the sound, although it was certainly the voice of a terrible monster, and no doubt the cause of the village's quick abandonment.

"We must pass through that jungle," said Lu Khen, his voice thin and worried, "even though some beast awaits us there."

Po Lee rummaged through oddments in one of the baskets and removed a beaten copper pot. He filled it from a stream and set it on a fire which Koy had built. It was the first time she had made a fire without being overseen by someone older, and she was proud of it.

While the water was heating, the old man and child pulled up their tunics and stuck the hems in their belts so they could wade into a pond, there to capture frogs. When they had several, Po Lee began to dress them out quickly, showing Koy how it was done although she was reluctant to try. With bellies slit and bowels popped out and thrown away, the rest of the frog meat was tossed in the boiling water.

"I've never had frog stew," said Koy, wrinkling her nose.

"You'll like it!" said Po Lee. He dug around in another of their baskets and found some wild basil which he'd saved from earlier in their journey. It had dried nicely and was brittle enough to shred between his fingers. He added it to the stew. He also added sweet bark taken from a cinnamon tree several days before, and there were four small, strong-smelling onions he'd found that very day.

As the stew cooked, it became more favorably aromatic. Koy took the knife Po Lee had used to clean the frogs, cleaned it in the pond by the stream, and used it to cut a wild fruit.

They had run out of rice early in their journey, but they had not gone hungry. In the weeks of travel, Ou Koy learned all that her great-grandfather knew of forest ways—or she learned a good portion at least. With his knowledge, she was able to see that the forest abounded with good food. People who starved in the wilds did so from ignorance!

She learned to make shelters and fires and judge the winds and weather, and how to keep to a certain direction. It was all much easier, once learned, than toiling day after day in a field or paddy.

"Great-grandfather," Koy asked while the frog stew bubbled, "why don't people wander the world like this all the time? It's an easier existence than building and repairing a house, sowing and caring for and reaping a crop."

Po Lee took a deep breath and screwed up his countenance until he looked appropriately wise. He explained, "People do not make houses and raise crops for ease and comfort. They do it out of greed. They build a house in which to store their possessions. They try to grow more food than they can eat in order to sell some of it and get money to buy more possessions to put in their houses. Once this way of things gets started, it's hard to turn it back around. People forget how to gather from the wild what they need to get by. They forget that life was easier before they developed a taste for excess. After a few generations, people even forget there was once a different way of living.

"Once their houses are full of these possessions, they have to stay close to home for fear of someone stealing their things away. They think they want to stay close to their family and the graves of their ancestors, but those are just excuses. If they wake up some morning and find out they've lost all the physical objects they've gathered through the years, they forget family and ancestors pretty fast and go somewhere else in a hurry.

"All of this is as true of poor people as rich people,

though for the impoverished, fulfilling greedy intentions is mere illusion. You'd think after a few years of trying hard and getting nowhere, people would stop believing in stupid things. But the existence of rich people merely keeps the poor hoping for the same luck, though in fact nobody ever got rich from luck; they got rich by making other people poor. And if they do get rich, it doesn't even make them happier than before they had anything, so it was all for nothing.

"I remember there was a time when nobody had a thing! It was during a famine that stretched to all corners of Ho. To survive, many people left their homes. They gathered what they needed along the way and it was enough, though there was nothing extra. The ones who died were the ones who stayed behind guarding their possessions, and those who went away taking the full weight of everything they owned in carts and on ponies and on their backs. They died because they were overburdened with these things, or because bandits killed them to take away the things that weren't necessary in the first place.

"But nobody learned from all this. They wandered about feeling miserable because they wanted to be wealthy. As soon as they could do it, when the land was turning greener, people started building houses anew, selling goods or produce, and accumulating lots of things which they only looked at now and then and didn't use. They had a whole different set of worries but basically they weren't nearly as well off as they believed, not happier and not healthier.

"The simple fact is that it takes more work to stay in one place than to hunt and gather one's needs while traveling about. But people say a vagabond life is laziness and they say laziness is sinful. It's just an excuse so they can feel better about themselves even though they're so greedy."

Ou Koy stirred the stew with a stick. It didn't seem quite done. She was having trouble accepting her great-grandfather's cynical views, although he related them as humorous things. On the other hand, she had trouble doubting anything he said, he seemed so wise from her perspective. Listening to him made her think things, and that was part of wisdom, too, teaching people how to think for themselves.

"Is that how you came to the Great Peninsula, great-grandfather? Because of the famines in Ho?"

Po Lee looked as though he didn't like this question. "Well, it was partly because of that. Actually, I left home before the famine, and was good at survival by the time things got really bad. I had already done a lot of traveling by then. Koy, it's my secret, but I was exiled from my home province for a while. I went back home once or twice after that, but couldn't stay there because things had changed, or I had, or maybe it was because things hadn't changed quite enough. It was a very long time ago. Please don't expect me to remember it all."

"If you were used to traveling around," said Koy, "why did you end up settling down on a farm, living in a house?"

"Well, did I say I was less greedy than anybody else? *Hmph.* Some people realize the world is wicked but they exempt themselves. That's foolish. We're all greedy, to tell the truth." Po Lee looked annoyed with himself, for he hadn't thought of this revelation for many years, though he had had it several times before. Thinking ill of himself because of his presumed greediness, he suddenly decided, "I think we can put everything we need inside two baskets instead of four!"

He had gotten agitated the moment Koy asked why he left Ho, and now he was acting vaguely senile, like he used to be. He started dumping out the four baskets side by side, then picked through things, deciding what they could do without. Koy watched. Po Lee rattled on:

"When people are wandering from place to place and life is free, they pass the time thinking how it would be nice to settle down with a family and build something for the future. If you ask someone who is getting old, or is already old like me, if you ask them, 'What was the happiest time of your life?' they will probably tell you it was when they were reckless and young and didn't have many obligations. But it doesn't seem that way at the time. People call a wanderer good-for-nothing and think he's lazy and a thief.

It can make you unhappy to have people make such accusations, especially if you're just trying to live your life and not be crazy like everybody else.

"It's easy to just stop one day, stop right where you find yourself and build a house and start a family. Now, I've met people of different races and cultures than our own, and some of them do indeed travel about in caravans with their whole families and never settle down and seem happy about it, though everyone who sees them pass says they're poor and dirty. As for our own race, we don't take to caravans for some reason. We believe that to have a family you have to settle down first, give up youthful wildness and frivolity and living free. What it really means is that you've got to be greedy like everybody else, stay in one place and start collecting things, because if you don't nobody will quite understand what you're doing and they won't trust you."

He filled two baskets and tossed the other two into the woods along with several articles he didn't think were necessary.

"The thing is, though," Po Lee concluded, "when a traveler finally does settle down, having always thought that was what he wanted to do, he keeps on dreaming about things, only now he dreams of wandering the world like the old days. Only he never does it."

"You've done it, great-grandfather."

"Why yes I have," he said, looking happier with himself. "It took me long enough, but here I am. I suppose that means nothing is ever lost for good! But really I think people are pretty bad most of the time. They make bad decisions. They do bad things."

"Was Lu Khen bad to neglect the family and run away?"

"I don't know about that, but everybody else was bad to make him run away!"

"We think the same about that," said Koy. "Since my brother isn't bad, then people in general might be better than you say. I don't think you're at all bad either. I think it's just a mood you're in."

"Oh, I'm bad all right, and so are you," said Po Lee.

"You think so? I try not to be bad."

"But we can't help it, Koy. We're the way we are. See, these were happy frogs a little while ago. Now they're all cooked up and ready to eat. It's very sad! Where are the bowls?"

"You just threw them away."

"Oh, well, run over there and get them."

She retrieved the bowls and they shared the hot soup and cool fruit slices. They sat on the ground slurping and chewing. Between mouthfuls, Po Lee tried to explain his feelings more clearly:

"Think of a squirrel." Koy thought of one. "A squirrel is closer to nature than you and me, and so devoid of sinfulness. It seems to act like a human being from time to time, it's true. It tends to mark a certain territory for instance, then gather a lot more nuts than it needs to survive the harsh months. As a matter of fact, it gathers five or six times more than it requires. All squirrels do it. There are no exceptions. People are just like that, only in the case of the squirrel, it's not actually being greedy. Unknown even to itself, it's planting trees! It buries its treasure and forgets where that place was, and a tree comes up right in that spot. Do you see? The squirrel puts back exactly as much as it takes away, even though it doesn't understand the scheme of things. When men store their riches, it's a different matter. A man does this only for himself and sometimes for his immediate clan. He gives nothing in return. That's what makes men worse than squirrels."

"But the squirrel *thinks* it's being greedy, great-grandfather," Koy ventured. "He doesn't think, 'I'm planting trees,' but, 'I'm sure finding a lot of things to eat and I want to horde them all for myself.' Maybe we're putting something back, too, great-grandfather. Maybe we're planting some kind of tree we can't see or don't know anything about."

"That's very good," said Po Lee. He sipped his soup loudly. "That's very smart of you. Everything is balanced in the end. We do give as well as take without knowing it, if you look at things hugely enough. But in the smaller details, things get mighty unbalanced."

"Maybe we're helping balance something by going on

this journey, great-grandfather. Maybe we're doing something important!"

"Maybe we are at that," Po Lee agreed. "But it doesn't mean we're good people. People are just bad, that's all; I'll tell you that. Here we are living an easy life and not taking anything more than we need, but we can't have any possessions this way, so are we satisfied? When this quest of ours is finished, we're bound to make the common error of building a new home, or else going back to the old one, and we'll have a harder time getting by after that, but we'll be afraid to live free again."

Koy shook her head and frowned. "Now that I know the forest, I could never leave it."

"That's what you say now. Maybe you'll do it like you say; it's not impossible. There are lifelong hermits and wanderers all right. But mark my word, you'll hear the voice at least, and the voice will be inside you saying, 'If I had a big high house, I could sit in the top room and see to that mountain. I could save things up in the basement. If I had a lot of children, they could take care of me when I get old. If I wasn't always traveling here and there, I could have something or another frivolous to keep in a box.' That little voice seems to make a lot of sense sometimes, but it's really some kind of devil talking, and it usually wins out in the end."

Harada lay half sleeping, half awake, shivering in the night, a few pitiful twigs and grasses posing as his covers. He tried to wake completely because he thought something or another was watching him. At the same time he tried to fall more deeply into slumber, requiring sleep's oblivion. He was so miserable, and so hungry, and so tired. Only the thought of the tomb gold, of eventual wealth, kept him going. He had become emaciated. He looked like the skeleton of Harada rather than Harada lying there shivering in the forest.

It was a warm night everywhere else, but around Harada the air was sparkling with frigidity.

The black cloud moved nearer and nearer the half-sleeping

man. Harada opened his eyes, saw the cold blackness above him, was certain it was only a dream, and closed his eyes again.

The black cloud whispered to him words of enticement. The black cloud suggested infamous crimes. *Yes, yes*, Harada's twilight mind responded. *Yes, I should kill the old man. I should kill the little girl.* But Harada was at heart a bully, a planner but not a doer, basically a coward. The black cloud gave him encouragement. It told him not to worry. Who could be defeated by a little girl? Who could be defeated by an old man? Besides, there were words people could use which were sharper than swords. He could bring the old man to his knees by reminding him of something he had tried throughout his years to forget about. Harada could make the little girl weep with sorrow and hatred for the old man by revealing the secret.

What is the old man's secret? Harada's mind inquired, eager for this weapon. The black cloud told Harada everything. After that, Harada was able to sleep less restlessly. When he woke up in the morning, he didn't remember the eerie dream at all, did not remember what he had been told. All the same, it lingered barely beneath consciousness, ready to lash out. The black cloud had planted ideas and knowledge that would come to the surface at a useful moment.

Harada quickly picked up the trail of the old man and little girl. They did not know they were followed and thus made no attempt to disguise their track.

The only thing Harada could find to eat that morning and afternoon were some wild grains, which he ate raw. The tiny seeds went through him undigested. His stomach growled. His bones ached. He was a weary, hungry, frightened man.

Even in the broad light of day, shadows seemed to hide wild beasts ready to jump out at him. After all, didn't the wolf always take the weak and starving first? Something was bound to leap from hiding and gobble him up! Harada tried to hurry. He drew his sword and cut branches in his path. If a wolf leapt out at him, he would cut that, too. The sword made him feel braver, but still not very brave.

He caught up with the slow pair early in the evening and had to drop back and hide. He saw them catching frogs and boiling them and eating them. When they were full of their stew, they broke camp and traveled on for a while. It would be dark soon, and Harada knew Po Lee and Koy would make their night's camp not far ahead. Harada decided to take over the abandoned camp.

He found a lot of things strewn about the camp. For some reason, Po Lee had decided to throw some things away. At first he had thrown out half of what he and the girl had brought this far, but in the end he had decided to abandon only one basket's worth of gear. They'd gone onward with him carrying two baskets on the ends of a pole, and Koy carrying one basket tied to her back. So Harada found the fourth basket and some other objects to put in the basket: a ragged towel, two wooden spoons, a tiny square box with a lid which smelled like pepper inside . . . items Po Lee had deemed useless. And useless they were, too, when judged practically; but in lieu of anything more valuable for him to accumulate, Harada was excited by the discovery.

The frog pond off to the side of the stream attracted Harada. He hoped to duplicate the trick of Po Lee and Koy, and make a nice meal out of frogs. But Harada wasn't a good cook. He had never dressed a frog in his whole life. He couldn't even tell a frog from a toad, and ended up catching one of those. He stuck a pointed stick into the toad's throat and cooked it alive in the rekindled firepit. He ended up devouring the toad half-cooked, innards and all, never knowing that a toad's back was poisonous.

That night he was deathly ill and vomited everything he had eaten that day, and sweated, and thought he was going to die. But in the morning he was no longer sick, though he was also not rested and therefore couldn't think very clearly. It was impossible to sleep in the sun, so he started on his way.

He was like a zombie staggering through the woods, a basket of items useless for his trip in one hand, a drawn sword in the other hand, his stomach growling, big circles under his eyes. What a monster he seemed! Toward noon he smelled something musky, and it turned out to be a root rat cooking on a spit arranged by Po Lee and Koy. It seemed they liked to stop and eat a lot and otherwise go along their way quite slowly. Even in his ill state, it was easy for Harada to catch up with them as usual.

He hid for a while, watching them sit and talk to each other as they waited for their meal to cook. He hated them and envied them and was afraid of them, too. He didn't understand how they stayed so healthy while he got skinnier and skinnier and sicker and sicker. It angered him that they weren't having as hard a time as he.

Something of his nightmare surfaced, some suggestion he had almost forgotten: *Kill them. Kill them.* It made him mad that they were such good friends. Harada never had a good friend like that. Watching them made him grit his teeth.

When Harada dropped his basket of useless articles, the little girl by the cookfire turned around and looked in his direction. At first she didn't see his hiding place. As he raised his sword and stood slowly from his crouch, her eyes became round with surprise, and she shouted,

"Great-grandfather! It's a monster!"

Harada charged out from the underbrush toward the cook-fire. His stomach was growling almost as loudly as his throat. He wanted to get to the freshly cooked meat, but Ou Koy stood directly in his path. His sword swung downward in a great arc, but Great-grandfather Po Lee leapt across the fire with surprising spryness and, swinging his staff expertly, struck Harada's sword sideways. The staff swung back in the direction it had come and smote Harada on the temple.

The starving man staggered backward, holding his sword before himself, afraid the old man would press the attack. But Po Lee only grabbed Koy and pulled her to the far side of the fire. The two of them huddled together, watching the stranger in their midst. Harada had lost so much weight on the journey that they didn't recognize who he was. He was so wild-eyed and dirty with unkempt hair and beard that they may have thought him one of the aborigines.

"What do you want!" Po Lee shouted, holding his walk-

ing staff straight forward as though it were a sword. Harada's
head hurt from the previous blow and he respected the old
man's stick-fighting ability. He tried to answer the old man,
but could only grunt unintelligibly. He approached the fire
like a hungry dog and took the meat from the spit.

He held his sword in one hand and gnawed the meat
ferociously, glowering at the pair beyond the cookfire. After
a while he tried to talk again, and though his voice was
hoarse from sickness and disuse, he managed to make himself understood:

"Don't you recognize me, old Po Lee?"

Po Lee still held his staff as a weapon. He squinted his
eyes and looked carefully at the emaciated man, but it was
Koy who recognized him first.

"It's Harada Fumiaka, great-grandfather!"

Realizing this was true, Po Lee lowered his staff and
said with extreme belligerence, "Evil man! Why are you
following us? Why try to kill us? How bad you are! How
insufferable! I should beat you to death with my stick!" He
stepped forward, moving around the firepit, and Harada
cowered, stepped backward, holding the gnawed meat close
to himself, not menacing anybody with his sword anymore.
Po Lee said, "The world would be better off without a man
like you! Some people just deserve to die!"

Harada dropped his sword and then the meat as well. He
pleaded, "Don't beat me! Don't kill me!"

"Why shouldn't I?" shouted Po Lee, his fist clutching
his staff so tightly that his whole arm shook. "How many
people have you killed? How many evil deeds have you
performed?"

"I've never killed anybody!" shouted Harada from his
knees.

"Hard to believe!" Po Lee snapped.

"Nevertheless, it's so!" said Harada, bowing and scrap-
ing. "I think about it a lot. I think about killing so and so
who makes me mad, or someone else who I can rob, but I
never do it. I've never killed a human being."

"Even a failure at being a villain, eh? If it's true," Po
Lee challenged, "why were you exiled from your island
country?"

"Not for killing anybody. I was caught doing things I shouldn't have been doing and was told I would have to commit suicide. I ran away instead. I've never been home since then. I'm not a good man, but I'm not a killer either. What about you? You want to kill me now? You've killed a lot of people, haven't you? You took justice into your own hands a long time ago, and you made a mistake!"

Po Lee stepped backward as though dodging a blow. His expression was no longer angry but upset. He looked quickly at Ou Koy who was listening to all this.

"You're an exile, too!" said Harada, crawling forward on all fours, unarmed but winning the duel anyway. "You're a worse man than me! You act righteous but it isn't me who killed a lot of people!"

"Shut up! Shut up or I'll kill you!" screamed Po Lee in a shrill, quavery voice. He raised his staff and smashed Harada on the top of the head. He smashed him a second time and Harada fell flat on his face, rolled himself over with difficulty, then lay groaning and staring up at the cloud-speckled sky. Blood was all over the top of his face.

Ou Koy grabbed her great-grandfather's arm before he could strike Harada a third time. "Stop it! He threw his sword away! Why hit him hard like that!"

Great-grandfather Po Lee had tears in his eyes, pouring out as though from two small red cups. His mouth was shaking as he looked down at his great-granddaughter. He dropped his bloodied staff, then fell to his knees beside Harada. The old man wailed with remorse.

Koy ripped strips of her own long tunic to bind Harada's head. He was barely able to move and wouldn't speak at all, but she managed to get him into a comfortable position and cover him up. When it seemed that he was partly awake, she gave him some water with local herbs mixed in. They spent the whole day with him, and stayed up the night to make sure he didn't die.

At one point during the long night, Harada shouted lots of crazy things. When there was a sudden breeze and the air became chilled, he became hysterical like a man caught in a nightmare, unable to wake up, screaming, "Liar! Don't

tell me that! It doesn't help me at all!" Then he was unconscious or else sleeping very deeply. In the morning he
wasn't speaking again. He stared at things which only he
could see. They couldn't move him and they couldn't leave
him. Things looked hopeless.

Po Lee moped and looked at his own hands and sometimes tried to keep busy. He set snares nearby and built their
lean-to large enough to house three. But he didn't complain
that they couldn't continue their journey for a few days. It
was his own fault.

After the third day, they still weren't sure whether or not
Harada was going to die. Before Po Lee went to sleep that
night, he broke the long silence between himself and Koy,
asking meekly, "Do you think I'm a bad man? What Harada
said was true, though how he found out I don't know."

"Everyone is bad, great-grandfather. You told me so."

It was a noncommittal reply, but at least she was talking
to him. Po Lee went to sleep feeling terrible. He hoped he
wouldn't wake up at all. He was old enough to die. He
should have died a long time before. He was ready.

In his dream, he went for a walk and met a girl along
the way. She looked like Koy but was older than Koy. She
was Po Lee's wife, looking like she did on the day Po Lee
married her. For some reason he wasn't surprised that she
was young again, and he wasn't surprised to run into her.

"I'm a bad man," Po Lee said to his wife. "I've killed
a lot of people in my time. I shouldn't have done it."

"You shouldn't be so hard on yourself," she said. "If you
were as bad as you think, it wouldn't be possible for you
to come here and talk to me." She took Po Lee's hand. He
saw their hands joined together, saw that his own hand was
as young and smooth as hers.

"Is this heaven?" he asked. He looked into the dark,
beautiful eyes of Fa Ling and said, "I'm glad to be here.
I'm glad to be with you again. I hoped this would be possible, but I didn't think it was very likely." He started to
cry for joy.

"This isn't Heaven," said Fa Ling. "I came to meet you
halfway, to tell you not to come yet. What would our great-

granddaughter do if she finds you dead in the morning! I wasn't alive when she was born, but I haven't neglected my duties as an ancestor; I've watched over her a lot. Glad as I am to see my husband here before me, I can't let you come live with me just now. You had better go back, don't you think?"

Po Lee frowned and looked like a pouting child.

"You've lived a long time it's true, and you should be allowed to die now that you feel like it, but you weren't given a long life for no reason at all. You can't give up yet."

"It'll be easier from now on," said Po Lee, looking happier now that he had thought it over. He was a beautiful young man, and when he smiled, he looked almost like a girl. He said, "At least I know now that we'll be together again."

"You won't remember any of this," said Fa Ling, keeping him from getting too happy. "But you'll do a good job anyway."

"A good job at what?"

"I can hardly tell you that, can I? You wouldn't remember it anyway. Now you go back the way you came, all right? Don't make me have to be mad at you!"

Po Lee bowed to his wife many times. Then he turned around and ran back the way he had come. In the morning he didn't remember this dream, but he felt better about living. A lot of things were worked out while a body slept, Po Lee thought. Even if dreamed thoughts and adventures could not be recollected, they had their healing influence. Koy was still as disillusioned with him as the day before, and it was hard to face it, but he would have to try.

During breakfast, he said to her, "Now you know everything about me, little Koy. Either you will love me as I am, or you won't. If you must punish me, it's all right."

She was feeding glassy-eyed Harada from her fingers. When her great-grandfather talked to her, he sounded so pitiful that it was hard for her to retain a hard expression. She glanced sidelong at him and smiled despite herself. "I love you, great-grandfather. It was bad of me to be cruel.

You were right that people aren't very good in their hearts. I haven't been good to you."

"It's not our hearts that are bad, Koy! It's our deeds. We have to work on making them better all the time."

Koy went with Po Lee to check the traps. He had caught a nocturnal civet cat in one. He was careful of its sharp claws when letting the scared, wild thing go free because it was no good to eat. It darted off, surprised to be left alive.

In the other trap there was a squirrel. Po Lee was about to break its neck and bleed it when suddenly he couldn't do it. He'd killed a thousand big and small animals in his life, and fed himself and his family on good fresh meat. He didn't understand why he was reluctant to kill the squirrel stretched between his two hands. It struggled to no avail, clicking its yellow incisors, unable to bite him.

He let the squirrel go. It didn't stay around to thank him. It ran off as fast as it could go.

"We can find a lot of nice roots and things," said Po Lee, feeling embarrassed. "Let's give up meat for a while, all right?"

"As penitence for our bad deeds?" asked Koy.

"For mercy's sake," said Po Lee. "Maybe it will be paid back to us if we need some mercy soon."

When they arrived back in their camp with a basket load of edible roots and wild fruit, Harada was gone. For some reason he had left his sword behind, yet he had taken the basket of useless things with him. He didn't steal anything of theirs.

They worried about him a little, but as he had enough wits about himself to disguise the direction he had taken, he must have been all right. Po Lee said,

"We never did find out why Harada was following us all this way. I don't think he meant us any good, though. He may try to follow us some more, but now that we've found him out, we can take precautions to lose him."

True to his advice, Po Lee led Koy down a stream, careful to leave no mark of their passing. There was no chance Harada would find them again. Po Lee had his two baskets and a pole, plus his walking staff. Koy carried her one basket, filled with things to eat. Also, she had strapped across her back Harada's sword and sheath. She looked like the littlest warrior.

When they cut back into the forest, heading northwest instead of west, things fell back into the old pattern, only now they rested less often because they had lost so much time. They made camp only after it was dark. They were up and on their way before it was completely light in the morning.

The next day they came to a place where there seemed to be a gash in the forest, or a mossy place without any trees. The treeless area was only a few feet wide, but it went east and west beyond sight.

"This is very odd!" exclaimed Koy, walking around on the spongy moss highway.

Po Lee used his staff to scratch away at the moss, then reached down and pulled up a large section of it as though it were a loose carpet. Underneath were stones placed close together. It was an ancient road.

"This is what I was looking for," said Po Lee. "This road goes right up to the capital city of the Lost Dynasty. There'll be no obstacles from now on."

As he said this, they heard a noise up ahead. Then they saw a number of aboriginal people step out of the forest and onto the road. They held spears and knives of bronze, and had tattoos on their dark faces. They stood very still and did not move to attack, but they were most assuredly blocking the route.

❧ FOUR ❧

White Tiger Forest

IT WAS FARTHER to the jungle than Lu Khen had imagined when first he glimpsed it from a high plateau. After days, they were still in the highland rain forests. The terrain lowered little by little, and Lu Khen was most confident that eventually the forest would give way to the tropical flora of the heated lowlands. This confidence became damaged only when he discovered that the land had begun to turn upward once more. Though the route never became steep, it was definitely no longer a downward incline.

Though the tropical country had previously been glimpsed from above, it was no longer in view, and had not been seen in days. Whenever the horizon was visible through the straight, tall trees, it was shockingly close, as though the world had grown smaller. Ou Lu Khen tried not to think about the possibility of his having gotten them lost, as he had lost them in the confusing network of watery channels earlier during their journey. He recalled the dreadful fear that the very mountains had disappeared; he did not want to repeat such foolishness by convincing himself a tropical jungle had vanished. He remained calm and kept to the forward course, even though they were climbing rather than descending. He was reasonably convinced that the too-near horizon would eventually fold back to reveal the jungle just as he had seen it before.

The weather was unique in this part of the rain forest. The tropical country hidden before them, the surrounding cool mountain peaks, and the apparent geographical dip they were in, conspired to hold all clouds at bay. The sky was therefore startlingly, beautifully, unnaturally blue. Yet, for all the lack of genuine rainfall, everything was awfully damp, as though morning were a constant event, providing dew with no opportunity to lift.

Gems of moisture clung to Ou Lu Khen and Yeung Mai Su. It made her look to be a holy being with stars in her dark hair. But Lu Khen looked bedraggled. "Someone might think we went swimming with our clothes on!" said Lu Khen, trying to cheer himself up. Mai Su gazed at him with something of admiration (not that he felt admirable) and something of a total lack of comprehension of his meaning (though likely she understood more than he).

Often the ground was mushy at their feet, as though they walked on sponge. Every footstep made the sound of wringing cloth. There was dampness everywhere and it combined the worst aspects of temperate rain forest and steaming jungle. Wetness lingered as in a humid jungle, but was clammy like a mountain rain. Unlike true rain, there was no getting out of it. The moisture filled the air, swept into their shelter, and condensed upon their hot skin. It was also extremely difficult to build a fire.

To look for some positive aspect to their present state, it could at least be argued that it was never unbearably cold nor miserably hot. The clammy dampness was merely uncomfortable. "I'm hard to please," confessed Lu Khen, half to himself since he was never certain Mai Su listened. "Once we find our way into the jungle, I will probably feel bad about the heat. Right now, though, I wish there were some way for us to dry out!"

He felt he might grow mushrooms upon himself. Or he

might begin to rot, just as the fallen logs they climbed over or around were rotten.

Yet Lu Khen was repeatedly overcome with a giddy happiness that made no sense at all. Being of a family that never lived at high altitudes, it could be that the thin air of the mountainside made him light-headed and nervously pleased. Then again, it could be Mai Su's presence which so delighted him, against all adversity. Things which were miserable he intellectualized and worried over; but this opposite feeling of freedom, of love, of delight and wonder . . . he could not intellectualize these so much, for none of it was logical. It was a thing he felt.

He wondered if it would last a long time or if, next thing he knew, he would be depressed.

At one point along the way, Lu Khen saw a gory patch of blood and bone. He saw it on the path not far ahead and tried to make a detour so that Mai Su, coming up behind him, would not see the terrible remains. But sometimes she would not be led. She brushed by, ignoring Lu Khen's efforts to change their route and spare her the vision. As a matter of fact, she acted eager to see the mess. This surprised Lu Khen, for the madwoman had always been alarmed at the sight or notion of a feast of flesh.

She stood over the horribly mauled animal, betraying no sentiment. It was difficult to tell exactly what it had been: a stout deer of one kind or another, judging by the hoofs. Its head had been half torn off, the skull punctured and crushed. The whole of its body was raked and torn, assuredly the markings of a powerful tiger's vicious claws. Spilled intestines steamed and palpitated, evidence of the kill's freshness. The poor thing had apparently put up a good fight, though it had been ill-equipped for anything but running and darting. Had the predator slain its prey slowly out of bestial cruelty, or been honestly incapable of performing its task with merciful speed?

It was curious that so little meat had been eaten. Cats wasted little, or so Lu Khen had always been given to believe. Whatever was left uneaten would be dragged off the deer trails and buried under leaves, or hauled into the crotch of a tree where bugs would not get to it quickly. There would have to be something odd about a tiger which killed, either cruelly or clumsily but at all events horridly, then abandoned the meat to scavengers.

It was possible the tiger left its feast due to the approach of Lu Khen and Mai Su. In that case, the predator would lurk nearby. It might rush out to defend the carcass. Lu Khen glanced nervously about.

Mai Su knelt at the mangled corpse's side and found an unbloodied patch of fur to stroke. Lu Khen thought her behavior most unaccountable. But there was much about her which evaded his understanding. It occurred to Lu Khen that Mai Su had never seen death before this moment, whether calm or violent in nature. She did not fear it, whether from her innocence or from a secret knowledge, he could scarcely guess. For someone who pitied animals too much to eat meat, it did strike Lu Khen as strange that she would register no more than the mildest, most abstract curiosity at the ruinous remains of a pathetic deer.

For a moment, he fancied it was himself dead upon the path, flesh rent from bone, and touched by a hand which bore compassion but no sorrow. It was a startling thought, for Lu Khen knew well enough that his love for Yeung Mai Su was generously requited; yet, would she weep if he were dead? He wondered. Naively fearless as she was, mystically protected by that naïveté, death well might fail to overwhelm her with regret. Whereas he, pondering the inevitable conclusion of every life, became unbearably sad.

Death required of everyone a certain resignedness, but he could fancy only one reason to embrace death gladly. Were Mai Su to die, he would not survive her by a single breath. He was certain of that. But he could not expect Mai Su to have feelings identical with his own, despite her love of him. The mystery of her was too complex, and her mind reposed far from ordinary response and limitation. Knowing this, he ached just the same, for it was hard to consider that his need for her might exceed hers for him.

In a few moments, she rose somnolently from her kneeling posture and continued along the path, unsettled by nothing. Lu Khen's own heart, by contrast, was greatly quickened. He looked to left and right as he followed the madwoman. He saw nothing, heard nothing, not even a frog.

He fell into old and easy patterns of fretfulness, deliberating on the likelihood of a tiger's assault, and the slim chance at success against such an animal. Truthfully, Lu Khen knew little about tigers. He had only once in his life seen one. It had been dead. It had come from a southern region, leaving a trail of terror to mark its passing, leaving a legacy of wondrously terrifying stories to be told. Due to its having obtained a taste for human flesh, nobody was likely to forget it for generations. Even when it had been slain, people feared the silence of the night and the tiger's savage spirit.

Four hunters of Lu Khen's and a neighboring village were the ones who set out to end the fiend's career. They succeeded in tracking it and, though killing it, two of the hunters died in the ordeal. Lu Khen was small at the time but not apt to forget the shining orange, yellow, and black of the fantastic beast's fur; nor could he fail to recollect its astonishing size, twenty times the weight of the fierce fisher-cats native to the canal region. Safe behind his mother's skirts, he had looked at that monster, while the whole village crowded around, gaping. No one had the nerve to poke it with a stick, for the tiger was majestic and awesome even in death.

The two hunters who returned with their lives, packing knives and curved bows, never had to boast. Others boasted in their behalf. Yet they seemed genuinely devoid of puffery, rather than falsely humble. Indeed, they acted ashamed of their brave accomplishment and refused to remain in listening distance of whoever bragged in their favor. It may have been that the loss of companions had been too dear a price. Or they may have respected their fallen foe too much. Whatever their mood or motivation, the surviving men never hunted again. They became simple farmers, refusing hunters' honors.

It was only a smart thing to be afraid of tigers.

"We had best be careful, Mai Su," said Lu Khen, hoping

she would understand without becoming frightened. It was enough for him to be afraid. "Tigers ought not hunt up here, but we have heard one roaring far away on a couple of different nights. That slain animal was still hot from the chase. We have nothing to fight with if it likes our smell and follows."

Mai Su looked over her shoulder at Lu Khen. She looked straight into his eyes, making him stop talking. It was not a sharp look, yet it slapped him somehow. He was surprised. She was leading the way again, as though she knew where they were going. She had been right a few times already, so he followed and kept still.

As it turned out, she had guessed wrong for once, or so Lu Khen would judge. Before nightfall, they came to an unexpected and quite alarming precipice. The rain forest came to an abrupt end, as though the world had been shorn away at that spot. The cliff on which they stood went left and right, curving out of view, revealing no descendable route. They were standing on the tip of an inconceivably monumental finger which pointed out over the jungle far below.

Looking down from the forested finger, Ou Lu Khen could not see the cliff's base. There was a cavernous hollow, the back of which he could not fathom. It was as though the rain forest drifted in the sky, nothing holding it up. Suppose the forest collapsed into the big hollow! It was a frightful consideration. But it looked like a pretty old forest. The trees were giants. The superlative overhang had not crumbled down in thousands of years. Surely their small feet would not damage things. "I always come up with things to worry about," Lu Khen thought, shaking his head at himself.

Mai Su did not join him at the ledge, so he pondered the view privately. The jungle was so near, yet only a bird could reach it. One step farther, and he would take a deadly plunge, and lie broken in the tropical land he and Mai Su were seeking. Lu Khen did not like to have this morbid idea. Was the drop inviting? Why would he think so? He had been raised in a sea-level country, and his head was unused to dizzying heights. The thin air made his thoughts occasionally wild. In his life, he had never had such an opportunity to look down from anywhere so high. What a startling temptation it provided! What a gorgeous spectacle and wonder!

A dark *something* whispered encouragement. The image of his straight, downward flight imbued his mind. How exhilarating! He might manage to catch himself on the feathery leaves of tropical flora and survive the experiment. That probably lacked the least possibility, yet the notion invaded his thinking and snuggled in.

Lu Khen's toes curled as he peered down. The skin of his face felt stretched taut. His eyes were big and round. These were not suicidal intentions which tugged at him from below, but a lunatic curiosity. *What would it feel like to fall?* It was a long drop and he would have ample moments to consider the sensations. If he changed his mind halfway down, it would be a useless sentiment.

He staggered back from the edge, oddly uncertain if he had ever been in peril. His face relaxed. His breathing was heavy, as though he had been straining against an inexplicable power. He tried not to look down again, but gazed outward, across the jungle's roof. Flashes of bright color were too distant to be definitely recognized as birds. The half-comprehended darting hues somehow eased his mind of darkness and illogical desires.

The sky was the color of a polished brass gong. The setting sun was the face of a golden mallet. In Lu Khen's excited imagination, the gong gave out a sonorous rumbling. It was the sound started by the creation of the universe. The world would cease to exist in the moment the sound ended.

Architectural wonders, halfway across the jungle's roof, were choked by vines and other growths, dwarfed by distance, yet remained startling objects poking up from trees. Lu Khen could almost judge the expressions on the huge faces of the thick, monolithic towers. Some of the faces were serene, while others glowered with menace. It was as though the buildings themselves were gods, raising their stone heads above the jungle. Those heads wore hats which were sharp, windowed spires, partly disintegrated and ragged on the sides. What evil haunted those spires? Surely, if the dreadful city of Tombs merited one one-thousandth of its ill fame, there were devils waiting!

"In that city waits my destiny," Lu Khen whispered, "providing I have one." There was really no reason for assuming his life or anyone else's had an unseen purpose; yet he had a degree of faith in this matter.

As the sun lowered, he turned away from the panorama to see what Mai Su was up to. She was clearing an area between mossy boulders. Having watched Lu Khen make their camps so often, she had learned to do it herself. This growing independence amazed Lu Khen. It was possible that in some corner of his mind he feared her increased ability to act of her own volition. If he felt this way, it was not to an overwhelming degree. But he had to admit to a twinge of regret at being less than her absolute protector and provider.

Another part of him was naturally relieved. Whenever she chose their path or gathered food or, as now, helped arrange a comfortable place for them to curl up until morning, his burden was lessened. His shoulders need not sag. Mistakes and successes could be equally shared.

Yet another portion of his mind wondered and sorrowed over the changes their journey had wrought, damaging Mai Su's aloofness from material necessity. Had he weakened the perpetuity of her meditative madness by changing the world around her? Or was there no change in her beyond surface aspects which were all his limited vision could observe? When he was thinking ill of himself, he wondered if he might be a subtle variety of devil—so clever that he could not recognize his own aim—with the devilish intention of tempting a saintly being away from the perfect path. Other times, when he felt forgiving of his faults, he considered the possibility of his having provided meritorious service to Mai Su and her Way. Whether devil or proper aid, the thing which was certain was that he acted unwittingly. If anyone were ever a true master of his life, it was not Ou Lu Khen; knowing this to be true, he wondered if he were manipulated by an outside force with designs of its own. Whether gods or fate or mere devotion set him dancing, he knew not, but he was mostly pleased to ride the wave of things, so long as Yeung Mai Su were near.

He watched her prepare the clearing, gathering soft ferns for their bed and moving aside uncomfortable branches. Then he approached her and said, "Mai Su." She looked up from her industry with such a curious innocence that he forgot what he had intended to say. Then she smiled in a knowing manner, as though some subtle communication had passed between them. If they had communicated something, it was too subtle for him to notice what it was!

He was more confused than ever, by everything except his love for Yeung Mai Su. Had their spiritual kinship sharpened on their journey? He felt it had. Perhaps for every rational move she made, his own reason was lessened an equal score. This queer notion somehow made him happy, to think they might become, by degrees, equal in their capacities to be sensible or insane. Yet he did not believe this deep inside himself. Mai Su's helpfulness was more instinctual than contemplated, whereas any slip of reason in his own actions set him pondering, and discovering, the cause. There was a difference between madness and stupidity. Lu Khen was merely stupid. Having figured this out, his happiness receded.

As darkness gathered, he tried to get a fire started from damp twigs and branches. The fire was smoky and unpleasant, and suddenly it went out. He talked himself out of disappointment. A fire was not necessary since the nights were not chill. Warm air wafted upward from the tropical land below. He and Mai Su could snuggle sweetly and be comfortable. But he had wanted the fire, if not to dry the clinging dampness from their clothing and hair, then to startle predators. He and Mai Su would be trapped on a precipice if the tiger came close.

They sat side by side, backs against one of the big rocks, and Lu Khen stared at the charred pit in which the fire had failed.

Mai Su stroked the back of his neck, soothing him of

fretfulness. "It is getting dark so quickly," he said. "Yet I am not the least bit tired." Lu Khen gave a long, soft sigh. He planned to keep alert the whole night. He felt himself to be too anxious to rest, and vigilance was necessary when a tiger dwelt near.

Lu Khen knew his body less than he supposed, for despite sleepless intentions, oblivion soon enough overtook him.

Upon the moon there grows a cinnamon tree of enormous size. Nothing else grows upon the moon, just this. Around it stretches the pockmarked surface of the moon.

At the base of the tree there stands a supernatural woodsman with an extraordinary axe. The axe is so big it is surprising the woodsman can lift it; but he has no trouble at all. With this axe, he tries, upon occasion, perhaps once in each millennium, to fell the cinnamon tree. Although the axe is mighty and the woodsman strong, the tree has never once been dented.

The rest of the woodsman's time is spent sitting high in the tree. He likes it there. The tree has no leaves. The trunk and branches are the color of blood. The woodsman is the color of bone. The tree is the bloodstream of something or other, the universe itself, or some god. The woodsman is only vaguely conscious of himself and does not think he is a god; yet that is what he is. If he were to succeed in cutting down the tree, the woodsman would bleed to death, his bones would crack. This god is akin to humanity in the way he tries to do himself harm.

He sits in the tree and looks to Earth, which is shaped like a coin, flat with human life on top. As he does not credit himself with much power, he believes falsely that the top of the cinnamon tree is near the Earth; for he can see the people very clearly. He does not comprehend how his own eyes work, for it is the nature of heavenly beings to know little of themselves.

He sees a young man and a young woman. They have wandered this way and that way, but presently they rest in a forest at the tip of a huge jut. Darkness is around them.

In another part of the same general area, he sees an old

man and a little girl. Their wanderings have mirrored the wanderings of the young man and woman. At the moment, they are held captive by wild natives and are filled with concern.

There is one other individual who attracts the woodsman's attention, if only for one-trillionth fraction of a moment. This is a dark fellow who is lonely and pathetic. He moves in a straight line between the mirrored paths of the four shining people, but he never gets very far.

The woodsman has no influence on anything. He only sees. He cannot stop the battle he knows is pending. Gods which are powerless are often fascinated with the doings of humanity. Powerful gods are more interested in themselves and cannot see as far. Seeing and doing are mutually exclusive abilities. The woodsman is the sort of god who sees. Consider him as the reader of an ancient book, but not its writer. He may have written it long ago, but has forgotten. He cannot at so late a time rewrite a single word. It is stuck that way, mistakes and all. Not one event can he alter for better or worse. Yet, miraculously, as he watches, things transmute of their own accord. Each time the book is read anew, it is the same but different, thus rarely tiresome. When it does become tiresome, he climbs down from the theater branch and swings his axe at the red trunk's base. Failing to ruin the tree, he will climb back up and watch things happen for another thousand years.

Certain dreamers say the moon was once a forest and the woodsman laid it to waste. There is a story people whisper to each other across gulfs of slumber, a secret story, about the multiple nature of the woodsman and his axe. As he is not much aware of himself or his nature, he is spared the knowledge of loneliness, despair, failure, and frustration. The day may come when he knows himself too well and becomes angry or upset. He will throw the axe to the Earth on that day (so the dreamers whisper). It will be found by a wood nymph and she will use it to destroy the land and the sea, until there is only one tree left, a tree without leaves but with sweet bark—a cinnamon tree. Having laid waste to all things but this, which is impervious, she will climb into the cinnamon tree and sit gazing at the moon.

This will happen at the end of time, but this will not mark the end of all things. The Great Earth Tree and the Great Moon Tree will grow while their inhabitants sit unaware of time. The Great Earth Tree is a different shade of red than the Great Moon Tree, indeed, in the proper light, the Earth tree is slightly blue.

Eventually the two trees will have grown so tall that they reach each other. The limbs of one will interlace with the limbs of the other. The nymph and the woodsman will kiss; it is the kiss which closes the circle of Ending and Beginning.

If the woodsman could find his lover by looking at the Earth, he would toss down his axe at once, so things would occur as they inevitably must, so he and she might embrace. But she is invisible to him, or beyond easy recognition, besides which the woodsman is too foolish to figure things out and would rather keep his axe.

Sometimes he has a pang of something akin to sorrow, not very strong, vague and uncomfortable. It makes him sentimental and he wishes that he could help the many lovers he has seen struggle toward each other, fall back, and try again in later lives. How he would like to show them the roads which are so clear from afar! He cannot do so, for he is the Watcher, not a god who can change things. It is just as well he cannot help. For there are other times when he does not feel the sad, longing sentiment. Instead, he feels a thing close to anger and frustration. This, too, is a mere echo of a stronger feeling and not the feeling itself. It is enough to make him wish he could thwart lovers, knock them apart, put walls between them. Thus it is a good thing he is a helpless god, and it is a good thing that gods with grimmer power are blind to Earth.

What this has to do with the story, none can tell. But it is a commonly accepted, widely held belief that the cinnamon tree is there, and the woodsman in it. If one gazes at the moon long enough, the woodsman will notice, and his eyes will shine into the earthly watcher's eyes and thus the moon gives madness.

No one knows where the Great Earth Tree grows, for it is not yet a presuming tree. It is supposed that the Earth tree can be recognized only by the dark-eyed nymph who at this moment sits in the branches waiting to receive the axe. It may sound as though sorrow will fill the world when she receives the axe and becomes the destructive spirit with a long red tongue and blood upon her lips. And it is true, it will be a sad time. But all things end and all things are reborn; someone has to fill this need and it might as well be her. When the world is laid to waste and the two trees connect across space, this will mark the rebirth of the world which before was tired and old. How the world will be recreated, and whether or not it will resemble the world as it now exists, the deepest dreamer cannot tell. Likely it will be a world of children who, through many lives, grow old, until the axe is found again.

The world grows older by the day but cannot end until the axe flies down from the moon. It is tempting to wish this never happens; but when things are very bad, one might rather pray it happens soon. Even if selfishness dictates that humanity wish the axe will never come, there remains a sad feeling for the woodsman and the nymph who are lonely but cannot find one another.

Gods have many avatars, as humans have many lives; and sometimes gods are merely human beings. Often these avatars exist several at one time; a god is able to meet itself and make rude remarks. These avatars die and are reborn at other times, past or present. Existence is less linear for them than for ordinary people. This being so, the woodsman is not necessarily and irrevocably trapped upon the moon. He may walk the Earth and other places with impunity, in many guises. The nymph, too, has many existences. And often does one meet the other. This relieves the pain of separation even though they know not who they are.

It is difficult for humanity to express happiness for the eternal lovers; for whenever they meet one another, in whatever guise, they come closer to their ultimate aim, which is the destruction and recreation of the world.

Fortunately, there is no reason to believe any of this has

bearing on reality. People believe extremely foolish things. Most of what they think is true happens to be false. The rest is false also. There is no one on the moon and no tree. In fact, there is not even a moon. The moon is a trick. Sometimes the magicians are careless and, out of the corner of one's eyes, the moon can be seen to disappear.

The world, too, is a trick. Sometimes everyone ceases to exist, though only for a moment. Our minds wander and things end. Then they come back. Every human who has ever walked the land—moreover, all those who ever shall—is the avatar of one or another god. We ourselves are the magicians.

There is a secret which explains how the trick works. The secret is quite simple. The thing which causes the magic to work is that there are people who care about each other and *will* it all to continue. As long as they care, things will exist in one fashion or another. The moment no one cares, the woodsman will cast down the axe, and the nymph will find it and become monstrous. If there is not one exception, if there is not even a woodsman or a nymph who cares, then the Great Moon Tree will be cut down, and the Great Earth Tree will fail to grow. The branches will not touch. The woodsman will not meet his bride. There will be nothing but stars turned black and blind. There will be no re-beginning.

It is important, therefore, to care about something, if only for a dog, or a dog's bone. A dog caring about its bone can help to hold the illusion together a while longer. Nothing can be destroyed from outside. It can only be destroyed from within. This is very hard to do because it is so difficult for that which does not exist in the first place to destroy itself. Unable to destroy itself, it continues. Throughout the whole affair, the woodsman and the nymph wander about in various guises, unaware of themselves, laying plans they do not think about, achieving ends they did not mean.

The woodsman knows part of this though he does not know it all. He sits in the Great Moon Tree and watches himself, in other forms, taking part in activities upon the Earth. He hugs his axe and watches. It is difficult to tire of a story when one notices himself a player. It will be another thousand years before the woodsman wearies of the vision and takes another swing at the base of the cinnamon tree.

They were awakened in the russet dawn by a horrifying, bestial shout. Lu Khen sat up beside Mai Su, shaking from his mind the most extraordinary train of thought his sleeping state had ever imposed upon him. He would like to look inside himself and strive to capture the thoughts before they were lost, for dreams are very hard to hold. But he could not think about it now and would never have another opportunity. He was looking in all directions, wondering at the shout, the echo of which had already faded. Mai Su was already sitting straight and alert, her eyes fixed in an upturned gaze.

Lu Khen was still too bewildered by recent slumber and peculiar dreams. He was unable to judge the degree of danger they were in. The passing roar was the same one they had heard on other nights. He had previously pondered how there was nothing to prevent beasts of prey, inhabitants of the hot jungles, from occasionally hunting in the cooler upper country. Such considerations brought fear upon him every time the roar was manifested. But over a period of days, he became jaded and less fretful of the sound, which had always been far away. He awakened, therefore, with small sense of urgency and with slow wits.

Mai Su certainly did not look the least worried, but was as ever placid. She had never in her life known fear, so far as Lu Khen was able to judge. She might well think the terrible sound was something of a pleasant melody. The closer the song, the more beautiful.

The sound did not repeat. Lu Khen dared to hope that his dream state had amplified the single roar, tricking him into thinking the predator was closer than was likely.

The last traces of sleepiness passed from his mind and Lu Khen followed the line of Mai Su's gaze. And his breath caught in his throat! He saw, standing atop a mossy boulder in the dim light of dawn, practically above their heads, a

huge white and black tiger! The tiger was ghostly, for it lacked any of the orange pigment behind its stripes. The dead one he had seen as a child impressed him as being the size of an ox. The present tiger, by its very life, imposed upon his sensibilities a still larger image. Glowering at them from above, Lu Khen could see the bloodshot corners of its eyes and the two rows of dry dugs along its underside. How menacing!

The she-cat's muscles quivered around the shoulders, as though she were tensing for the leap upon Mai Su and Lu Khen, eager to tear them part from part. Weaponless, Lu Khen moved a hand toward a stone. It would be a feeble defense. Yet he resolved to save Yeung Mai Su even if the stone were insufficient to save his own life. He would bash the tiger between the eyes over and over and over, even while its claws tore the flesh from his bones! He raised himself from his bedplace of ferns and moss. He stood in a crouch, the stone held in a tight, white fist. With his other hand, he motioned Mai Su to remain still; she did not pay attention to him yet did not move.

The eyes of the huge tiger looked directly at the couple. Then she looked beyond them, as though something far away had caught her attention. Her tongue lolled and saliva dripped. She panted heavily, as though she had run to this place; her attention remained fixed on a distant height. Suddenly, the tiger wobbled on her front limbs and fell on her own chin with a crack of the jaw. She rolled awkwardly from atop the boulder and plunged to the ground, limp at Lu Khen's feet.

He raised the stone above his head. He did not understand how a powerful beast could have fallen so clumsily, but he knew he might never have a better chance to crush its skull.

But something grabbed his arm. It was Yeung Mai Su's slender hand, stronger than he had ever imagined. She would not let him slay the stricken cat. She pulled his hand down and made him keep his arm at his side. Then she turned her affectionate gaze to the creature with black stripes on a pure white field, rib cage clearly outlined due to hunger and old age. The tiger lay, eyes open and glaring, chest heaving. Mai Su knelt beside the stately feline and petted her flanks.

Though the beast was without apparent injury, she was dying all the same, for she could battle Time no more than human beings could quell the ravage of passing years. Mai Su's compassion for the pitiable tiger was communicated to Ou Lu Khen with a single glance. He let his stone fall and roll away between ferns.

The sun rose slowly, causing the sky to go from rust through bronze on its way to gold. Sun shadows moved through the forest. No wind stirred the leaves. Yeung Mai Su raised the cat's huge head into her lap as she began to sing. The young man who stood nearby thought he might swoon to the song's intense sorrow.

Though it was a sad melody, it did not seem so much for the dying as for those who must remain. Ou Lu Khen could not know the words his beloved used, no more than he could guess how she knew such words or why she used them only in her rare music. Yet he could sense the meaning. And he was moved to tears.

The huge cat growled deep inside herself, then peeled back wide, frightened eyes, apprehensive of the singing woman. But as Yeung Mai Su was fearless, so too was the she-cat's confusion lessened. The tiger rocked her head feebly in Mai Su's lap, and Mai Su, sitting on a carpet of moss, continued to stroke the cat's fur, to sing to her, to ease away all fear and all pain.

When the white tiger died, Mai Su ceased her song and did not move. Bright sun sparkled between wet leaves, scattering specks of rainbow.

Just as Lu Khen was gently tugging Mai Su away, the roar of the white tiger came once more, though she lay dead before them. The roar filled the mountain forest. The voice of the tiger raised itself into the sky, then faded away to heaven.

In the crook of a tree squatted a strange monkey which was not a monkey but a weird, wiry little girl. She had become lost in the forest when barely able to walk. She had no remembrance of when or how it happened. She remembered living in the wild as though it had always been so.

It was miraculous that she survived, though such things have been known to happen in other places as well. She had been helped by a bear with a sun-yellow crest and tufted ears, a beautiful she-bear. It had taken pity on the needful girl. The she-bear had lost a cub, so maternal anguish made her receptive to the unexpected creature crying among the underbrush. The feral girl suckled against the bear's warm belly for long days and nights, though rather old not to be weaned. She and the bear traveled about in the evenings, foraging, but the girl preferred to suck. The bear was not the biggest of animals, but big enough to ride. When there was danger, the child would cling to the bear's fur and hang on tight; and the bear would run swiftly.

Later, the bear had second thoughts about the furless cub and got rid of her. The child continued to survive.

Somewhere along the line she found her way to the place of her origin. It half awakened memories of infancy. She had small recollection of anything but the forest. Her mind worked like a beast's, taking things as they came, disposing of the rest, learning without remembering, or remembering that which was essential to another day of existence, nothing more.

Yet there was something about the sight of the village, and the creatures who strode upright, that cast a veil of nostalgic magic across her senses. She ought to run away from the place, but could not. She squatted among the ferns and brush outside the village, peering in. She had seen such animals before, without realizing she was their kind. She thought herself related to a bear. The ones she had seen before were hunters and she feared them, hated them, hid from them, and never tried to find out where they lived. Now, curiosity overcame doubt. She mimicked their upright posture, a dirty apparition standing where she might be seen. She felt vulnerable and crouched down at once.

She lurked about the edge of the village for months on end. People caught glimpses of her but could never catch her and soon gave up trying. A sad woman would come into the forest from time to time, to shout a certain word that caused the feral girl's heart to stretch forth and ache.

But she never went to the call, never growled reply, never imitated such sounds.

The sad woman began to leave food in the forest. This encouraged the feral girl to come about, grabbing things to eat. It was interesting food. She never approached anyone nor let them approach her. Yet she became a presence at the periphery of the villagers' lives.

Time was meaningless. The new routine became eternal. Then, to her surprise, she came one day looking for food, and there was a lot of it there, more than ever at one time, and she ate so much it made her belly round; but it was to be the last of it. The village was deserted.

The people had gone off somewhere, for what purpose, the feral girl could not begin to calculate. If they had caught her and beaten her, it could not have injured her more. She gazed into the empty village, panting hard and noisily, eyes wild with disbelief. She had never realized how much they meant to her, how much she counted on their presence despite her refusal to be tamed. Maybe it was the food that made her want them. It had certainly made life easier; survival would be hard once more. But the fluttering panic in her breast suggested they had meant more to her than easy meals.

She was forlorn, just as she had been when the she-bear snarled and would not let her suck again. The feral girl went into the village for the first time, crouching, crawling, jumping from one insufficient hiding place to another, but there was no one there to see her. She searched for the sad woman. Surely the sad woman had remained. But there was nobody. The child sat on her haunches in the middle of the village and made long, wailing laments. The whole night, grief tried to kill her. Yet she was a healing kind; she had a beast's pragmatism. Come the new day, she hunted food.

That very evening there came two strange travelers to the abandoned village. They were unlike anyone she had ever seen. One of the strangers spied her and tried to steal her dinner (or so she was convinced) but he failed. She had not eaten anything substantial since she caught that fat, arboreal rat.

Today she smelled meat. She crouched in the tree and saw where the meat lay. Before she could get it, those same two travelers happened along. The female of the pair sniffed at the carcass, crouching by its side, but apparently found it an unacceptable meal. The feral girl waited in the crook of the tree. She was perfectly still, sniffing the air. She waited until the strangers went along their way. She waited until it was dark. The tiger which had killed the deer, and the two people who had looked at it for a while, never came back.

The child came down from the tree, lank and quick as a gibbon. She struck the ground lightly, sniffing left, sniffing right. She knew about the tiger which had come up from lower lands, and she wisely feared it. She took a circuitous route toward the deer path, then leapt out onto the dead animal and began beating it with a rock. She beat at the haunch until the thigh bone shattered. Then she tugged violently at the loosened leg until stretched ligaments tore.

The feral girl ran madly through the forest in search of a safe place to sit and eat.

The small wind had dropped, leaving a deathly quiet and all the shadows still. The faces of the aborigines were streaked with tattoos that looked like trails of dark, glistening fluid, forming intricate designs. They wore nothing above their waists, not wishing to hide their stomachs and shoulders, which were decorated with intriguing whorls. They wore about their hips an array of tails from deer and civets and other wild beasts, hunters' prizes. Their pants were of coarsely woven cloth, but brightly embroidered with the same whorl designs which adorned their bellies, shoulders, and cheeks. Wherever their flesh was not stained, they were the color of copper.

There were seven of them, wiry men, and strong, each with spears of hardwood and brass. They had planted themselves like solemn sentinels upon the moss-grown, ancient highway, as though waiting specifically for Koy and her great-grandfather. What brooding, silent figures they seemed in the forest's gloom!

There was no escaping them, no sense trying. They led Koy and Po Lee away from the highway which had taken Po Lee so long to find. Po Lee whispered, as much to ease his own apprehensions as hers, "They are hunters and not warlike. I had some experience with their kind when I was young. There is no reason to be afraid."

Koy had not been particularly frightened, though she felt she ought to be on guard, especially as it had not looked accidental that the hunters found them.

Po Lee knew something of their language, yet could not get them to talk in more than guttural commands, nasty-sounding syllables which meant "That way!" or "Go!" The guttural intonations were used only when addressing whom-ever they considered inferior. When they chattered among themselves, it had a more pleasant ring, sounding much like excited geese.

"What are they saying?" asked Koy.

"They talk too fast for me to follow," said Po Lee, shrug-ging his shoulders. "Also, it has been a long time since I heard their tongue. But I can tell they are not surprised to have found us."

Koy said, "Here is Harada's sword strapped to my back. They only have spears and might not know what a sword is. This one looks like a fancy stick when it's in its sheath."

"Oh, I should think they know it is a sword, all right, even though they lack the skills to forge anything but copper and bronze. They respect such things, and will not take it from us unless they have to."

"I think I should stay close to you," Koy said, "in case you have to draw the sword and fight them."

Po Lee's brows raised at the notion. Koy had gotten rather too adjusted to the idea that her great-grandfather knew how to kill. He said, "To be sure, I have used swords in my life, but none like Harada's, and never against seven. If they meant harm, they would have taken everything away from us by now. Best if we cause no trouble."

All the same, she made sure the handle of the longsword stuck above her shoulder in the direction of Po Lee.

They came eventually to an encampment which was alive

with activity. Trees shaded the area. A brook wound through a clearing on its way to a nearby lake. Swift, clean water burbled over rounded stones.

The hunters kept Koy and Po Lee hemmed between them. They bowed to equally tattooed women but did not bow to anyone who had fewer tattoos than themselves. Koy was surprised to note that more women than men had the prized if gaudy pigmentation added to their skin. It appeared as though women had several ways to earn the desired tattoos, but men must risk their lives as hunters to earn many markings. Some of the young, unstained men appeared content at the bottom of the tribal hierarchy, but hunters did not bow to them.

The tribal costume was pretty similar for men and women, though few women bared their breasts unless to reveal encircling tattoos. The women tended to wear more layers of the coarse cloth, and had better, denser embroideries. Several members of the tribe had pretty feathers in their hair, hanging downward, held on with nothing visible. They were slender people, probably handsome, though Koy could not judge whether they were good looking or not, so alien were their costumes and their marked skin.

Another thing Koy observed was how these poeple probably were not generally nomadic. They were only slightly better prepared than herself and Po Lee for an extended journey. There was a makeshift look to the camp, as though they had not had a great deal of experience raising their temporary dwellings. The ground had been cleared haphazardly. The hastily constructed huts were sloppy, undersized, and inadequate. The huts barely qualified as shelter, consisting of long leaves of a palmlike plant, bound together to make a roughly cone-shaped structure like a huge rain hat. Each such structure might house one or two people. A good wind could knock them down with ease. These were veritable throw away houses, easy to make from new material at each stop.

Po Lee tried to explain some of this to Koy, speaking softly as they went with the hunters, but it did not strike Koy that her great-grandfather was entirely certain what was going on. "These folk were settled until recently," he said. "They used to live a bit west of here. Something has frightened them from their usual place."

As the tribe was on the run from something, they had few possessions to slow them down. There were weapons, but nothing more aggressive than hunting spears. There were small, simple looms which apparently belonged to untattooed men who were the tribal weavers. Women alone were the embroiderers, though; some of the oldest women sat on the ground, chewing sweet bark, embroidering coarse cloth, and gossiping. Their small eyes watched Koy and Po Lee pass by. Koy saw someone carrying water in a cupped leaf, and someone else eating off a leaf with his fingers, so few things they had brought with them.

But the uprooted people did have one impressive object which they had been unable to part with, and which they had brought with them on their unexpected exodus. This one object was soon revealed to Koy and her great-grandfather.

Eight stout men with only a few tattoos on their arms and chins carried a transportable, wooden temple into the camp. They eased it onto a newly cleared patch of ground, keeping it very level. The vehicular temple had turrets and curving roofs. Its walls were painted with shapes which betrayed a degree of sympathy with the tribe's tattoo and embroidery patterns. Under the eaves were gargoyles with bloated bellies, grimacing faces, and webbed feet, carved in attitudes of holding up the roofs. There were lots of small windows in odd places, and the door was hardly big enough for anyone to crawl through.

Koy looked upon the structure as a marvelous toy, a pretend temple, scaled down but intricately done, made to look haunted but too small to be truly frightening.

"It's so pretty, great-grandfather! I would like to climb in there." She thought about it again and added, "On second thought, it is pretty strange."

Po Lee's aged brow drew up so that his wrinkles had a pinched look of consternation. Regarding the wooden structure carried into the middle of the fresh camp, Po Lee said nothing.

The bright dyes and mud-based paints gave the temple a showy aspect which eased it of some of its eeriness. The carved devils under the eaves, with fierce red faces and long, lolling tongues and sharp teeth were the scariest part. Except for the teeth, they looked like peculiar toads.

The hunters urged Po Lee and Koy nearer the small temple. The men who had carried it were presently squatting to left and right of it, taking rigid ceremonial postures. Several women strutted up with self-importance, their faces tattooed so much they looked to be peering out through the eyeholes of masks. They acted as though the temple were more theirs than anyone else's. Their blue-black faces showed an immeasurable egotism. Their shirts were slit down the front to reveal the dark designs of red and blue encircling their breasts. The embroidery of their costume was thick and heavy. Others watched these women as though they were the tribal beauties, though Koy found their haughty, stained faces horrible.

These women gathered into a group and raised their hands to the temple and began to hum a repellent dirge as though to hail the dead.

Po Lee was rudely batted in the back of his knees with the butt of a hunter's spear. He plunged to his knobby knees in forced obeisance to the temple, and dropped his walking stick. A quick sidelong glance warned Koy to kneel quickly lest she be treated roughly, too. She knelt close to her great-grandfather and asked,

"Is Buddha inside?"

"They know little of Buddha," Po Lee answered. A dark hand slapped his pate to silence him.

Three of their seven captors approached the shrine and spoke humbly, reporting about Koy and Po Lee, no doubt. Po Lee concentrated, but Koy could tell he was able to make sense of few statements. Were they explaining things to their god? She wondered if their god really was in there.

The hunters withdrew when their speech was done. The humming women continued their strange music with greater fervor.

"What will happen?" asked Koy.

"Shush," said Po Lee, then grinned at the guard near his

shoulder, averting another whack to his pate. The aborigine actually smiled back; it might have eased a lot of tension, except that with his face exquisitely tattooed, it was hard to tell if it were a friendly smile, an evil one, or a grimace.

Koy's breath caught in her throat when she saw movement at one of the windows of the temple. Something moved back and forth, wobbling oddly. The temple did not look big enough to house anyone. But if Koy doubted the shadow, she could not doubt that two women hurried forth to open the small double door.

Po Lee took Koy's hand without looking at her. It was comforting.

Something was crawling out of the miniature temple. At first Koy saw only a nest of white hair and two bony arms. Women hovered near, to help the stick figure out the door and to a standing position.

It was a tiny old woman. She was skeletal and had a strange gait. She held a polished wooden staff with a black knot for a handle. Her eyes were pale and vacant. She turned her head one way and then another, listening. Among her tattooed people, the old woman was ghostly, her skin devoid of artificial pigmentation.

Po Lee told Koy in a most hushed tone, "She is the tribe's oracle. They are often blind, coddled, and protected by their worshipers. She rules them after a fashion, but you need not be afraid of her."

"I'm not," said Koy, but she sensed Po Lee's unease.

In a slow, cracked voice, the blind crone spoke in the tongue of Koy and Po Lee, though with the oddest accent. "Why were you on the Forbidden Road?" she demanded. "You must go another way, or my people will not let you go at all."

Po Lee replied in a clear, slow voice, so that the oracle would understand his every word. "Why is that road forbidden? I have walked it once before."

"Have you?" said the oracle with disapproval. She hobbled forward, toward the sound of Po Lee. She was quick as a spider, bracing herself with her cane, followed by attentive women eager to support her if she lost her odd, wobbly balance. "You cannot disobey me," she warned. "As you see, my people are many, and you cannot get away. If you insist on that road, I can have you tied up, to be taken along with us. It would be for your own good."

"In that case," said Po Lee in a calculating manner, "we will go straight back the way we came."

"That's right," said Koy, enjoying the opportunity to tell a good lie. As she was ordinarily such a truthful girl, misleading someone was quite thrilling. "We were only lost in the first place."

The blind woman ignored Koy. But she had stopped right in front of Po Lee. He had his staff upon the ground before his knees and she had her cane; Koy thought they looked eager to fight one another. The oracle stretched her white eyes wide—a monstrous effect—and said, "You do not sound truthful to me. But you do sound familiar. Are you my lover from a long time ago?"

Po Lee looked stricken and his complexion flushed. His mouth dropped open in surprise. It took him a moment to find his voice, but find it he did, and said, "How could I be such a fellow?"

"I think you are," she said. "I think you are Po Lee."

"That's you, all right, great-grandfather!" said Koy, interested in the new revelation about Po Lee's youthful conquests.

Po Lee gave her a hard look to silence her.

"I remember you," said the blind oracle. She reached out a hand to touch Po Lee's face. It was like an insect crawling over his forehead and down his cheeks. "Not so handsome anymore," she said, drawing her hand away. "What a pretty man you were! I liked you a lot. Do you remember? Was I beautiful, too? In my darkness, I thought we were a perfect pair. Tattoos mean nothing to an oracle who is blind; I could overlook the opinion of my people. You could have stayed but you would not. I knew from the beginning it was not meant to be. But a young girl dreams. Even I had dreams; I who see the future and should have few illusions."

There was a weight of responsibility in the old woman's

blind expression, and a sorrowful memory that made her look less threatening and less homely than the moment before.

"Some of these young people," said the oracle with unexpected quickness, "are your relatives. Can you believe it? But your daughter died many years ago. One of our hunters is your grandson. You have several nieces and nephews. I bet you are surprised!"

"I did not know we had a child," admitted Po Lee.

"You did not stay long enough to know!" she said with mild reproach. "She had a good life, so you need not feel guilty about her."

She shooed away the men who were acting as guards. They went off, looking dejected. But one, probably Po Lee's unknown grandson, stood nearby. This hunter was not a young man and he was greatly tattooed. Po Lee did not look in his direction, but Koy was curious about this new relative. They stared at each other.

The oracle turned back toward Po Lee, speaking again in the coastal tongue, "I told them not to be rude to our honored guests. As you are family, there is no need for them to watch you so closely. A happy reunion! Do you agree?"

"A happy reunion," Po Lee said doubtfully.

The rawboned hag raised one hand over her head and made a declaration in her own language. The people bowed to Po Lee as a result of what she said. Everyone began scurrying about, planning a feast and a celebration.

Koy had not thought anyone had been especially menacing to begin with, but now they were downright fawning. Wives came forth to stroke Koy's glistening black hair. They spoke with kind intonation, as though to a child half Koy's age, but she was not annoyed. One of the women hooked a feather in her hair; it was bright green and hooked at the quill's tip so that it would not fall out. Tribal children gathered at a distance and looked at her poutily, as she was an unexpected rival for attention. Po Lee looked about in continued uncertainty, but Koy did not see a reason for him to fret. The hunter who was Po Lee's middle-aged grandson continued to stare.

As fires grew larger and food became plentiful, revelry became more heated and noisy. But in a rare, quiet moment from the ensuing celebration, Po Lee was alone with Koy, and said to her in a soft voice,

"I knew that oracle when I was a young fellow, as she said. I must say I am surprised to see her still alive. I will tell you something else, Koy. She can see pretty well, though not with her eyes. It will be hard to get away from her. These new-found friends who are being so nice to you and me are yet our wardens. Unless their oracle can be convinced to set us free, we are in a sorry situation."

At the onset of their journey, Koy thought her great-grandfather was infallible; she had since learned of the mistakes of his life, and he no longer struck her as superhuman. It is the strange part of growing up that Giants become, by imperceptible stages, smaller and smaller, until they are no longer all wise, but rather similar to oneself. This being so, Koy was no longer predisposed to credit her great-grandfather's discomfort regarding the tribal people. They were harmless and kind.

Koy was yet a child, and more prone to emotional extremes than to mature observation. Her naïveté was impervious to disillusion. The Giant in her life, the once-infallible adult, had become utterly mistaken about *all* things. If he jumped and ran for fear of his life, she was less apt to follow, but might look around to see what worried him. She no longer assumed he knew best. Yet she loved him every bit as much as before. She could forgive him anything and was not condescending about it. It never occurred to her that the perfect being she had previously thought him to be, and the eternally incorrect man she now perceived, were equally childish visions.

So she disbelieved there was danger among these people, who laughed, who enjoyed life, who prepared interesting meals. There was mad dancing, and Koy learned their dances. There was weird, wailing song, and Koy learned the easier parts, without getting the meaning. There were a lot of fish caught from the nearby lake, flashing scales becoming dull

upon the fires, fresh and moist and sweet and handed to her
on the ends of sticks. She ate many. She ate unusual cakes
made from mashed palm hearts.

She clapped her hands and hopped comically and crooned
eerily with the rest. The tribal men and women laughed at
her antics. One heavily tattooed woman with a stooped back
came up to Koy with an embroidered shirt and pulled it
over her head. It was red and green and bright. Koy liked
it. She hugged the stooped woman and felt, indeed, these
were distant kin of hers, for how could she not be related
when Po Lee had a grandson and nieces and nephews and
cousins all about?

All the while, as the sun descended and the fires licked
high, Po Lee remained reticent. He joined none of the events.
He ate quietly. He sat beside Harada's sword and the baskets
of traveling gear. He hugged his walking stick and rarely
moved. He kept his eye on Koy every moment, as though
afraid she might be dragged into the forest when it was least
expected, never to be seen again. But he did not try to spoil
her good time. He did not tell her to settle down or to be
careful.

Upon the porch of the vehicular temple, the scrawny
blind woman sat with her legs crossed, looking to be a
starved but holy being. A heavily brocaded robe had been
wrapped across her shoulders. Her guardian women, priestesses perhaps, were never far away. Her white eyes reflected
the bonfires. She was at once severe and pleased in her
countenance. She listened to her reveling people and was
well satisfied with their noises.

There was someone else who did not join into the state
of things: It was the tattooed hunter, Po Lee's bastard grandson. This fellow crouched in a shadow, watching his grand-
sire as a cat watches a bird on a limb. He embodied all that
was unhappy about the tribe, lost and forlorn, torn from
their traditional land with slight understanding of the cause.
Koy barely took note of this. She was getting too much
attention to suspect the least misfortune.

Children were not usually allowed at the center of things.
Koy was a special exception, an entertaining imp from an-

wendy
wees

other part of the world. The tribe enjoyed everything she did in their company, despite that some of her behavior would not have been tolerated in their own children.

As for those children, they observed the shenanigans of their rival, always at a distance, with grim disapproval. They played their games separately from the adults. They had their own miniature pecking order in imitation of their elders. They glanced time and again at Koy, and she at them.

After a while, Koy pranced off to join them. They were grudgingly friendly, though jealous of her privilege. They taught her a game played with smooth stones from the brook. Ordinarily it would have enthused her endlessly, but there were distractions. Now and then the children were a bit rude. She alone had the freedom to join the center of adult doings. She did not have to withstand the least nastiness from her own age group if she did not want to. Though she did not consciously intend to create a situation of power and demand, in fact she manipulated the feelings of these children with ruthless abandon. She would join them, withdraw from them, join them again. They bid at once for her friendship. Then they would try to exert their authority over her, for they alone were proper tribal children, therefore superior. By turns they were self-effacing in her presence, then haughty as young royalty.

It was emotionally stressful despite that everything was fun and exciting. The evening became night with no hint of the festivities letting up. Koy had to rest from so much running about. She joined Po Lee, who was sitting with their gear and munching a roasted eel someone had brought him. As he was not enjoying himself, Koy wanted to cheer him up. But her first question put him on the defensive, though she had meant to be conversational.

"Was that old blind lady your first wife? Before you met Great-grandmother Fa Ling?"

As Koy already knew so much about him, there was no sense in secrecy about this. He scratched behind his ear and gazed awkwardly around. These were evasive postures. He looked at the small temple which was the centerpiece of the festivities, and at the oracle seated on the deck in front of the tiny doors. What a deathly goddess she appeared!

"I guess that would be true," Po Lee finally confessed. "Among these people, though, only women can ask for marriage favors. Your great-grandmother was the only woman I ever personally asked."

"Is that so?" Koy was glad to hear it. She had never known Fa Ling except as an honored ancestor, but there was no ancestor she thought of more highly or more often. Even her own father was more ghostly and unreal than Koy's long-held fancy of the ideal great-grandmother.

"I think I remember right," said Po Lee. "Actually, maybe we asked each other at the same moment. I forget. But to be honest, I did rather like the oracle. Does it mean I was unfaithful, even though in those days I did not know my future wife?"

"I suppose that would not count," said Koy, her expression serious as she patted Po Lee's weathered hand. She looked toward the oracle, and thought the oracle was looking straight back, though that was most unlikely. Koy was very curious about that old woman's previous relationship with Po Lee. Koy said matter-of-factly, "It is a hard thing to imagine."

"She was very attractive," Po Lee assured her. "It may be hard for you to picture, but it was so. She looks like a feeble bag of bones sitting over there so high and mighty, but she was beautiful once, though her eyes were always just like now. I think I looked pretty good myself in those days, though to these aborigines, I was a bad choice for a lover, lacking status and tattoos. If I had had special sight, it would have been all right. But I was very alien to them. I almost got tattooed so they would like me better, but evaded it somehow."

Po Lee's eyes grew misty with remembrance. He said, "She was a romantic girl, too! I seem to remember she was. But she was kind of pitiful due to so much responsibility. People could not do anything without consulting her first. She made every decision. Loving me was her one rebellion. She certainly is different now! Not just because she got old, but because it looks as though she enjoys authority. It was a burden before. She dreamed of running away with me."

"But she never did run away," said Koy. "She let you go by yourself."

"Responsibility is like that," said Po Lee. "I was not eager to convince her to come with me, either. I liked her, but I was also frightened of her, to tell the truth. Not constantly, but there were moments. I finally convinced her to let me go. I could never have gotten far if she had refused."

"Then you can convince her again."

"I hope I can."

"As you were just like a husband to her, she has to obey you!" said Koy with indignant certainty. "Tell her not to interfere with our important mission! It's easy."

Koy thought this a sparkling notion, but Po Lee winced. He said, "Husbands do not have the same say-so in this tribe as they do among our people. Men are sort of like second brothers and uncles; even fathers and eldest sons receive no special admiration. Men make cloth, cook, watch the children after they are weaned. Women fish, hunt birds, gather fruit, and embroider. The wives are more like what we think of as patriarchs. The only exceptions are the hunters, honored for their physical strength and bravery, and even they obey their wives. If I talked too big in such a place as this, I could get in trouble. Some women might drag me off and teach me a lesson."

"Not only that," said Koy, "but you are faithful to great-grandmother, despite that she is dead so long. That makes it hard to act like the husband of someone else."

"That might not quite apply in this situation," said Po Lee. "But I have indeed been faithful to Fa Ling up to now."

Koy had an odd thought and asked, "If I decided to live with these people, would that mean I could be head of the family, like an eldest brother or a father?"

"You have just the meaning of this place!" said Po Lee. "See, it is not hard to understand."

Koy looked at all the dancing and singing going on. This new information made her see everyone in a different light. There was a group of women singing and swaying back and forth, and some men were hopping and dancing in front of them. It had a different meaning altogether when one considered women the leaders of the tribe.

"In that case," said Koy, "when we find Lu Khen, we should all come back and join the tribe."

Po Lee smiled in spite of the distress he felt about their situation. "You would like so much responsibility?" he asked. "It hardly made Lu Khen happy. He might be glad enough to obey you for a change! But, to earn the responsibility, a lot of work would be involved for you. You have to earn a lot of tattoos by catching birds and fish and decorating the rough cloth, and other things. Every time you do something valuable for the tribe, they reward you with pins and dye on your skin. About the time you look like a blackberry instead of a human being, they proclaim you an important lady."

Koy scowled at the thought. "Maybe some other tribe is less excited about tattoos," she ventured, trying to fashion a more ideal system.

"Maybe," said Po Lee teasingly. "I could tell you some funny tribes you might like better. There is one near the borders of Ho where women have a lot of power and fight in battles. They think they look best when their heads are shaved and their ears cut off."

Koy gasped, clapped her hands to her ears, and looked horrified.

"No need to worry about them, though," said Po Lee. "They never come so far south on the Great Peninsula. In fact, if we fail to get free of *this* tribe, we may never see anything or anyone else! Also, I hope the oracle will not expect me to do anything like in the old days."

"What kind of things?"

"Oh . . . things," said Po Lee. "I am not up to it nowadays. Besides, she is too old for me! And what would Fa Ling think? But I must be kind to the oracle in some way, or how will I convince her not to keep us here? This is a hard predicament, Koy."

"I'm not worried," she said, confident in her great-grandfather even if he did seem mistaken about things.

He said, "Well, in the meantime, you might as well enjoy

the party. See there, a new batch of fish are cooked! Get one for me, too. Then you can dance some more, if you like."

When the reveling and wild dances were done and the blazing fires drew in their tongues, black night impinged with all its attendant gloom. Koy had been so worked up over the day's excitements, and the evening's festivities, that it was now difficult to court sleep. But the aboriginal people were going off by ones and twos, burrowing into their temporary palm-leaf huts. One such hut had been designated for herself and Great-grandfather Po Lee.

As the leaves were not bound together at the base, all one had to do to enter the confining, simple structure was to part any pair of leaves. Koy and Po Lee crawled inside and huddled close. It was too small a space to stand within. "If we move around too much," Koy whispered, "we will knock our house right over!"

"As long as there is no rain," rejoined Po Lee, "that would not matter. Isn't it more an umbrella than a house?"

"A big umbrella!" Koy agreed excitedly. "An umbrella drooping right to the ground!"

They laughed together a while, then strove for comfortable positions. Po Lee drew his legs up so that he could fit within the confines. Koy was able to stretch out full length. They had put their few belongings in the center of the structure, between one another. Koy reached around their gear and touched her great-grandfather's head. Pretty soon, Po Lee was snoring, but Koy was wide awake.

She heard a noise outside the palm-leaf house and tensed for fear of trouble. Then she heard a child's stifled laugh. In a moment, two dark-visaged brats parted a pair of palm leaves and peered in, unconcerned with the privacy of the occupants. Other children looked over the shoulders of the foremost two. There were five children in all. One of them, a slender girl and older than the rest, motioned for Koy to come out. The children grinned with mischief and the promise of adventure. Koy pulled on her new, colorful shirt and strapped Harada's sword to her back, where she was getting used to having it, and crawled out to see what the tribal children had in mind. She stood among them like an elfin warrior, alien and proud.

Whatever they had planned, it was being done without the permission of the elders. They made shushing signs to her and to each other. They went crouching among the quiet huts and dull embers of dying fires, so as not to awaken their parents and relatives. When one of the boys giggled as he had done earlier, the tall and lank girl who was eldest smacked his forehead to warn him into silence.

The lank girl was the only one who had her first facial tattoo. The tattoo streaked from one side of the left eye to her chin, an aesthetic curve suited to her particular jawline. The girl was harsh but attractive and the tattoo made her more so. Yet Koy felt there was a limit to how much tattooing could be appealing, and personally found some of the men and women of the tribe perfectly grotesque, when *they* found each other prettiest. She tried to imagine the lank girl a few years hence, her entire face striped like that.

There were whispers between the children, but Koy could understand none of it. She followed them beyond the camp, along the brook, and toward a lake not far off. As they went, everyone gathered smooth stones from along the stream. Koy gathered a few also, without knowing the purpose.

When she saw the lake, round as a bowl, she was overwhelmed by the beauty of the place. The moon lit it with subtle magnificence. Feathery, drooping trees rustled about the shore. The brook splashed down a steep incline, a tiny waterfall sparkling into the round lake. A group of night lotus were opened to the moonlight, diadems of midnight dew strung about the flower petals. Koy wished to pick one of the violet lotus; they were close enough to reach if she were to climb down to the bottom of the moist bank. Also, the pads were so big, one could imagine walking on them. The sight was like a dream!

From one lotus, a menacing black beetle with shining garnet eyes glowered toward the group of children. Then it withdrew into the heart of the plant, as though the stem were a hollow tube leading to the bottom of the lake.

A fisher-owl swooped down and away, carrying a fish.

The children squatted along the upper bank, pointing toward the center of the lake, their arms long and thin and their elbows knobby. They poked each other and jabbered. Koy stood up tall to see what they were pointing at, but there was nothing.

Then there was something after all. There was a swirling *presence* far out under the surface of the water. The small waves were made luminescent by the moon, every ripple lined in silvery light. The giggling boy was whacked on the forehead again. All the children grew silent. The lank girl pulled at Koy to get down, and she squatted amongst them.

The lank girl passed out strips of leather. She gave one to Koy, who did not as yet know what it was for. She soon enough learned. First the oldest girl and then the others each put a stone into the saddle of the leather strips and began to whirl them around their heads. These slingshots took more skill than most of the children evidenced. The lank girl's stone was the only one which went straight toward the unseen presence under the surface of the lake. Some other stones went in that general vicinity, but most were wide of their object. Everyone tried again. They were most serious in this endeavor.

The slingshots were really for bird hunting and Koy did not understand the sport, even as she imitated the others. She whirled the thong over her head, aiming far out in the water. Her first stone slipped out and went backward into the woods. The boy who liked to giggle suppressed making fun, as he was not doing so well himself. Her second stone splashed right below them, dampening the children squatting nearest the edge of the embankment. Her third try was lucky. It skimmed over the surface, hopping the whole distance, finally sinking at the stirred and frothy area of the lake. The giggler got his head whacked for the third time. This time it made him mad. He gave the lank girl a good kick in the shins, disregarding her authority. She grimaced fiercely and shoved him backward. He stumbled down the bank and right into the water, lily pads buckling under his weight.

It was only knee deep, but he fell on his butt and sat with water above his waist. He was too terrified to get out, though Koy saw no cause for his alarm. His eyes turned toward the center of the lake. He opened his mouth as though to shout in fear, but nothing came out of him. The lank girl, as a result, had to climb down the steep bank to the water's edge, then wade out to get him. It only wetted her below the knees, but the boy was soaked and muddied. He was done with giggling and sat away from everyone, hugging his knees and looking chilly.

"You spoiled it for him," said Koy. The lank girl looked at Koy without understanding, the curve of the tattoo making the girl's face appear long and expressive.

They threw more rocks, all but the boy who was soaked and sulking. The water became more turbulent, as though something were getting very angry. Whatever was out there in the middle of the lake, it kept moving from one side to the other, trying to get out of the way of the projectiles plopping into its domain. But rocks occasionally found it, no matter what it did or where it went.

Koy was getting the hang of the slingshot. It was fun. She hit the target a second time (out of about ten more tries) and saw a distinct response in the roiling water. Then she was out of rocks and joined one of the other children, crawling around in the darkness and feeling for more stones near the brook.

While she was busy stone hunting, she heard the wet, huddled boy give a mild squeak. He leaped to his feet and ran away through the forest, fast as his legs would take him. Koy looked up. The lank girl was pushing the other youngsters away from the embankment, suddenly concerned lest another one slip into the water.

There was a V-shaped ripple on the water's surface, rather than the previous swirl of random waves. The V cleaved reflected moonlight and aimed its point in the direction of the harassing children. It was coming swiftly. The lank girl wanted everyone a safe distance away. But they did not follow the coward who fled, terror stricken. Rather, they picked up bigger rocks in their fists. They stood poised, ready to throw the rocks, ready for anything.

Everyone was silent. Even their breaths were still. Koy put the leather thong inside her shirt and picked up a good-sized rock, like the others had done.

The wedge of ripples came very near, until all evidence of it vanished amidst the lily pads. The water became smooth and quiet.

No one moved for the longest while, including the thing beneath the water.

The lank girl whispered a stern command, affecting the guttural tones Koy had heard the hunters use. One of the boys inched forward a step at a time, then heaved his stone into the water.

Instantly, the beast reared up! The boy wheeled around and ran screaming into the forest. Koy kept near the lank girl, as did the two other remaining children. Koy comprehended that the frightful game was of the eldest girl's device, that she was less surprised by events. If the lank girl did not run away, Koy felt certain she could herself be brave.

But what a horrific thing it was to see! It reared up against the moonlit sky, a fleshy, serpenty, flabby thing like an elongated frog, quivering half bonelessly, and oozing slime. Its face and general shape had been echoed in the gargoyle carvings on the tiny temple in which the blind oracle was carried around. Koy had not thought whether or not the gargoyles were taken from life or legend, but here loomed the definitive reply to the unconsidered query.

It roared awfully. Water flooded from its wide, toothy mouth. Koy thought it hovered out of the water for ages, but a scant moment had passed before it was already collapsing under its own weight, unable to remain long above the water, having rubbery bones and no experience with land or air.

The lank girl gave another guttural command. One of the other children, a dark-eyed girl who started to run away but had come back, answered the leader's command, going forth and tossing the rock.

The monstrosity lurched upward again, roaring louder with increased hatred. Its piggish wet eyes shone balefully. In the night's stillness, its shout struck Koy as deafening;

but really the sound was only a croaking that, off in the woods, would sound like nothing more fierce than an especially obnoxious toad.

It waved degenerate arms back and forth like a crazed fat man trying to get attention. Then it splashed down at the bottom of the embankment, half out of the water. It began to ooze itself forward, struggling to climb the bank, to get its hated foe. It was not having much luck climbing, but the odor of its scummy flesh was sufficient to defeat bravery.

It became very flat on the land. It looked as though it could barely carry its weight. Its small forelimbs were not designed for anything but stuffing things in its mouth and were practically useless. Behind, it dragged long legs. The feet were still hidden in the water, beneath the lotus pads. The legs were already twice as long as the fat, mushy body and not yet completely visible.

The violet lotus blossoms had closed against the horror of things, and their color had grown pale.

The lank girl gave one more command. But the last two children had run off. There was only herself and Koy. She looked hard into Koy's face and repeated the command.

Swallowing hard, Koy took one step toward the bank and lifted the rock above her head, prepared to throw the rock right between those shining, piggish eyes. But in that moment, the gigantic toad-beast drew its long legs completely from the water, stood on huge webbed feet, and raised its fat body the full height of the embankment! At the same time, a long tongue shot forth from its toothy maw and snatched Koy around the waist!

It collapsed to the foot of the bank once more, but its long tongue still held Koy. She dropped the rock, shouted, and fell to the ground, grabbing onto a bared root. The lank girl leaped forth to grab hold of one of Koy's arms, trying to help. There was no longer any of the certainty which had marked the tattooed girl's eyes until that moment. There was none of the commanding self-possession on which Koy had set her faith.

The toad-beast used its small forelimbs like a pair of

hands drawing in a rope, but the rope was its own tongue, and Koy was dragged off the edge of the embankment, toward a big ugly mouth. Its eyes gleamed with victorious malevolence. The lank girl lost her grip on Koy's arm. Koy lost her grip of the root. She slid down toward the vengeful monster.

She had Harada's sword, but it came loose from her back and she was being drawn away from it. She managed to grab the hilt, so only the sheath was lost to the higher bank. As she plunged downward, she chopped blindly through the air beneath her, hoping to strike the beast. Its tongue was severed by sheer luck; the monster lurched straight up into the air, a hideous hop which made it come down on its back upon the water.

It thrashed madly as black blood gushed from its mouth. It croaked pitifully.

It took the lank girl's aid to get the adhering end of the tongue loose from Koy's waist. The tongue really wanted to remain attached. Despite that Koy was scared and muddy, she managed to look calm as she cleaned sticky blood from Harada's sword, then got the sword's sheath and cleaned that, too. The kicking toad-beast floated away, dying from the injury to its tongue. Despite that it was horrible, Koy felt sorry for the thing.

She found herself leading the way back to the camp, for the lank girl was much cowed, and had gained a lot of respect for the tough little outsider. A couple of the children had only been hiding in the forest and they came out and followed also. It had doubtless been the intent of these children to scare the girl who had gotten so much attention during the long day, while the native children got no attention at all. But they had scared themselves better. In the end, Koy had come out looking like a monster-slaying hero and not a mere stranger to be put roundly in her place.

But she did not feel as though she were a hero. She wished she could speak their language so as to make her feelings known. The rest of the children hung around the edge of the camp, waiting to regroup; even the soaked boy reappeared, sheepish, his white teeth flashing. Before everyone slunk back to their palm-leaf huts for the remainder of the night, Koy told them, although they could not understand, "It is wicked to tease animals." She chastised herself as much as the others. They sensed only her dissatisfaction with events, and their eyes were lowered.

Koy slipped back to the leaf hut and crawled inside to rest. To her surprise, Great-grandfather Po Lee was not there. Had he gone in search of her? She did not know whether or not he had done so. Surely he would be back soon. Maybe he had to pee and it would only take a few more moments.

She wanted to stay awake until he got back. But the day had been long. The night felt longer. She was bone tired. She fell asleep, still unaware of Po Lee's whereabouts.

The toad-monster drifted in the black lake; and a blacker cloud—could it be the soul of the toad?—issued from its tortured mouth. What an evil soul the monster had!; if indeed it were a soul and not a weird parasite. The black cloud drifted over the water, over the floating, bloated corpse of the monster, turning all to ice. The black cloud pulsated, shimmered, wishing that it could expand over the face of the world, bringing an age of Ice and Despair. In fire, the cycle ends in a heavenly unity; but in the hellish coldness, the souls of things past and present are held captive. The black cloud radiated frustration and anger, the coldest of emotions.

A fisher-owl passed through a wing-shaped appendage of the gleaming black shadow. At once the taloned hunter dropped onto the surface of the lake, cracking the ice which had formed beneath the cloud. The bird was stiff and dead.

At length the black cloud became less agitated. As it quieted within itself, it began slowly to dissolve into thin nothingness.

❦ FIVE ❧

The Winged
Man

HARADA FUMIAKA TRIED to remember where he left his
sword. Had he put it down somewhere recently? Had he
lost it several days ago? He looked in his basket, but that
was stupid. His sword was three or four times too long to
fit in the basket. What was he doing with the basket? He
could not remember where he had gotten it or how long he
had been carrying it around. Probably it was stolen, he
decided, and was at first proud of himself for stealing it,
then felt ridiculous for not having stolen things more useful
than what was in the basket. He was not thinking clearly
at all! He had to find his sword! He looked everywhere. It
was not behind any trees. It was not on that rock. It was
not by the pool where he had gotten a drink of awful-tasting
water.

He was lost in the forest. So was his sword, for all he
could tell. He tried to retrace his steps to see if he had
dropped it along the way. But he was uncertain which direction he had come from, or which direction he was going
for that matter.

It had been his father's sword and it would not do to lose it. His father would beat him to death! No, that was impossible; his father had been killed by somebody a long time before. Besides, Harada was bigger than his father. Everybody remarked on it. Harada was big like the priest his mother often went to see. Despite being bigger, he remained scared of his father. He was still scared after the mean-hearted fellow died. Awful man like that was apt to hang around and cause mischief out of spite! His father never seemed to love Harada, so Harada was all the more pleased to get his father's sword after the old coot was killed. A good son would avenge his father, but Harada felt more inclined to avenge himself. Keeping his father's sword was revenge for himself against his father! If he lost the sword, he would have to start all over again, seeking revenge.

Harada's head had ached for days. Someone had beaten him up. He had not felt well since. He remembered how his father used to beat him up. He remembered sitting up in a peach tree, and his father, a famous warrior when younger, was standing under the tree saying, "Come down here and let me beat you up!" Little Harada refused to come down. "It will only go worse for you if you refuse!" his father shouted, drinking from a ceramic bottle. Harada grimaced and held onto the limb so he would not fall down where his father could get him. "Haven't beat you up for several days now. About time!"

As Harada kept refusing, his drunken father became genuinely mad. He had not been mad before but only wanted to have a good time terrorizing a fat little boy. But a son should be obedient even if his father intended to beat him up for no good reason. Disobedience seriously annoyed Harada's father. He threw the bottle down, drew his sword, and bellowed red faced, "Down here at once!" Harada started to cry noiselessly. His father took a fine, proud stance, raised his sword at a high angle, and sliced at the trunk of the tree. He cut halfway through. The trunk started to crack and lean. "Momma!" cried Harada. "Momma! Momma!" His father said, "Here comes the tree right down, you little brat! Get you now!"

But Harada was not a little boy in a peach tree. He was a grown man lost in the forest, and just as scared as when he was little. He would feel better if he had the sword. Where could it be? That old man must have taken it! Yes, it was the old man who had beaten him with a stick, just like Harada's father used to do. "I've never killed anyone before, but I'd like to kill that old man!" thought Harada. "Maybe I'm not much, but I can take care of that old Po Lee!"

He decided on a direction, and started off in search of Po Lee. By nightfall, he was so disoriented and hungry that he fell down under a conifer and tried to eat some pine needles. They got stuck in his mouth and made his gums bleed and he could not swallow them. He sat on the ground picking needles out of his mouth one at a time, feeling as though there were no end to the things. He forgot how they got in his mouth in the first place. It was like a bad dream, all this stuff in his mouth!

He lay down under the tree and became extremely chilled. "Look at my hands," he said wonderingly, holding them upward. "They have turned perfectly white! My fingernails are blue!" He did not have anything with which to cover himself. "Hard to move my body. Feels tied up."

In a moment of lucidity, he realized he was not going to be able to go anywhere from then on. He was too weak. "I'm going to die," he said, quite aware of the effects of prolonged exposure. "Life is like that," he mused, staring upward through limbs at a starry sky. "A man wants to succeed and be rich and have respect, but he dies by himself like this. His enemies have a party and spend the money that should have been his. What a cruel trick life is! But I'm ready. Take me right down to Hell, I don't care. Can't be much worse."

His bold resignation gave out; his courage fled. He regretted death. He remembered his mother, her long arms, her dark hair as she brushed it and oiled it. "Want some? Want some oil?" She put oil in his hair, too. She combed his hair. Wasn't he happy then? It was hard to be sure. If he had been happy, then surely he had also been gentle and brave and confident and filled with prospects: an innocent boy playing underneath a fateless peach tree in the yard, watching the blossoms fall, laughing gaily. Had it been so?

So there he was in the house beside his mother and she was combing pleasant-smelling oil into his hair. How nice! What bliss! Then in rushed his father, staggering, coming home from someplace. He shouted, "You're making him a sissy!" He kicked the aromatic oil across the room, spilling it on everything. He slapped his wife across the mouth. The little boy flung himself at his father and bit deep into a thigh. That was how Harada lost two of his lower front teeth.

"Momma," Harada whispered, looking up through the pine. She was an old widow now and not well off. Maybe she was dead. How would he find out? He blinked moist, red eyes. A dirty beard hid most of his grimace. What if his father were waiting for him in Hell? That was a terrible thought! Were there peach trees in Hell? Would he have to sit in one, with his father waiting below?

Harada made pitiful grunting noises, wondering how he came to be such a man. Weren't all villains people who loved their mothers and hated their fathers? No, true villains hated their mothers, too! That was what Harada figured out. He was a failed villain. He was unfilial enough to be a cad, yet too filial to be a truly, effectively cruel man.

Maybe it was untrue he hated his father. He was afraid of him all right, but some part of the child envied the man. The innocence of a child was only half beaten out of Harada. The other half was corrupted from within himself. Didn't cruel people always get their way? There was a nice man who went around begging for things to eat, rattling his bells, and look what people fed him! But Harada's father made huge demands. He was not nice for a minute at a time. He ate the best things in the house, not that these were the best things anyone could have. Better than Harada and momma had, at least! So Harada wanted to be more like his father, whom he admired and envied and—loved. He wished his father would like him a little bit, that's what! So there sat Harada, getting oil combed into his hair, and he was caught being a sissy! He crawled away in a corner and watched his father beat his mother very badly. Harada wept tears, but never came out and bit his father at all. Harada did not lose his two lower teeth by biting anyone. They were knocked out of his mouth when the peach tree fell down with him in it!

"I *would* have bit him," thought Harada, "except my mouth was already swollen." But that wasn't true either. The incident in the peach tree was several days later. He had strong teeth at the time but was afraid to use them to help his mother.

Harada wondered if only villains changed their memories around so they could feel better. Did honest people lie to themselves? He was not very likely ever to know how honest people felt about things.

This was where it all ended, though. That much was certain. Lost in some foreign country, flat under a tree in a forest where nobody was likely to find his bones. Everyone ends up a corpse no matter what, but it was extra pitiful to think nobody would do anything about this one—not so much as the basic prayer of the sort mumbled for homeless beggars who drop dead in the streets.

Harada's body temperature had dropped a long way, but he was too weak to shiver. He closed his eyes, though he knew he would die within moments of falling asleep. He muttered a terrible prayer, expecting it to be his last: "Buddha is nothing to me. If there are any devils around here, why don't you help me out? You'll have me someday in any case. I'm not ready to die. Will Hell be bitter enough if I've no memories of something more pleasant?"

It seemed as though someone or something heard his prayer, even though he had spoken so badly that it would have been unintelligible to human ears. Harada forced himself to open his weary eyes, for he heard a strange crinkling sound run through the pine. He saw that the tree limbs had turned white with frost. He saw a black, shimmering shadow passing through rimed branches. Had he seen that thing before? Had it given him some useless advice that only caused him injury?

If the previous information had been a trick or a mistake, then it might have been because Harada had failed to pray earnestly. This time he had asked for help, and was heard. Even if it was only a devil that cared about him, that counted for something.

The chill cloud began to shrink inward, to coalesce into a thing more compact and substantial, taking specific form. A writhing *something* shaped itself from unsure vapor. Harada watched as from a nightmare of petrified terror. The writhing he witnessed was not that of agony, but of sensuality, as though the thing manifesting itself in the world did so as an act of rape, degrading the very atmosphere it displaced, penetrating the cosmos with unwholesome desire. When all of it that was vaporous had been drawn into solid form, the thing ceased its repellent, sensual movement and stood fully made and quietly observant.

The creature was half again as tall as the biggest man Harada had ever seen. In Harada's slow state of mind, he thought what he witnessed was a sable giant in whose arms was held a load of white snow. Such coldness shone about the miraculous vision, it did not at that moment seem illogical or absurd that the thing carried snow.

This giant might have been carved of obsidian, but that his shimmering skin was pliant as a snake's. His face was hideous yet mesmerizing and intriguing, thin lips protruding as though striving to emulate the contours of a wide-beaked bird. The nose blended into the upper lip; the eyes were exceedingly far apart and glowed with malignant silver fire. Vertical, transluscent membranes served as eyelids which closed and opened at long intervals.

It had no hair, this fiend, and no clothing. Its genitalia were sheathed like a serpent's or a bird's, noticeable only as a triangular bulge under dark, taut skin. Its hips were narrow, its legs long. The shoulders were extremely wide and strong, the arms incongruously thick and short compared to the long, slender legs.

Behind the fiend's shoulders, Harada perceived enormous wings. They faded into the shadows of night so that the dying man was at first uncertain of the wings. They

were like the wings of a bat, though without fur. He would have thought them false wings, such as are worn by costumed dancers at a carnival. The left wing was indeed so perfectly still that one could easily imagine it to be a cleverly attached invention. But the other wing was rising slowly, dreamily, its tip going up among the branches of the frosted pine; there was something pensive about that motion, as when a common man raises thumb and forefinger to chin.

The monstrous winged man, who moments before had been a vast and intangible blackness of vapor, was now able to take a long step forward. Harada was beyond movement. No degree of terror could have animated him, so near to death was he. He lay at the thing's taloned feet, staring upward with unblinking eyes. He wondered if he were about to be gathered up and taken into the vast hollow of the world, tossed by the winged fiend into damnation.

Yet there was something approximating concern in that weirdly birdlike and reptilian face. Harada was emotionally bolstered by the idea of a monster's sentiment for a lowly man. It was a better fate than to have nobody and nothing to care about one's last repose.

"I," said the monster in a deep, watery, frightful voice, "am the Garuda."

The Garuda blinked his silver eyes, closing the vertical membranes for a thoughtful moment. Then the silver light shone forth again, and the Garuda looked about himself, at his surroundings, before settling his wide gaze once more upon the prone man.

"You," said the Garuda, "have called me more fully into the world."

Harada was too weak and deathly pale to utter denial or confession.

"I am grateful," said the Garuda, but there was a rueful edge to its horrid voice. "As you have called upon me for aid, I have brought you a warm coat."

The fluid resonance of the Garuda's voice shook Harada to the depths of his being and strangely energized him, hauling his spirit further from death. But he still could not exercise the least of his muscles. His vision became better and he realized the Garuda was not holding anything so unlikely as snow. Over the fiend's arms was draped the fur of some animal, white with black stripes.

"With this," said the Garuda, his voice and body insinuating upon Harada, "you will be strong as the tiger. You will be able to hunt with the tiger's cunning. For so long as you are within its coat, you will *be* the tiger. Nothing in the jungle before you, to which you must go, is stronger than the tiger—excepting the elephant. By no means let one near you."

The Garuda bent forward and laid the white tiger pelt over the quiet man. Harada felt the fur's power course through him, and he began to move. His arms fit into the forelegs and clawed paws of the skinned animal. His legs fit into the pelt's hind legs, as snuggly as into warm leggings.

The tiger's skin clung to his.

His head fit into the hollow skull which had not been removed from the pelt. He was able to see through the eye sockets of the tiger's skull. He saw differently and more acutely than he ever had with his own eyes. There was less color in the world, but sharper edges and outlines, and smaller things stood out with importance, and the starry sky was blazing.

He smelled through the skull's nostrils. What he smelled was the fear and horror and death of creatures other than himself.

He felt the tiger's cunning just as the Garuda promised. Harada wanted to question this gift, to doubt it, the gift of a fiend. But what choice had he besides this new found strength—or death. And already his mind was becoming subject to a more bestial way of thinking and perceiving. He felt everything as a tiger feels. It was invigorating. Harada's intellect was easily, almost gladly overwhelmed by this simpler but immeasurably intense feeling of authority in the wilderness.

As the Garuda expanded and dissolved into sparkling, insubstantial nothingness and vapor, and rose into the dark sky, Harada was already on hands and knees, strengthened, but hungry, and eager to hunt. He tried to rise to his own two feet, but the four legs of the tiger's pelt preferred to stay hunched down. Thus Harada shambled forth, part man, part tiger. Then he sprang through the flora after something he smelled.

Lu Khen had for some while despaired of finding any route down from the heights of the gargantuan overhang. He paced near the dangerous edge. The moon whitened the palms far below. There was a stillness over the world that rendered all but his own breath beyond certainty. For all that he could perceive, he stood within a painting depicting night in an alien land. Everything was static, dreamlike, agonizingly beautiful, with something ferocious lurking underneath. He shook his head, then felt his face to see if he were himself more than a phantom.

He felt weary of this whole affair; at least in that moment he felt so. And he doubted his quest was reasonable or plausible or meaningful or apt to come to any particular conclusion.

"If we find a way down there," he thought, "and make it so far as the Tombs, what will we find? Old ruins, likely enough, with nothing in them of any sort. Who ever heard of finding madness sealed up in someplace? Isn't madness rather lurking in oneself? Is it less than absurd to think of finding it, like a berry, and swallowing it down?" He shrugged, not knowing if he were being more or less logical than usual, more or less morose.

He did believe there was something sinister about that distant architecture, invisible by night, but not once out of his mind since the first moment he set eyes upon it. Possibly he tryed to convince himself that arrival would prove meaningless, so that he could hold at bay his own superstitions. It was a strange way of thinking, to fear success, and to worry about failure, to be left, thereby, without purpose.

"What will I do if I find madness? What will I become? Maybe I am afraid to know myself so deeply as that. Maybe the madness hidden in me is a homely thing, or a vicious thing, or an empty and churlish thing. Maybe Mai Su is not truly mad at all, but people have misunderstood her and misinterpreted her actions. If so, my finding madness would make me less like her, not more like her."

Maybe this, thought Lu Khen. Maybe that.

"Maybe I'm a coward. Maybe I'm a fool. Maybe I'll be sorry."

His appalling reverie was interrupted by a warmth near his belly. It was the feather of the flame dove, in his tunic, glowing brightly. He reached into his clothing and drew it out, the light coloring his nose and chin and cheeks. He had come to think of the feather as a kind of spiritual link between himself and Yeung Mai Su. It must mean something whenever it glowed as now. He hurried the few paces to the site where they had been camping, but Mai Su was not where he had left her dreaming. He saw her off to one side, down a slope, standing among some old and twisted trees.

How she shone in the moonlight! Her posture was just so, demurely perfect. Lu Khen was struck once more by the sudden thought that Yeung Mai Su might be a heavenly spirit. He hurried down the slope to where she was standing. He saw that the twisted trees hid a narrow cave. Mai Su stepped into the opening.

"Maybe some monster lives in there," thought Ou Lu Khen. "Maybe there is a pit and we will fall into that."

Mai Su stepped further back, into blackness, tempting him into the unknown. Unless Lu Khen followed with the light of the feather, Mai Su would surely lose her way.

"Maybe she knows what she is doing," he supposed.

He followed. The shining feather held back the inky darkness. It looked as though he held a candle's flame, without the candle, between his fingertips. He saw that he and Mai Su were on a stairway carved into the steep floor of the narrow cave; a stairway carved by human hands, or devils'. And the place was ages old, a mystery never to be resolved. The stairs wound downward.

There were side passages into which Lu Khen would hate to wander, into which the feather's light failed to penetrate. From these passages or rooms came the sounds of breathing animals great and small, ordinary and supernatural. Some-how Lu Khen felt the unseen beasts had lain slumbering in their chambers for incredible spans of time. The thought of waking them chilled his spine, for surely they had not been restless since the Forgotten Dynasty was devoured. The thought that the chambers might actually be empty, despite the sounds of breathing, chilled him more.

It was a haunted cavern, to be sure. But the ruddy glow of the flame dove's quill was just the thing a ghost or monster would avoid. In this, Lu Khen took heart, and kept near to Mai Su. Though she mainly led the way, it was he who bore the light.

The vaulted ceiling sparkled in that ruddy light. They were passing through a vault inlaid with crystals at the top and along the walls. He could not tell if the crystals had been carved and set in place, or had grown there naturally. With so many, surely they were not made by human hands.

From within or beyond the myriad crystals, bizarre faces peered out, reflecting upon each other a billion times. And yet, the faces were so tiny, Lu Khen was unsure he saw a thing. Were they the faces of curious watchers, like gods, or readers of a book through which he trod? Were they the faces of the forlorn? the lost? the tortured? the saved? He dared not peer close enough to learn, for fear his own soul would be sucked out and held fast within those rosy, faceted gems.

It was not a quick route down. They went for such an interminable period, Lu Khen began to fear they had gone below the level of the jungle without finding a way out of the caves. Down and down they continued, hoping they were on a safe route, though there was nothing to insure they were not in actuality on their way to a kingdom darker than the Forgotten Dynasty's . . . the kingdom with which those unknown rulers had imprudently aligned themselves, to the detriment of reason and soul.

Were they the souls of cruel dynastic citizens trapped within the crystals?

When they did come out of the cavern at a lower place, Lu Khen was not aware of it. The enormous overhang blocked the moon and sky. The feather blinked out, for the way was done. Lu Khen gasped, and held in his fright with great effort, having no way of knowing that they were safely

down. The only new sensation was of a thick, warm, aromatic breeze. Then, in the darkness before them, he saw
the faintest outline of tropical flora, gray and spidery from
their gloomy vantage point.

The stairway of carved stone had likewise ended. They
were walking on loose shale. It clattered beneath their steps.
Lu Khen was clumsy, for he was unable to see. But Mai
Su walked as though well-sighted; who could know what
her dark eyes were capable of seeing? When they came to
a point where the sky could be seen, Lu Khen's sense of
reality strengthened, and he felt better. The lip of the overhang cut heaven in half and Mai Su suddenly stopped at the
edge of two worlds, refusing to go farther.

"It cannot be but a day or two more," remarked Lu Khen,
sounding much calmer than he actually felt. "Should we
camp here, or continue by moonlight?"

Usually Mai Su would manage to make her own pref-
erences known; Lu Khen studied her face for reply. But she
did not notice him. He saw something in her eyes he had
never seen in them before. They were tears. They were
flowing in long streaks over her high cheeks and toward her
chin. Her gaze wandered slowly from side to side as though,
for the first time, she had lost her way. Then Lu Khen
thought he saw in her expression a reluctant remembrance
of things past. What could she remember? Lu Khen could
not know.

Her gaze fell on something, but when he looked out into
the jungle, he saw nothing. As he could not induce her to
move from the spot, and since he was himself very tired,
he set about clearing an area so that they might comfortably
repose. But Yeung Mai Su would not join him at rest; when
he awoke at dawn, she was standing in the same place,
looking in the same direction, weeping in silence. It was
noon before she was her imperturbable self, by which time
they were deep into the stifling, misty jungle.

When he came to his own awareness, he was at the side of
a stream. The white tiger pelt lay over a rock near the banks.
Harada's arms and face and the front of his clothing were
drenched in blood. Several fine hairs from a furry beast

were wedged between his teeth. He did not remember what
he had killed, what he had eaten, how he had eaten it. He
felt ill and disgusted; the nearer he came to remembering
the climax of the hunt, and the crazed feast afterward, the
more unsettled his stomach felt.

He went weak-kneed into the stream and washed the
blood from himself. He spat and spat the vile taste from his
mouth. In a moment, nausea overtook him. He heaved bits
of hot raw meat into the water, perhaps half the contents of
his belly. It was carried away in chunks and shreds and
clots. He turned from the sight and tried not to let his
stomach empty itself more. The problem was that he had
eaten too much, gorged after the kill, and then had failed
to rest. If he looked too long at the material coughed into
the stream, the sight would cause him to keep retching, until
there was nothing left to nourish him, and the degradation
of the hunt would have served him nothing.

He sat at the stream's edge, gazing sometimes at the
swift clean waters, sometimes at the pelt. His heart was
racing. Harada was not so foolish as to trust devils, nor so
smart as to know he might himself become one. There were
always strings attached to things which appeared to be free.
Harada trusted no one, nothing.

The Garuda had warned him of elephants, but of nothing
else. Suppose the pelt itself were dangerous, and the Garuda
had maliciously left off such information! Some part of
Harada was perfectly aware of the danger. But in his life,
truth had been easy to ignore. He had lived with lies so
long that he could no longer recognize wisdom, especially
in himself. He could make himself believe whatever was
easiest.

Disgusted though he might be by the half-remembered
slaughter, another part of him remained, even now, enamored of what he had done, attracted to the strength that
had been his throughout the night. He grappled with conflicting feelings regarding the pelt. Should he go his way
leaving the pelt where it now lay? A quavering hand reached
forth and stroked the pelt lovingly. It was soft and miraculously clean. In its present limp state, it was no more
frightful than a fine, plush rug.

He dried himself in the sun and against the pelt's plushness. He tried not to think much about it, but the forest was so silent, it invited thought. He wondered why the Garuda should have favored him. He could not think of a good reason. He did not believe in idle patronage, not even from gentle gods. A devil would be even more apt to want something for his troubles. "I must be resigned to serving the Garuda in some way," said Harada. Thinking that he could be of some aid to the monster eased Harada's doubts but did not fully alleviate them. For, if there were no conceivable service he could render the fiend, and the fiend had been aware of Harada's general uselessness in all regards . . . then, what could the pelt be except a trick, and his demise?

One way or another, chances were the pelt would destroy him. "Even if I make myself useful, would a devil be reluctant to use and then discard someone like me?"

But he had to grasp at some shred of hope. His hope was that there was honor in the black heart of the Garuda, however alien its reasoning might be. He hoped that if a lowly man sincerely tried to render good service to a fiend, then the fiend would not reveal an apparent blessing to be a curse.

There were good reasons not to abandon the Garuda's gift. Harada figured he could wear it to increase the distances covered in his journey. With it he could see in the dark of night. By the pelt's aid he could overtake Po Lee and Koy or Lu Khen and Mai Su. He could arrive at the Tombs before them, if he desired, running with the tiger's senses and agility.

Also, he would be hungry again, and no better able to fend for himself except for the pelt's magic. Harada's uppermost desire was to survive.

Thus, wishing to survive, his mind wavered again, the pendulum returning. How could he believe there was no danger inherent with the skin? It, more than any terror the jungle could throw at him, was a threat to his survival. He had not been himself during the hunt of the night before. The tiger intellect had not wanted to be the sniveling, frightened, unsure Harada Fumiaka ever again. Whether it was actually the tiger's spirit eager to possess him, or only his own dislike for being himself, the outcome was the same: he might wrap himself into the pelt and never get it off again. He would cease to exist separate from the tiger's will. He would be neither a man nor a beast, but a weretiger forever, combining not the best of each life, but the most inimical.

Having arrived at this conclusion, he decided never to wear the skin again. He would survive without it. He resolved to leave it where it was, over the rock, for scavengers to tear to bits, for small mammals to line their nests. (As he made this resolve, his hand continued to stroke the softness of the fur.) So what if he would be hungry again? He did not want another repellent meal like that in any case! Did he? Well, blood did have a certain fascination. He hated to admit it. He refused to admit it. He could not understand how it could be so.

For all his resolve, already he was folding it neatly to carry away with him. "Might as well have it for a bed," he thought, and invented other silly reasons. "It doesn't mean I will wear it." He held the folded pelt near, hugged it in his arms. The beast's hollow head leaned upon his shoulder like a lover.

He did use it for a bed, and slept the greater part of the daylight hours. When he awoke, he was hungry, and not fully awake before he fitted himself into the skin and hunted for the second time. How he could run! How strong he felt! The skin's glamour was an addiction, and he no longer gave it thought. He did not consider how each time he became the tiger, it would be more and more difficult to become himself again. The twilight beast required action by night, and Harada slept by day. When did he have the chance to exercise his own personality? Why would he *want* to be himself? Was it not better to be keen sighted and extraordinary?

He cleaned blood from himself the next morning. His stomach was easier this time. Already he was used to it. The pelt, as usual, was clean, though his own chest and chin and arms were gore spattered. He was less appalled than on the previous morning. He no longer deluded himself into thinking he had the will power to deny himself the glorious, sensual, self-assured existence of a great cat.

As he lay down upon the black-streaked snowy pelt to sleep the long day through, he made a simpering prayer of thanks to the Garuda. He cast off the last shadow of doubt in favor of the deeper, blacker shadow of a devilish faith.

High in the crook of a tree, looking down at him, was a child, crouching like a monkey. She was dirty. She blinked moist eyes. She had barely evaded him the night before. When she was certain he was sleeping, she hopped from one branch to another, swung down to the ground, and ran noiselessly on.

Po Lee had been roused from a scant hour's slumber. As the first hour of sleep is often the deepest, he was especially dim-witted about the interruption. It was a hunter's tattooed face that peered at him, a tattooed arm that reached out and shook him awake. It was, in fact, the man pointed out to him as his own grandson, a man as old as the father of Ou Lu Khen would be, were he still alive. With so many markings on his face, it was impossible to tell if the fellow resembled Po Lee or his family. The fellow seemed entirely aboriginal. Po Lee felt no kinship for him.

In his dazed, sleepy state, a jumble of thoughts raced around and around: This fellow is as close a relation to me as Koy or Lu Khen; but really that is not so; he is an aboriginal man, born and reared, and no part of me; blood does not define a family, for an adopted son is as much a son as one of blood; customs and likenesses and mutual understanding of a way of life defined a family; this fellow shaking me awake is a stranger to me, nothing more; and furthermore, he is a stranger who has watched me most of the night and here he is bothering an old man who would rather sleep; and why was that?; why was Po Lee being roused and stared at by that awful face?; surely it was not a pleasant conversation the tattooed man sought. *Perhaps,* thought Po Lee, *I am in danger.*

The hunter said a single word. It was not in the guttural, commanding tongue, but in a deferential tone, and this relieved Po Lee considerably. He searched his memory for the meaning of the word the hunter had spoken. It meant: "Tryst."

A tryst. Po Lee was being called to some tryst. The hunter poked him gently, gazed on him with wide, strange eyes, and encouraged him to get out of the hut. As Po Lee began to crawl out through the palm leaves of his shelter, he was suddenly fully awake, for the realization of Koy's absence had stricken his heart with worry.

Once Po Lee was on his feet outside the hut, he saw that three tribal women were waiting to lead him away. Po Lee gazed back to see the hunter standing next to the palm-leaf hut, a motionless and mysterious figure.

Po Lee went with the women, tribal priestesses who were wildly stained and half naked so as to show off their every artistic marking. They took him by a circuitous route which led ultimately to the very center of the camp, to the miniature temple in which the oracle lived. They encouraged him to bend toward the double door and to climb in, but he balked. They were insistent, and he gave in. The temple looked too small for even one occupant, but actually it could hold two, though not very comfortably. He went halfway in on hands and knees. The first thing he said, in the aboriginal tongue or a poor approximation of it, was "What have you done with my great-granddaughter?"

The white, blind eyes of the oracle gleamed with a gauzy light, reflecting the bit of moonlight which came through the narrow windows above their heads. She acted legitimately surprised by his query, but peeled back her weird eyes as though to check on matters, and answered in Po Lee's language: "Koy has slipped off with some of the children to play. She will have an adventure but no harm will come of it. Please come the rest of the way in. You are showing your bottom to the priestesses outside."

"There is too little room," he said, but this was an excuse.

"You will find it not so bad," she said, and added, "Please speak in the language you taught me, so that my curious people will not bother to overhear. They are eager to know about my business and will have their ears to the walls as they guard my residence."

"The more reason not to come in," he said in his own tongue. He was sweating, though the night was not warm.

"You need not fret about appearances at all," she said. "They already know who you are. You are a famous story told among my people, though only I am old enough to have known you before. My people like to see me wistful. Come in. Come in."

Since she insisted, he pulled his backside in, and the three priestesses sealed the door, sealed him in with the oracle, and began to hum a strange, sacred song so softly he could barely hear it from within the tiny temple. As it was pitch dark, all he could see were the oracle's blind eyes like shining pearls. Po Lee shuddered when he considered the malevolent potential of this bony woman. He must be polite to her at all cost, for it was essential to win her to his purpose, lest she refuse to let him and Koy leave the tribe.

It was very close indeed, cramped next to the oracle in an exceedingly intimate fashion. He was surprised to recognize her odor, as clean and pleasant as when they both were young. When his eyes adjusted to the miniscule amount of moonlight at the small windows, he could not see well even then; the temple was simply not designed to house the sighted. Yet the oracle began vaguely to appear before him as a gray ghost, all her bony edges and wrinkles smoothed out by the limits of his vision. He could half imagine she was the young woman he had met so very long ago.

The oracle was forced by the limited amount of space to put her arms about Po Lee. Her voice was as girlish as a carlin's voice can ever be as she asked, "Isn't it nice?" Now there was no doubt in Po Lee's mind as to the oracle's intentions.

"It is roomier than I imagined," he said evasively, patting one of the walls with the flat of his hand. "If it were my house, though, I should have had it made taller. It would be nice to stand up in it once in a while."

"Oh, I can stand in it if I want to," she said, adding coyly, "But there is no reason to stand just now."

Her hands fondled at his tunic and around his neck. For her own part, she was almost naked. He was surprised that she did not feel skeletal. She felt like a slender girl. Her skin was soft, for she had never had to work hard for her tribe, at least not in the physical manner.

"You do not feel like an old man to me just now," said the oracle.

"You do not feel like an old woman," he admitted.

Yet he was more embarrassed than he had felt in half his life. He had been chaste since the death of Fa Ling. Besides that, he was not even certain his body was interested in such things anymore. Gently, he removed her hands from his clothing, for she was trying to get his tunic to come off. Her voice was small and injured when she asked, "Is something the matter?" She seemed to think they could pick up where they had left off an entire lifetime before.

"In my heart," he said softly, apologetically, "I am wed to a woman named Fa Ling, who is dead for many years."

"You never mentioned her before," said the oracle, slightly petulant.

"I met her after you," he said. Sensing her sadness, which he thought easily might turn to anger, he said, "If you had wanted to leave your place among your people, I might never have met Fa Ling. Life might have been different. But you adhered to your way of life, and I returned to mine. It cannot be rewritten."

"But it can be remembered," said the oracle. "Or, is it an excuse to evade me? Am I too old for you? Well, are you so young?"

"To tell the truth," he said, "you have the same gentle touch as when we were handsome together. Were I still a virile fellow, who is to say, maybe I would not be faithful to my wife. Maybe I would say, 'How can it matter since she is dead?' Maybe I would want a last fling in my life, to recapture something of so long ago. But if you would be so kind as to allow me to think better of myself"—and here Po Lee pressed his palms together in a holy gesture—"I should prefer to say it is for Fa Ling that I abstain."

"Too bad for me," said the oracle. "You were a most vigorous man, all right. I guess I had them bring you here so I could feel young again. I never did forget you, after all."

This made Po Lee infinitely sad; for truth be told, which tonight it would not be, he had not thought often about the wildwoman of his youthful exploits. His mind had dwelt on other people, on other adventures. If he thought of her over the years, he remembered that she was something strange and beautiful which had existed briefly in the busy, far-off years of a young man. It was odd to think she had been left with such huge impressions of their affair. Perhaps it was only because she was so utterly bound to her responsibilities, a leader of her people, locked in her position of importance and power. She had second sight, needed by her people who otherwise must perish in a terrible and haunted land. These things limited her life, no doubt. His visit, a minor occurrence in his varied life, was a rare and momentous occasion in her own.

She must have wanted him to leave, too, for otherwise she would have mentioned that she had carried his child. He had had a daughter he had never known; that daughter grew up and died never setting eyes upon her father. Had she been stigmatized as the bastard of an outsider, or honored as the oracle's child? He was afraid to ask. There was a melancholy about the tattooed man who was Po Lee's illegitimate grandson; this melancholy made Po Lee suspect the hunter had seen his mother live a difficult life. Perhaps the hunter blamed Po Lee, and so had watched the old man the whole evening long, with a curious mix of interest and anger.

The oracle said, "I have lived a very long time knowing you would come back someday. It was not merely a girlish longing, as you know. From the beginning of our affair, I saw to our future and final meeting. It made it easier for me to let us part before. And I had hoped the foreseen reunion would have meaning for you as well. I will not say I lived so long only for this moment! That would be foolish indeed. But it was one of the things that made too long a life easier to bear. Otherwise, there would be only frightful purpose to longevity, its climax being my tribe's exodus. I will die soon, but not before I have found a safe place for my people. Can you imagine the burden? But at least I always knew I would see my Po Lee once more!"

How embarrassed he felt! She insinuated herself on him again. Awkwardly, he said, "I never thought any friend of my young days would still be living. From what you say, I gather that you had no choice, but had to live so long to see your tribe through some crisis."

"There will be," she said softly, seriously, and clung to him not with ardor, but a fearful need to hide in his embrace, "a clash of hideous strength in the center of this ancient land, where stand the houses you call Tombs. I have seen it in the future since I was a little girl, glimpses only, but horrid to all extreme. How far away I thought it was! Now the time draws near. That is why, when I sensed your presence and the child's upon the ancient highway, I sent my hunters to search for who it was, to avert anyone stumbling into the vortex of terrible power. For your sakes I had you captured. How glad I was of my second sight, finding out that it was you upon the forbidden road! I saved you from an awful thing, though you may not believe it. And you have met your grandson, too; you have family here. I think your great-granddaughter likes my people. She has the makings of a priestess, I should say."

There was an edge in the oracle's voice that lacked conviction but merely wished to convince Po Lee that staying was a pleasant choice. He said, "You have lived so long a life for a definite purpose. I think I have done so also, though what purpose I have never known. You insist on keeping me from visiting the tombs of the Lost Dynasty; but kin of mine are nearly there, and I must follow. Since you have special vision, surely you have seen my course cannot be shaken. It is tragic if you stop me."

"I have not been able to see to the very end," the carlin whispered, clinging more tightly to Po Lee; he rested his long hands upon her. "Dark powers blind my mystic sight. Yet I cannot help but know that pain alone awaits you there. You would beg me not to interfere, I know. You speak well in saying I have no right. But knowing there is danger, have *you* the right to risk the little girl?"

Po Lee's breath caught, and he stiffened. There was something calculated and manipulating about the oracle's argument, yet she had struck the blow perfectly, to a sensitive spot. He said, as softly as she had spoken, "If my sweet Koy is doomed by what I have started, and that doom can be averted by turning from the path I chose for her and me, tell me plainly that you see the way to improve her fate, and I will do your bidding. But listen: Upon the remembrance of the love you felt for me long ago, tell me only truth and not your speculation. If Koy's life is in the balance, you shall have your way. If you cannot see the slightest injury, then be silent about these matters, and set us free tomorrow."

The old woman was still for a while. Both of them were sweetly in one another's arms. Then she said, "Do you wish me to search for your fate as well as hers?"

"Only hers," he said vehemently. "For myself, I require no prognostication. I have lived long enough already. It may well be that I prefer to die on a lonely trail."

"Then I will tell you nothing," she said, and there was an edge to her voice half angry, half resigned.

Po Lee was overcome with gratitude regarding her change of heart. Her hand reached up and felt a tear upon his cheek. She said, "On the morning, you are free to take your own direction. As for me, I have seen my death. It is not far off, and it is peaceful. I will be taken to the site of my choosing by my devoted people. They will place this tiny temple in a certain place and make of it a mausoleum for my bones. It is a good fate for me. Whether or not it is a better fate than yours, perhaps I am not a fit judge after all, even were I able to see everything more clearly."

"I am grateful to you," he said gently, and nuzzled her with his face. Belated memory of all that was good about her overwhelmed him, and his heart swelled, and they embraced. He said, "In the morning, Koy and I will go our way. As for you, surely you will seek your destiny as blithely as do we of lesser vision. And tonight, we will see what we can do, and be young a final moment."

"Life is someone's nightmare," Harada decided, panting and shivering, lost in the highland forests. "Whoever it is, I wish they would wake up."

It had been troublesome getting the skin off this time.

His own skin itched and burned from wearing that of the tiger. He was worn out and disoriented, though after previous hunts he had felt invigorated and well-satisfied.

He had learned early on that it was a bad idea to try to remember whatever he might do as a tiger. In the first place it was frightening to recollect that point of submergence into the savage personality of the tiger's ghost, uncertain that his own personality would survive. Besides that, if he remembered the act of killing, it upset him.

Harada's repugnance, even without memory, was especially keen after this hunt, yet he was not as drenched in blood as on previous occasions, nor did he feel as excellently sated. In fact, he was as hungry as he had been before donning the striped pelt. The spirit of the tiger, it would seem, had failed to catch and hold anything.

But there was *some* blood on the pelt, that Harada cleansed easily, since the fur repelled soil of any kind. So something was nearly captured; it had not caused any injury to Harada as a tiger, though it must have escaped somehow, or else Harada would not still be famished.

There were conflicting emotions as he folded the pelt and started along the narrow animal trail. He wanted to don the pelt again and get something to eat this time. But he feared to do any such thing. In the few days since he had acquired the pelt from the Garuda, he had overcome the greatest portion of his trepidation—until now. Something of his original fear had come back and was intensified. He could not, therefore, don the skin at once, but preferred to keep his hunger for a while.

Though knowing it was both difficult and unrewarding to remember his adventures as a cat, that it would make him sick if he remembered too well, today his curiosity was acute. He battled with this feeling.

Though he liked the vague remembrance of power and certainty, at the same time he could not adjust his consciousness toward an acceptance of a cat's cruel way of killing, for cats tease their prey and are as vicious as brave men. Harada was cowardly by nature and thus not as vicious as other men, or tigers. He did not like to recall the methods of wounding some pathetic beast, terrorizing it so that it would bleed itself dry, and finally rending and devouring what might yet kick and whine. This was acceptable only under the glamour of the pelt.

Even so, curiosity tugged. He wanted to know what had escaped, why the cat had failed, or, if it had not escaped, why it had not been eaten. Harada's mind wandered back, back, back along the route of the night before . . . but memory rebelled.

Then he saw a trail of blood upon the path. Had the wounded prey escaped the tiger and come this way? No— it looked as though something injured had been dragged. Harada's two personalities linked momentarily, so that he recalled holding something in his teeth, dragging it along this trail, turning off the trail up there on the weedy incline. What had he done next with the dying prey? Another momentary connection between his cat-self and his true self revealed to him the sensation of leaping powerfully into a tree, the carcass in his jaws, in the jaws of a cat's skull attached to his own face.

He followed the bloody track into the dense foliage, looking hard at the ground. "Do I want to remember it?" he wondered. The trail came to a halt near a big tree. Harada crouched and looked about the ground for signs of the track, but it went nowhere. He realized this must be the tree into which he had jumped.

He turned his gaze upward from the ground.

He shouted and fell back.

He scrambled away from the tree, scooting on his butt, pulling with his hands, pushing with feet, trying to get away from the terrible tree.

He wept and grimaced. He lost all the strength of his limbs and wiggled feebly and ridiculously. The tiger's pelt lay on the ground, several arm lengths away from him, a more hideous thing than he had known it to be a moment before.

"I won't wear it again," he said, and his mind filled with panic. "I won't," he said, and again, "I would rather die in the forest than put it on again." But he found strength enough to throw himself onto the pelt with an almost catlike pounce, and to draw it close to his heart. "But I don't want to die at all," he said, turning tearful eyes upward once more and rubbing his cheek against soft white fur.

"Villains always hate their vices and perversions," he said softly, shaking his head, seeing deeply into his heart. "But it's hard to give them up." He saw that he cared about himself very little, selfish though he had always been, and probably cared less than most men for his own life, hard as he pretended to preserve it. If he was concerned in a larger sense, he would have taken better care of himself from the beginning. He would have been a more honest man, if only slightly so, and kept in better health.

"I would rather be this tiger and feel no guilt forever," he cried. "It is not what this tiger has done that appalls me, but myself I find so strange. Why shouldn't a tiger live by any means? It should do so! But why should I continue to exist? I cannot think of any reason!"

Whether he said these things or thought them; whether they were as lucidly considered as that, or were vague feelings; whether or not he knew what he was doing scarcely mattered. His skin tingled with desire for the pelt. And he wished for oblivion. Perhaps he knew and said, "If I wear the tiger's skin once more, it may adhere to me, and not come off." Or he may not have known this at all. In either case, he would not care, not in such a state as he was in. "Oblivion," he thought, and put his legs into the legs of the pelt. "Oblivion," as his arms fit snugly into the pelt's forelimbs. The pelt pulled snugly against his spine.

He remembered now how he had fought the tiger's personality, kept it from eating its fill; remembered escaping from the deed, tearing the pelt from himself with an effort of will greater than he had evidenced at any other time in his life or would evidence again.

"Oblivion," he murmured, his eyes still filled with tears.

He pulled the skull over his head and then, while gazing upward into the tree, he saw things differently, felt them differently, evaluated them with dispassion.

Lying across the branches, dangling from above, was the corpse of an aboriginal child, the feral girl who had been *not quite* agile and expert enough to avoid the horrific weretiger. Her fingers pointed down; dry blood stained their ragged tips; and into the face of a hungry cat her blind eyes stared.

When a tiger learns to kill a human being, it is rarely satisfied with less clever prey or the taste of other meats. A death tiger, whose spirit has walked as a ghost in hell, and been recalled to dominate the weak will of some pitiful man, is apt to be a more frightful mankiller than any other kind. Yet the tribal people were far away, a seeress having predicted terror on the land. Where, then, could the beast find meat?

Wandering into the rank, humid lower country, the weretiger spied monkeys and likened them to the dirty aborigine that had been so hard to catch. The macaques were swift, and mean, and clever. They were tainted with some hideous inner evil that was part of everything of the jungle basin. But none were exactly what the feline intellect was seeking. It must find prey that was more fully like that other. It must be patient, and it would find what it required. In the meanwhile, to honor fierce unnamed gods obliquely worshiped by the wildest and most malevolent of beasts, the tiger fasted.

In the midst of the hot, green country the weretiger encountered a gigantic elephant with three heads, and more legs than a cat's mind could calculate. It knew of elephants, and it knew that this one was larger than others. The cat slunk backward, arched its back, and hissed mightily; but the monstrous elephant was carved of stone.

The three trunks curled upward, the end of each holding rainwater and supporting aquatic beetles, water striders, and floating plants. The cat decided that the three-headed elephant was dead, if it had ever been alive, and thirsted toward one of the miniature pools. Six dull eyes from three faces made the cat uneasy. Six long tusks swept over the cat's head.

It almost drank, but not quite. Startled by a sound or thought, the weretiger made a great leap into the foliage and vanished without a sound.

In time, the tiger, hunched down on all fours and loping

in a manner not fully feline and by no means human, entered a fabulous and forbidden place, the ruins of a dynasty forgotten to the world. The tiger knew or reasoned or expected this to be the handiwork of some high being, the type it had longed again to taste. It passed beneath a southern gate, in the shadow of an enormous wall that was actually the long body of a stone serpent; the cat was spared the sight of its head.

The tiger passed between temples and tombs, through lesser gates that were broken and collapsed, over large and small pieces of masonry. The forest had long ago entered the city, and objects appeared suddenly from between aged trees. The tiger glowered, panting, at marvelous statues of beasts and monsters, of gods and dancers. It gazed overlong at a particular statue, of a dancing girl whose limbs were bent at odd, sensuous angles and whose face was serene. In its feline manner, the beast's mind knew, "This is what I'm after, but not quite this." Like the three-headed elephant, there was no smell of life past or present, no motion, no threat, and no fear. But surely all that the cat was seeking would come with further patience.

It found a dark place and settled down to rest. Weirdly, it began to rumble, a deep-throated purr of contentment. No hint of humanity was visible where it reposed in a curled position. It slept. It waited.

Po Lee and Koy were again upon their chosen road, an ancient highway sloping gently downward, into an increasingly dense and tropical land. The fauna became green-black and dripped moisture; the very air was green, or would appear so. Koy was overheated in the red embroidered shirt the aborigines had given her. Between her and Po Lee, there were only two baskets now. Po Lee had rigged up woven lengths of straw rope so that they could tie their baskets across their shoulders like a pack. Po Lee had his walking staff, that could double as a weapon, but his weaker leg had grown stronger with exercise and he took long strides in a less ungainly fashion than before. Koy, with Harada's sword strapped alongside the basket at her back, also felt invigorated, now that the trail was easy. They each went at a fine pace.

At a resting place, both took their baskets off and sat upon a pair of squat stone idols of the sort common along the side of the ancient, cobbled highway. Koy doffed the aboriginal garment that kept her too hot, folded it, and put it in her basket until evening. She got up from the idol and peered at it, realizing at length that, beneath its jacket of lichen and moss, it was the stone carving of a homely frog. It made her think of the toad-creature of the lake, though this stone frog was not nearly so grotesque.

Koy had not told her great-grandfather about the adventure of that startling night with the tribal people, and he had not told her where he had stayed during that same night. They had secrets from each other, therefore, but Koy did not mind. It had been different when great-grandfather had secrets while she had none. Then she had been shocked to find out everything about him on their revealing journey. There was a balanced feeling to their secrets now. Didn't everyone wish to be a little bit mysterious? There was no sense being seen through all the time and feeling very simple because of it, too easily understood by everyone.

She wondered where her great-grandfather had been, but did not ask; rather, she took pride in thinking he must wonder where *she* had been. She thought, "We are mutually mysterious people." It was a good feeling.

They did not rest long. There was an excited feeling about closing in on their destination. "A day or two longer," said Po Lee, and Koy had a feeling it might be the "day" and not the "or two." How horrible and thrilling! In broad of day, she was able to ponder the notion of hideous monsters leaping out of the Tombs. Come night, it might be more wholly frightening. But just now, with her leather thong of a slingshot tucked into her clothing, and Harada's sword at her back—and never mind that she could not use either one with particular effectiveness, for what child considers herself less than inherently skillful before tested—it all felt to be a good adventure. Hadn't she killed the toad-creature without effort? Surely there was more than luck in doing that. Hadn't Great-grandfather Po Lee proven himself strong at stick fighting? She was a precocious girl, to be sure, but still prone to a child's fancies. At that moment, it felt perfectly reasonable that a tiny girl and a thin old man could, with stick and saber, defeat the worst conceivable monster or foe without the smallest price.

They passed another of the mossy stone frogs. Upon its head, between its stony eyes, sat a real frog. It peeped and jumped back into the jungle, a jade trinket sprung to life, then vanished.

"I haven't told you a good story for a long time," said Great-grandfather Po Lee, who had quietly pondered many adventures of his early life in Ho, before he became a far-wandering exile and a pioneer. In his life he had heard or experienced many wonderful things, which in some cases became changed around for the sake of an ideal or a better tale. Even with his regained clarity of mind, he was not always certain what was his own experience and what was one he had overheard, or what was the absolute truth and what had been embellished. All he knew was that his mind was filled with beautiful and strange memories. These made him his clan's best-loved storyteller, until he had gotten into the bad habit of mixing things up or wandering off without quite finishing what he had started. His memories were treasures and now they had been dusted off. Without them, his life would be nothing; with them, he felt himself to be a giant, and a part of something even greater than himself, no matter how far he wandered from that greater thing that was Ho.

Though Koy had not known him in the full glory of his storytelling prowess, yet she recollected being dandled on his knee, she and Lu Khen hearing the most extraordinary events of far Ho, that would become mixed up in her own dreams and perceptions to become a part of her. It was this remembrance of an ancestral home that made their community decidedly apart from native peoples, civilized and wild alike, for family legends in many ways defined their ethnicity in the newly tamed provinces of the Greater Peninsula so far south of Ho. It was hard to imagine a race that could exist without something that was similar, a people severed from the heart of the world—a people, perhaps, like those that were erased from the annals of history and whose capital was now but a green-black jungle.

"Do tell me the story you are thinking, great-grandfather. It will help to pass our day."

She walked briskly at his side.

"I would like to very much," he replied.

And he told her the story of the Master Ventriloquist who could throw his voice a hundred miles and was made into a god when he was dead; and of a woman slain who returned to life long enough to save her province from war; and of a rabbit who pretended to be a dignitary of Ho. He told her moral stories passed down from priests, and stories heard elsewhere that perhaps a little girl had better not have been told, but she liked them all. The day progressed swiftly, and her brain whirled with wonders of a magic place, so that the grimmer magic of the thick jungle passed her half unnoticed.

Po Lee's stories reconfirmed that neither he nor she were truly part of this accursed jungle and they could not be injured by it. If, now and then, as dusk gathered around, small Koy looked askance at shadows and the evil-looking amber eyes of odd-appearing monkeys, how could she be afraid while Po Lee whisked them both away to the great lands of Celestial Ho? Even the cold, dark shade against the stars could not affright her then. And wasn't that red star a happy omen?

They would sleep in the jungle that evening. Even Po Lee's final tale of a sorrowful ghost haunting the well of a temple, compelled to devour lovers, filled Koy with less dread than cultural affirmation. Early the next day they were to enter the weird city, the city with a past erased, and to a girl whose history was strengthened, the monoliths would seem shrunken, and the horror no great mystery at all.

But in a tomb, the beast was purring.

❧ SIX ❧

Light and Dark

HOW CAN A poet convey with all their glory and pathos the varied destinies of humankind? It cannot be done. It can be written that someone died and someone else was changed; that yet another rose above things while this one was plowed under. Paintings can be made to show it and songs can be sung, but no one understands the simplest of matters, not wholly. As to the complicated things, why try? Yet try we must, all of us, to convey and understand. Why else have any of us existed? Either there is no reason at all, or this is our reason. The sad thing is this: The harder we try to meet our purpose, the further astray we go, as though we have no hands but sharp sticks, poking at a round, smooth thing and veering from side to side. Success is met by more obtuse means; the greater truths are hidden in myths, our total and accumulative selves, and in the things we say profoundly in a rustic way, or refuse to say at all.

You will see the thing, or have it described to you if you are blind, or feel it with your hands—but understand it

better if it is never seen, never felt or described, but taken
into oneself like a dream. For this reason should the story
of Lu Khen and Mai Su, of Koy and Po Lee, of Harada the
man-tiger, and of one other mortal you may not have seen
. . . their story should end here. You should know no more
about it, and by this means, understand.

But we are foolish beings and must describe things out
of existence, to be done with them forever, to move on to
the next thing to be described and forgotten. We must think
we know everything and so know nothing. We must dance
for our friends until we collapse and die, wondering if we
danced at all. It will be studied minutely; the poet will lead
you astray trying with sad sincerity to show you to the
middle. The lines of the map will be more comprehensible
than the world that has no lines; and everyone will know
precisely the thing that should never be precise.

And here it shall be said with all precision.

The jungle lay like a jade sea beneath a coral sunset. Night-
blossoms were already releasing their pungent invitations
to jewel-winged moths. Bright parrots nestled one against
another in the tops of palms. The dancing silhouettes of
bats fluttered against the gorgeous hues of heaven.

Yeung Mai Su and Ou Lu Khen stood amidst the frag-
ments of a fallen archway at the city's northern entrance.
Dusk's shadows gathered around them like half-seen spirits.
Behind, the verdant wall swayed to and fro under the touch
of a humid breeze, and great fronds whispered. To each
side of the broken arch, the walls of the city, all but invisible
beneath creepers, swept beyond sight. Before them: the City
of Tombs, so thickly invaded by the jungle that only two
strange buildings stood in view, and even the two were
obscured by vegetation.

The tomb nearest and most visible was square and squat
but its surfaces were intricately carved, worn bas-reliefs
portraying wars and wonders. Further on, less visible through
palms and branches, a more peculiar building rose up and
up, higher than the trees, though its mountainous peak could
not be seen from the gate. A god's face peered out from

the side of the thick stone tower, staring through the branches and through the gloom toward Lu Khen and Mai Su. On each side of the tower were similar faces watching east and west.

From their vantage point they could not guess the enormity of this place of tombs and temples. The buildings were spaced far apart; only small sections could be explored in a day. Great courtyards and stone fences gave each area a sense of being apart from all else. Even had there not been a thousand years of jungle reclaiming much of the ground between fabulous buildings, the ancient inhabitants must have felt isolated from other places in the city, no matter what estate they chose.

The roads were wide and paved with small square masonry, some parts broken and overgrown, other portions finely preserved. Mai Su and Lu Khen strode forth along the main avenue, still barely guessing the size or the layout of the Lost Dynasty's capital. In Lu Khen's mind at that moment was wonder, and also fear, both of which would treble as he understood the city better; followed, very likely, by a lessening of these feelings ... for the human mind inevitably adapts, much as a glib, thoughtless mouse can live anywhere, with anything, and danger all about.

From the moment they stepped around the rubble of that broken gate and into the city, Lu Khen felt that they were watched. At first he tried to dismiss it as his imagination, or as an instinctual dread of anything associated with the Lost Dynasty. And the great towers of the temples, with their carved and scowling faces, could only inspire a sense of observation.

But the eyes he sensed were neither stone, nor fancy. Soon he could not deny his suspicion. He and Mai Su were observed by malignant monkeys.

A macaque stood upon the twisting branch of a thick, huge tree, the roots of which embraced a little tomb. Lu Khen had thought it nothing until its yellow eyes glinted and it showed its teeth. When the weird sentinel jumped toward the ground, it passed through shadow, and vanished into the network of bared roots, or possibly entered the tomb to which the old tree clung. Lu Khen had not heard it make a sound, and did not see it again; but it was difficult to find consolation in the fiend's easy disappearance.

He quickly saw another macaque, a female with a deformed back, nursing an infant that had inherited the spinal abnormality. It sat on the head of a large stone dog; it leapt away when spied by Lu Khen. Its homely infant fell and rolled away, squealing a moment's surprise, then ran after its parent. It stopped once, looked back over its malformed shoulder, tiny yellow eyes gleaming and conveying subtle, cruel emotion.

He and Mai Su continued along the avenue of the ancient capital, passing hideous ruins, passing courtyards enclosed by stone walls, gates guarded by statues of dogs or deities. The few temples and tombs that had escaped the roots of the silk-cotton trees were not severely damaged and did not look their age.

Mai Su chose a side path that had no cobbles, but apparently was used, if only by the macaques. Lu Khen followed, as their long adventure had taught him was the only thing to do. As building after building leapt from shadows, Lu Khen never quite adjusted to the monstrous excesses of the architecture. No walls of any building were left smooth, but were covered with bas-reliefs telling unfamiliar stories, showing scenes from events and mythologies Lu Khen could not fathom, or which were familiar only in the most obscure fashion.

And everywhere there were macaques, on roofs, in trees, sitting or squatting on side paths or beside walls, or shoulder to shoulder with the smaller statues so as to be difficult to detect until practically upon them. Always they were watching the two invaders with an aspect of mistrust. At first they would scurry away and vanish whenever noticed, but as it became evident that more and more were accumulating, it was also evident that they were becoming increasingly bold.

They were silent at first as well, but with dusk becoming night and their ranks swelling, they became excited. They chattered disagreeably with each other. They would shout at Lu Khen and Mai Su, or bob their heads and peel back their lips with expressions supremely chilling.

These monkeys had scraggly, short, bent tails and fat, ugly, hairless bottoms. They had long arms and long fingers and long nails. They made fists, or beat the ground with the backs of open hands, or shook the branches. Their teeth were long and as yellow as their eyes. Their voices were piercing. And when many were screaming at once, Lu Khen shook with fright.

And all the while Mai Su led an insistent route and did not care about the monkeys. Lu Khen had grown partially accustomed to the mystery of her knowledge, and trusted her to find her way; but her disregard for the fiendish macaques was not greatly reassuring.

The colors of the world were now leeched by extreme gloom. The sky shone gray; the first stars winked into existence. Lu Khen followed Mai Su, close at her heels.

A particularly large macaque—as big as Lu Khen were it to stand straight—whose fur was grizzled and scarred by old bites was evidently the leader. He had appeared from time to time, always upon the ground, but never let Lu Khen catch him moving. Only when Lu Khen looked away and back again did the old one cease to be where he had been. And always he would appear again, ahead of them, waiting like the serene veteran of many a wicked victory, a veritable Buddha of a dark aspect, who could not be stared down, whose motion was outside the perceptions of normal vision.

About the fifth time Lu Khen saw him, the old male was squatting low on all fours, teeth bared, right on the path Mai Su had chosen. Lu Khen was so startled by the chief's extraordinarily fierce posture that he grabbed Mai Su's arm and spun her around almost violently, meaning to retreat. But there were dozens of the fiends sitting on the path blocking any retreat, waggling their tongues and flaring their nostrils. Mai Su did seem curious at that point, though only mildly so; she wanted mainly to watch the one Lu Khen wanted to avoid. She turned back to see the chief of the macaques . . . but he was gone.

Lu Khen followed her further on, until they came to something of a clearing. There was a wide stone path leading to a particularly large temple, and the path was guarded along the way by enormous stone dogs. At the edges of this vast courtyard, the silk-cotton trees reached inward with gnarled, twisted limbs. And as Lu Khen's vision adjusted to the night, he was able to see the macaques standing, hanging, sitting everywhere at the fringes of the courtyard. They were among the trees and in the bushes, and upon the roof of the enormous building at the far end of the paved approach, and on the backs of the stone dogs. Their numbers were shocking!

The veteran appeared again. This time he was not motionless. He strode on all fours, out from between two statues. His knuckles pressed the walkway. The fur around his shoulders bristled. He took one of his frozen positions, daring Lu Khen or Mai Su to approach the looming temple.

It was the monkeys' city and the veteran's menacing posture was a territorial behavior not far removed from normalcy. Yet a greater malignance hung about this simian population, touching Lu Khen's soul with icy tendrils. Something of an ancient evil was in them, absorbed or inherited; Lu Khen could not quite put a name to it.

The vast tribe of macaques began to press forward from all sides. They poured into the clearing. Even nursing infants were malevolently attentive. Mai Su stood sweetly, quietly, unconcerned, while Lu Khen's teeth chattered though the atmosphere was thick and warm.

There was something nonchalant about the monkeys now. They closed around, but did not seem inclined to do more than watch, as though leaving the worst actions to their leader. As for the chief macaque, he remained in his stony posture in the one direction not blocked by the furry devils.

How menaced Lu Khen felt! How absolutely helpless!

Gathering a moment of bravura, he screamed at them to run away.

He shook his hands at them, a gesture he had seen them make.

His feeble efforts to return to them an iota of his terror resulted in a greater intensity of chatter. Mai Su looked askance at him, and he felt a fool. The macaques were laughing at him, or talking about his actions in a manner that sounded like laughter. They certainly weren't frightened by his antics, but shook their hands right back and snapped their teeth rapidly. Lu Khen gave up and became motionless. He was more afraid than ever.

"Whatever happens," he promised himself, "I will protect Mai Su." He envisioned himself defending her with his body, holding her against a wall, stoic and immobile despite that monkeys tore his spine to pieces. "Mai Su must be kept safe," he said; but inside, he felt himself to be a perfect coward. He was unable to make another motion one way or another. There was nothing he could see to do. He was paralyzed, except that his knees quivered and his throat tightened.

What was it about the macaques that made them so peculiar to Lu Khen? His eyes met theirs, from one face to another, and he knew it was their eyes that made them weird. Something in the gaze of each was not merely cruel but also melancholy. He detected an unwholesome glint of intelligence such as he had never seen in the eyes of beasts. They were like the eyes of villainous men!

With horrific dawning, Ou Lu Khen realized that the essence of men and women gazed out from the faces of those imps. In that moment of terrible insight, he knew the souls of an extinct race were being punished with rebirth, forever and forever, in the bodies of macaques.

The infamy of the vanished people lived and glowered in the eyes of beasts, glowered with hatred, and sadness, and vengeance—vague vengeance against anything not suffering as they must suffer, anyone not punished for so long.

"They will kill us," said Lu Khen. "This is their city, where once they ruled as men. This is the last fort of their accursed spirits. Murder is the least of their most infamous deeds, the most easily accomplished."

And as he resigned himself to the helplessness of the situation, the monkeys grouped nearer. He heard more of them plump to the ground, one here, two there, a half-dozen barely out of sight. They crept forth on hind legs or on all fours. Their expressions were increasingly malevolent, their teeth flashing promises of pain.

Now did Mai Su take real notice of the small monsters.

She had noticed especially the leader, though momentarily she passed her gaze along the closing ranks of the others. And before Lu Khen could move to stop her, she stepped forth into the thickness of their bodies.

She stood amidst them like a priestess among children. And the monkeys began to shout in unison. It was like a sutra, a drone; their long, thin arms reached out. Their malevolent expressions dissolved into tears of self-pity. The monkeys wailed. They grew thicker as they pressed nearer, harder against the legs of Yeung Mai Su and, by then, Lu Khen, though disinterested in him.

The king among them had vanished from sight, but reappeared, and Lu Khen saw him coming. He slapped his followers this way and that way. He snarled when they moved too slowly to please him. He bit carelessly, at random. And they parted to let him through. His followers drew back, and suddenly he stood before Mai Su, his arms reaching out to either side as though expecting Mai Su to enter his embrace, like a father greeting his daughter, an emperor his princess. . . .

Then his arms began to shake, then lower, a look of human agony upon his gargoyle face. He fell backward with a pitiful scream. When Mai Su reached out to touch him, he recoiled as from an awful fire.

He seemed to recollect himself, like a warrior on the verge of terror and just in time rallying new courage. He stood his ground and raised himself on hind legs, nearly as tall as Yeung Mai Su, at whom he gazed sadly; then he turned about and led the terrible troops of monkeys away.

They withdrew far more quickly, and more quietly, than they had come.

In a little while they were nowhere to be seen, nowhere to be heard. Whether they had scurried to the jungles beyond the city's circling wall, or kept themselves well hidden, Lu Khen only wondered.

Before him and Mai Su, silhouetted against a starry heaven, the grimly visaged temple waited. Even before Lu Khen had regained a semblance of calm bearing, Mai Su walked forward on the path, the stone dogs her protectors.

* * *

On the surface it may seem queer that Po Lee and Koy could have camped beneath the curve of a huge, convex wall, protected from the frequent rains, for an entire week without catching the least hint of the presence of Lu Khen and Mai Su. The old man and the child had explored various paths through the city day by day, but found no footprint, no evidence of another camp. "It is not possible," Koy said worriedly, "that we beat them here by so many days." Her great-grandfather nodded his head with unspoken sorrow. Neither would come right out and admit what each was thinking: Lu Khen and Mai Su may have died along the way, never having reached the Forgotten Dynasty's capital.

Their problem stemmed from the city's division into three distinct sectors. The enormous convex wall was not the city's edge as Koy and Po Lee supposed. It was merely an enormous partition. It may have been raised over some political disputes or the sectors may have housed different castes. At so great a distance of time, the reasons could not be guessed. Whatever the purpose, the effect was that the ruins sprawled in three portions, each separated from the others. Koy and Po Lee had never fathomed this condition.

In gloomy spirits, having secretly decided she would never see her brother after all, Koy went off alone, taking with her the scabbarded sword that had been Harada's. She liked to wear it across her back. It would have been delusion to consider herself capable of using it with much effectiveness, but she considered it to be at least a talisman against the evil shadows of the city.

No evil had as yet manifested itself; and a week is like a year to a child. If nothing happens in a week or a year, chances are it never will. So a child will say. Po Lee continued to insist they stay clear of the ruined buildings and not go knocking at the doors of any tomb. But he, too, apparently lost many of his doubts about their safety. Hence Koy was able to wander at random, whenever she pleased, being careful only to avoid certain shadows.

She had arranged a set of rules for herself, abiding by them always. The first was that she must never step into a tomb's shadow. That was of primary importance. The temples' shadows were all right, being too big to avoid anyhow, and it being absurd to make up rules that could not be followed. The smaller shadows of squat mausoleums were more easily circumvented. If Koy accidentally stepped foot into such a shadow, it was not the end of all hope, for she would put her hand above her head and touch the top of the sword's hilt and count to three. That was the second rule. She believed this was sufficient to counteract any ill effects of having stepped on the wrong shadow.

It is wrong to dismiss such a childish scheme. Koy certainly was a child and prone to fancies, it is true. But if the matter is considered carefully, it can be observed that the world is full of unavoidable traps. Hardly anyone would make it to adulthood with all limbs intact were it not for good luck. What is luck but magic? Children are full of magic. It is unnecessary for children to learn complicated spells of a particular type, for magic is instinctual and it is strongest in the young. Children forever make up rules for all kinds of problems and situations. This is what heightens their good luck. Touching the top of the sword's hilt and counting to three may not seem a spectacular spell of much influence during moments of peril. But nothing had gotten Koy in a whole week, and that is something.

She walked along the convex wall, one hand brushing soft vines and white flowers. The air was heavy and aromatic. She took deep breaths, like sighs. There was a lot of rubble up ahead, where two big buildings had been torn to pieces by the roots of silk-cotton trees and fallen over. As it was hard to get through that area, Koy had not explored it during the first week. It was also difficult to avoid the shadows of a cluster of tombs in that area. But at the moment the sun was high, the shadows small. Koy began to climb upon shattered masonry, an ant upon a pile of rocks. When she obtained the top of a huge stone block, she saw something that surprised her. In fact she saw a couple of surprising things. But the one that had her attention quickest was the wall's true nature.

The wall by which she and her great-grandfather had

been camping was not merely convex, but tubular. She could see it distinctly from her present vantage point. The tubular wall went out into the jungle, where it did not merely end, but rose straight up above the trees and flattened out.

It had a gargantuan hood. Around the rim of the hood were numerous eyes and mouths. It was a Naga, a multi-headed cobra, bigger than Koy's worst nightmare might conceive. Happily it was only made of stone. That was bad enough. It was such a startling vision that the importance of a second revelation nearly passed her by.

She could see across the wall to a whole new section of the city—a section she and her great-grandfather had not suspected. Koy climbed up the incline of leaning masonry that took her to the top of the Naga's back. For a while she could not look away from the back of the Naga's hood. But there was a terrible odor coming from the ground on the other side of the wall, and the buzzing of millions of big flies. Her gaze altered as she tried to spot the source of the terrible odor.

She wanted to resolve everything before running back to tell her great-grandfather. She ran along the Naga's spine, toward the awful smell. From one point she had a clear view of a wide river dividing the city again. Thereby she resolved to her satisfaction that the city was divided into three parts by means of the Naga and by a river. Across that river she was able to detect a faint column of gray smoke as from a cookfire. Hope burned anew in Koy's tender heart that she might find her brother after all.

Below, near that wall on which she stood, there were numerous tombs sitting in long rows. One tomb had a collapsed roof. Around the broken tomb were numerous small corpses and scores of bones. For a fraction of a breath Koy feared Lu Khen and Mai Su had been captured by something that lived in the tomb and had been eaten. But she quickly realized the corpses were not big enough for grown people. They were slain monkeys. Something had moved into the broken tomb, a predator living off the flesh of macaques.

Koy was no bigger than a macaque. The possibility of danger did not escape her thinking. When she saw, moving upward from the shadows of the tomb's crumbled parts, a furred head of white and black, and red eyes glowering, she turned quickly and ran back along the Naga's spine. She ran toward the leaning masonry that had been her ladder. She leapt to a piece of fallen temple and slid downward on her bottom, the sword rattling in its scabbard, the backs of her legs scraped raw—but she did not cry out.

As she ran through the shadow of a tomb, she touched the hilt of the sword at her back and said, "One, two, three." At the same moment, the tiger roared.

The man-tiger came slinking from its den, stepping across rotten meat, approaching the wall. It gave one powerful leap upward but could not achieve the top, rebounding with a fluid motion to the ground. It shouted once, sounding more tiger than not, betraying little of the man snared within the fur. It paced back and forth before the wall, its haunted skull mad with dark animal thoughts. It had seen the very prey that was its great desire. It had seen the favored meal. But the game had fled. The wall could not be measured by leaps alone.

Pacing, pacing, pacing that short section of wall as though in a cave, the tiger tried to conceive some plan. Foresight was not its finer ability, not even in such cases where instinct proved insufficient to an aim. So the tiger strove to draw upon deeper cunning, sought conference with its human part, lest the wall remain unresolved mystery.

The human part did not wish to offer clue or information. It wished to sleep without awareness. It was beyond struggling with the tiger's personality, beyond concern for its selfhood, incapable of asserting itself merely to be confronted by so many sinful occupations. But the tiger's will insisted. Awake! Awake! There was war within, and the human part could not hope to win. Weak as it was, frightened as it was, desirous as it was of internal slumber, the human portion was partially aroused. A sleepy, whining thought suggested to its grimmer aspect: *Every wall must end. Seek its end and you-I-we may go around.*

The tiger started toward the head of the gigantic Naga,

out into the jungle, to find its way around and nearer to its dearly wanted meal. How cleverly it moved about, as though expecting challenge at every corner. The internal companion made the tiger skittish, anxious, wary. Its taste of death added to its sense of easy oblivion. By the time it had found the campsite of Po Lee and little Koy, the place had been abandoned. But a tiger cannot reason out a complex situation and could not guess that Koy's information about the city's other sectors had sent them packing, in search of Lu Khen and Mai Su. The tiger assumed the prey would return to its camp at least by nightfall. So the tiger slunk into the deep, long shadow of a tomb, far enough from the camp to rest undetected, but close enough to keep watch.

Only the tiger's eyes shone from that shadow where it lay down in the hot, late afternoon, panting. The big cat slept, and in sleep acquired surer affinity for its human portion. It dreamed strange dreams of human frailty and feline mightiness, of oceans and jungles, of cities, villages, canals, and wilderness . . . all fused into a bizarre yet highly focused universe of impossibilities and unlikelihoods.

Into this impossible dream-environment of houses and wilderness, boats and ancient ruins, of helplessness and absolute power, a winged presence came and spoke angrily to the tiger and the man, or to the confused amalgamation they had become. "Foolish pet," said the Garuda, reaching out a loving hand that turned into a fist. "Get up and go upon your hunt. The time is now." And the tiger stood instantly, and instantly the human part was suppressed and the dreamworld replaced by cruel, sharp reality. It was night, and night is beloved by tigers. It leapt into the campsite, scattering the palm-leaf bedding, then the ash of past fires, eager for a sleeping prey. But there was none.

The beast stalked toward the tail of the long Naga, guided by a thought or a direction taken from the dream. It crossed familiar territory where it had hunted macaques for several days. It came to a river and stood before a stone bridge built like half a drum upon its side.

Atop the bridge, almost invisible in darkness, was a human form. It was too black even for the keen eyes of the cat to see in detail. The tiger leapt at it, but it was gone. The dark spirit was now visible along a path. The tiger tried again and missed, and was led thus upon an eerie chase, without the least concept of ghosts or devils. At length the tiger came by a back route to a temple surrounded by weedy courtyards, motionless guardians in the shape of dogs, and sickly fruit trees with a few shriveled fruits, these trees defining vaguely the circles of long-vanished gardens.

The fur of the man-tiger pricked and sparked. Its ears became erect as it listened to the soft murmurs of scores of sleeping birds. It slunk closer to the ground and moved with an almost serpentine grace, spoiled occasionally by an apish tendency to rise unexpectedly on hind quarters only to slink down again.

It circled the huge building, observed by carved faces. It drew back on its haunches and leapt through the entry, into the corridor. It stopped. It listened. Its round eyes gleamed.

The sweet voice of a blind goddess spoke: *This is but a dream; you are part of me.* Lu Khen rolled onto his side, dreaming. The sweet voice said: *There is no danger if you do not exist;* and Lu Khen's eyes opened. He stared upward into darkness. He listened for the faint, far communication, but there was nothing more.

He and Mai Su had lived for several days in the ruin of the huge temple. The building was dangerous, he knew; it was strewn with parts of deeply carved engravings broken from the ceiling. But there was never such a thing as making a decision for Mai Su. For all her apparent passivity, he had long understood that the majority of their choices had been hers. They had taken possession of a particular chamber for which Mai Su had a strange affinity. It was about as comfortable as the monastery wherein Lu Khen once sought a moment's insight and found only reason. But in some unreasoning corner of his mind, some hidden memory of another life, the temple and the grounds surrounding it had some affinity for him as well. He felt an odd joy by living in this place.

It was dark in the cell even at broad of day; at present, it was deep of night. All was still and black. Beside him, Mai Su slept upon the makeshift pallet he had made for them. They lay beside one another as brother and sister although, when Lu Khen was honest in his thinking, or had dreamed something embarrassing, he confessed to himself that he did not feel like Mai Su's brother.

He sat up in the dark, gazing around himself with blinded sight, as though expecting to see something other than Mai Su shining with subtle luminescence. There was only her. Beneath the beautiful glow of her skin were traceries of lightest blue. Lu Khen leaned over her wonderingly, his heart swelling, and he saw that her dark eyes were open.

"Mai Su?" he whispered, but she did not reply. She was gazing at something he could not see, gazing at some dream, or into a void beyond sane comprehension. Momentarily, without once having wakened, her eyes closed, and she breathed more deeply.

A tiny, heatless fire could easily be mistaken for a shining heart beneath Mai Su's garment. At Lu Khen's heart, too, was such a light, the flame dove's feather uniting him and Mai Su whether close or distant. He touched the spot between her breasts, lightly so as not to rouse her, then touched his own heart. Then he turned his face away, to gaze into blackness, emptiness, or emotions of indeterminate meaning. He was confusing even to himself. He was full of innocence and sinful wishes. He was like anyone at all.

He had to pee. He rose from the comfortless pallet and walked from the cell into a long corridor, footsteps echoing from the vaulted ceiling in the hollow of the mountain-shaped temple. At the far end of the corridor, starlight and blue-gray shadows filled the shape of the doorway. He touched his hand against the wall to keep his balance, fuzzy-headed with drowsiness. His fingers traced the convoluted patterns on the wall. Behind him, he heard soft padding, but made himself believe it was moisture dripping. Before him, the swirling grayness of the exit shrank and swelled as might the maw of a breathing giant. He tried to shake the illusion from his cloudy mind.

Outside under the starlight, he heard parrots and other sorts of birds roosting uneasily. The courtyard had become a sanctuary for birds in the week since his and Mai Su's arrival. Lu Khen walked far away from the doorway and stood behind a big stone dog, upon the shoulders of which an owl no larger than a sparrow perched and watched Lu Khen's business.

The gentle goddess whispered in his brain: *Everything is part of me*.

"Who is it?" said Lu Khen, embarrassed, covering his penis. He turned full circle, and the miniature owl squeaked, "Who?"

Somewhere distant, there was a sutra murmured by a deep, insistent voice . . . the voice of a monk or priest. The hairs at Lu Khen's nape pricked. In adjusting to his unusual life in the City of Tombs, Lu Khen had begun to forget that such a place must certainly be haunted. For the first few days of trepidation, he had pried at tomb entries and found entry to a few, expecting dangers or wonders, and hoping especially to find the madness for which he quested. But the ancient capital had offered no monsters, no ghosts, no promise of insanity. The greatest danger was that some damaged structure would fall upon his head.

The eerie architecture never gave up its malignant mood; but it had begun to seem as though the evil of the place had paled over the millennium. Its villainy had grown impotent. Lu Khen's quest had been rather metaphysical from the start; so he had to admit that a part of him had doubted all along that madness was an object to be discovered under rocks or worn like a mantle. As it was true that he had never whole-heartedly believed in his proposed goal, what ulterior motive had he hidden from himself? He had sought Mai Su's company. That was all. And however frustrating and unfulfilled their relationship must be, he had few regrets. So he had given up both his hope and his fear of terrible hauntings; he gladly took into himself Mai Su's evident delight of the ruined temple and its surroundings; and he gladdened himself further with her happiness with his company.

If it were somewhat short of a healthy affair, Lu Khen

did not mind. He put limits on his selfishness and adapted well.

But the sound of the sutra shook at the recent and infirm faith that the tombs were unhaunted. They had to be haunted. He should never have doubted it. The sound of the priest's calling reverberated unnaturally, tugging at Lu Khen in a physical manner. It was no hermit or lost pilgrim praying, but a supernatural agent.

Did he want to go in search of the voice's origin? Was he too afraid to move from his spot? Had he given up his quest for madness, or had he not? Did he want the special enlightenment of the mad, and so be Mai Su's husband, or was he satisfied with safety and a chaste arrangement?

It was, he felt, unsatisfactory to remain in their present stasis. If desire did not demand more, then a warped kind of conformity demanded holy consummation. That, or it demanded he withdraw from the terrible road already taken. It was far too late for that option. So his quest had been sincere after all.

The voice may have beseeched some god, but it felt to Lu Khen as though it called to him, promising reward and sweet terror. He strode among the silk-cotton trees and palms, starlight barely penetrating to the ground. He found his way through the damp, warm night from one building to the next. The priest's incantation became clearer and more insistent in Lu Khen's mind.

He came to a squat, dark tomb from which a deep, blue light emitted. Lu Khen could not be certain if it was a tomb he had seen before, as darkness had made his bearings uncertain. It did seem to him that it was a tomb previously sealed against him. Now it stood without any door to block his view of the interior.

Run away, he told himself. *Flee!* Then he thought: *This is what I came to see, what started me out in the beginning.*

He bent his knees and moved stealthily to one side, trying to see into the open doorway without getting too close.

Within, sitting cross-legged on the floor with a pot of blue coals placed before him, a priest in black robes with a beatific face and half-closed eyes sang his unusual sutra and tossed a handful of dusty resin in the pot. The pot flamed. The blue fire burned cold. It was as much ice as it was fire. The incense drifted forth to Ou Lu Khen, drugging his senses, making him simultaneously bold and too languorous for action.

Momentarily, the priest's lips ceased the incantation. His eyes opened—dark eyes that reminded Lu Khen of his beloved, reminded him of madness—and the priest said:

"Come forth." His voice was commanding.

Lu Khen shook his head from side to side, but was too fascinated to run.

The priest glowed with the same chilly blueness of the pot of coals. How strange he appeared! Yet he was strangely pretty. He said: "I have that for which you seek. With a single act, I can render you insane."

He gazed upward at the ceiling of his tomb, then sideways at its walls. He said, "I was trapped in such a place as this for a thousand years. A silk-cotton tree freed me by its insistent roots. But there remains a guardian against me. You have brought her to me."

Devils only lie, whispered Lu Khen's secret goddess.

"Devils only lie," said Lu Khen. "Mai Su is no guardian. She is simple. She is mad."

"So am I," said the priest, smiling sweetly. "In my simplicity, I want revenge; in my revenge, I acquire freedom. Tonight, the spirit of the immortal dove will be destroyed, enslaved for a thousand years as was done to me. Whatever was beautiful about the world until today will be horrific after the dawn. You will know when the forgotten prophecies are done, for that feather near your breast will turn to ash. Your beloved, as you know her, will be dead. What else is required to bring you madness?"

The seated priest began to stand in a flourish of dark robes. He stood slowly as though he were a weighted being. As he stood, the robes turned into wings. His head twisted halfway around, until the beatific face was replaced by the face behind: half human, half bird of prey. His voice became terrible.

"Remember, it was *you* that brought her to meet destruction. *You* were an instrument of the Garuda's revenge. *You* stole the boat that belonged to another . . . another who felt compelled to follow after and whom I have transformed into a werebeast stalking, at this moment, the one you love. All this will give you madness, the reward for your shameful quest."

Before Lu Khen's eyes, the Garuda became blue mist, then empty blackness that seeped upward through the cracks in the tomb's roof. The black vapor rose above the trees and spread like a malignance over the city, blotting out the stars. Lu Khen was left facing the stone seal of an unopened door, as though it had never been open and all that he had seen was but illusion.

From the temple, where he had left Mai Su, he heard the squawking of numerous parrots upset from their slumber, followed by the rustle of innumerable wings in sudden, panicked fright. Lu Khen wheeled and fled along the path, but lost himself at once, retracing his steps, running another way. How like a dream it was! The worst he ever had! The more essential he felt it was to rescue Mai Su, the more inaccessible she became! His very eagerness made him inept; he could not concentrate on the difficult task of holding the proper paths in the newly starless darkness.

He wanted not to believe the creature of the tomb, but what adage is more common than, "The attainment of one's desire is the end of one's purpose"? Wasn't he on the cusp of the madness he had sought? Or was this only hysteria on his part? Would he know madness when he found it? By what better means might madness be found than through actions that harmed Yeung Mai Su?

By the time he found his way to the edge of the courtyard, all was silent, the temple a mountainous shape, the birds far gone. Such quietude! Lu Khen could hardly breathe.

Ah, it was dark, and for the first time in days Koy was frightened. She lay against her great-grandfather to keep warm, their backs to a broken fence of carved stone. Night in the derelict capital had grown unexpectedly, unnaturally cold. In the sky was neither star nor cloud, but a shimmering canopy of malignance. She and Po Lee had been searching through previously undiscovered portions of the city for the whole day. Darkness found them away from their familiar camp. Koy's stout sensibilities were injured. She could not keep herself from fancying strange things.

"I cannot sleep," she whispered, and sighed. Great-grandfather Po Lee tightened his arm around her. Staring at the weirdly starless sky, he said, "Nor can I."

"I won't sleep all night," she said.

"I don't know if I will or not," said Po Lee.

"Tell me a story," said Koy, thinking it would fill the time and distract her from dreadful worries.

"Something scary or something sweet?"

She ought to ask for something sweet, she thought. But it would be so out of place. Usually she did not like sweet stories that much.

"Something sad," she said.

"Are you sure?"

"Yes."

"Have I ever told you of 'Tsi Hwa's Civet Cat'?"

"I cannot remember that you ever told me."

"I will tell it, then," said Ou Po Lee.

"Please," said Ou Koy.

"Tsi Hwa raised the civet cat from the time it was a kitten," began Po Lee. "It grew to be the size of a dog and menaced everyone but Tsi Hwa. It had a long, thickly furred tail; a long, lean body built equally for running or climbing trees; and long, needle-thin teeth for catching, holding, tearing. Tsi Hwa named the civet Stink Monster, on account of the scent gland that it used when frightened. But the civet had not been frightened of anything since it was small, so 'Stink Monster' was less appropriate for the grown civet than it had been for the kitten it once had been. To the neighborhood, therefore, the civet was simply Monster, nothing more nor less.

"Stink Monster had long before rid the neighborhood of rats and mice, birds and game, and had seriously curtailed the population of dogs and cats. The carnivore was king of the district and Tsi Hwa was proud of his strong pet, oblivious to the complaints of his neighbors.

"One day an infant was found in the back yard of an influential family. The infant had been torn to pieces.

"'Stink Monster was right here the whole time!' said Tsi Hwa to the magistrate's questions. But everyone had had enough and pressed the magistrate to pursue the matter. Tsi Hwa was arrested and severely beaten, but refused to change his story. 'Stink Monster was with me! Stink Monster was in my lap!' The magistrate's men beat Tsi Hwa harder and harder, until all he could do was moan and grunt his denials. 'Stink Monster . . . did not . . . do it . . . Stink Monster . . . would not eat a child.'

"As he could not be budged, they let him go. His kind-hearted grandmother came and helped Tsi Hwa home, where he passed out and was fevered for many days. His grand-mother nursed his swollen joints and sliced back. Because he was so ill, he didn't know that during his imprisonment, the neighbors had set traps for Stink Monster, killed him, skinned him, and made the skin into a hat.

"'Where's Stink Monster?' asked Tsi Hwa.

"'Outside catching rats,' said his grandmother, wiping sweat from his brow.

"In a few days he was better and found out what had happened. Tsi Hwa walked up and down the streets of the district for an entire night, shouting, 'Stink Monster was innocent! Stink Monster didn't kill the child!'

"After the skinning of Stink Monster, people started to notice a terrible aroma. They hadn't smelled anything so awful since Stink Monster was young and small and afraid of anything that moved too fast.

"Tsi Hwa sat in his house all day. He stroked the fur hat that had once been his pet. 'Nice Stink Monster,' he would say, keeping the hat in his lap. 'Good Stink Monster.' Some people said he was hit too many times in the head by the magistrate's men. But his grandmother replied, 'You shouldn't have killed his civet.'

"The neighborhood began to smell worse and worse, as though the very houses and the earth were dead and rotting. Then one evening, a big dog was stopped from killing a child. The dog was chased away with sticks and rocks. Someone said the dog had been seen in the vicinity in the past, but Stink Monster had always chased it away.

"Now the dog came whenever it pleased. It came at night and everyone had to be careful about their children. No one could figure out who owned the dog or where it came from. It was too smart for traps. It wouldn't eat anything that had been poisoned. One night it maimed an old man who was drunk. It ripped off an arm and bit out an eye. People heard the old man screaming and came out of their houses to chase the dog away. It was clever and escaped. It only attacked people who were helpless and alone. It hurried away when there was more than one.

"Meanwhile, the air around the neighborhood was so bad that people didn't even want to stay alive and breathe. They didn't know what was worse, to be haunted by the fearful odor of Stink Monster, or to be terrified by the vicious dog that had claimed the neighborhood as its territory now that Stink Monster wasn't alive and on patrol.

"At last it was necessary to visit Tsi Hwa to beg his opinion. Tsi Hwa was still not in his right mind, whether from the beating, fever, or grief; all he did all day long was sit and pet the hat. Several neighborhood advocates beseeched his forgiveness.

"'Now we know that mean old civet of yours was secretly protecting our district from a terrible dog. We are deeply ashamed and wish for you to overlook our evil actions. Monster's ghost is still around, punishing us with a sickening stench. Could you pray to the spirit of Monster and make him forgive us? It's bad enough that we must fight that dog, without having our health dragged down by that odor, too.'

"'Stink Monster,'" said Tsi Hwa petulantly. "Not 'Monster.'"

"The advocates went through their speech a second time, saying 'Stink Monster' instead of 'Monster,' and behaving twice as humbled.

"Tsi Hwa then replied, 'Stink Monster only makes an odor when afraid. He hasn't been afraid of anything for a long time. Therefore he wouldn't be making such a smell as you describe.'

"'All the same, would you ask him to stop it?'

"'I will tell him I don't believe you a bit,' said stubborn

Tsi Hwa, and he began right away to stroke the civet-fur hat vigorously, saying in a loud voice, 'It isn't you, is it? No, it isn't you.'

"The advocates went away mumbling to each other, 'He's a loony. He won't help.'

"But that very night, when the dog came again, howling in the street as though he owned the whole neighborhood and frightened people peered out the cracks of their windows, a ghost-civet appeared in the sky. It gave a fierce growl as though it were a lion, and swooped down to bite the head off the dog. Then the ghost-civet sat down on the corpse of the dog. He licked his paws and long tail. When all the windows along the street were filled with startled faces, the civet looked at them and said, 'I have answered your prayer in this way, saving you from this dog, who always was my enemy. As for the odor of the district, I cannot help you, for it isn't mine. It's yours.'

"Then Stink Monster rose in the sky and was never seen again. The next day, it was discovered that Tsi Hwa was dead, and the fur hat was missing. But the neighborhood never did stop smelling."

When Po Lee finished the story, and after a moment of silence so that his small ward could ponder all the events, he asked, "Was it sad enough?" But when he looked at the great-granddaughter in the crook of his arm, she was sound asleep, and never heard the story's end. Po Lee smiled, his mind wandering away through dim corridors of memory, toward bittersweet dreams and slumber.

Lu Khen calmed his breath and stood looking along the dark path toward the stairway to the gaping entry of the temple. When his breathing was quiet and his heart no longer raced, he took one step forward. With that step, he heard the sound of stone rubbing stone. He stopped, listened, but the sound did not repeat until he took another step. There was the grating sound again, ceasing when he became motionless. He turned his head left, then right. His ears wiggled slightly. But only when he took a third step did he hear the sound again, and he was alarmed.

Near the top of the temple's entry, a stone slab had lowered three handlengths. Lu Khen had not previously noticed any mechanism for the lowering of a door; it must have been well concealed. But he remembered too well the magically disappearing and reappearing door to the priest-Garuda's tomb, and Lu Khen's nerves began to itch and tingle with dreadful speculation.

Given that the door was slipping down to seal Mai Su inside, how could he restrain himself from a quick effort to reach her? He had to give it a try and so ran five steps forward only to bring himself to a sudden, anguished halt. The door had lowered an additional five handlengths.

The shimmering sky made a sound like dry leaves trampled under a soft tread. Was the overhanging presence laughing?

Lu Khen took one step backward, but the process was irreversible. The door remained in its position. When he took the same step forward, the door lowered another handlength.

He dared not step backward again, for he would only lose irretrievable ground. He tried to estimate the distance he must cover and the space each of his steps caused the door to lower. He gauged that the seal would be nearly completed before he could reach the door.

He dared not move in either direction.

Nowhere on the ground could he detect a trap or trigger. There was no physical connection between himself and that door. It could only be the Garuda's doing, a cruel jest. Lu Khen could scarcely imagine himself so important to the scheme of the universe that he was worth the bother of teasing. It must take a lot of effort to cause him so much suffering. Creatures of amazing power surely had more interesting things to do.

But what could he possibly know about the nature of the universe? It might be that all things were arranged so as to do injury to anyone sensitive enough to appreciate the situation, to understand the meanheartedness of wheels spinning, wheels crushing, wheels slaying, wheels blocking simple paths. The simplest individual might exist solely to be harmed. The very gods might suffer, and siphon off their pain into lesser things, a hierarchy of anguish with people at the bottom.

Or he might really be something more than he thought himself to be, someone really worth singling out for major or petty attack. Demons feared him, fought him. Demons admired him, hated him... for his own sake, or for his affinity with Mai Su and her divine madness. Gods might watch with pity and no action, while demons were free to do as they pleased.

Then again, he might already be half mad and all his speculations idiotic. There was no reason to assume an incredible connection between demons, himself, and that doorway threatening to seal itself forever.

But if the notion of such connections was unreasonable, so too was his notion of a binding force between himself and Yeung Mai Su. Love certainly united them; he believed this. Since love could be such a binding factor, what other intangible forces webbed the entirety of the universe for the sake of good or evil or indifference?

If there was no connection between himself and that lowering door, then there could be no connection between himself and Mai Su. But there was, and there was. Evidence of sinister power was proof as well of things that are bright. Thinking this, testing this, he took another step forward, and the grating rock lowered another space. Darkness wished to sever the thread of light between the chaste lovers.

And there was nothing for Ou Lu Khen to do.

His face twisted in agony. His eyes pinched shut. He asked himself over and over again in a whisper, "What can I do? What can I do?" Then he cried out: "Mai Su! Mai Su!" In a moment, the partly shut doorway filled with a ruddy glow. For a moment, Lu Khen saw the flame dove fluttering near the exit. The bird took no notice of Lu Khen before it withdrew within.

And Lu Khen heard Mai Su singing for the first time in days and days, singing to the flame dove.

"Mai Su!"

But she would not answer, would not come to the door. He could not make her come out. Yet if he tried to go to her, he could not make it in time, the door would be closed for a thousand years. . . .

He knelt to pick up a rock twice as round as a fist. A dry limb was also close to hand. He had to take a step forward to reach it; and the doorway lowered one space further.

Now he leapt. He sprang as far as possible. The doorway still only closed a handlength. He stood motionless, pondering, seeing that he could minimize the door's descent while maximizing the ground he covered.

At such hope, the starless sky replied with crinkling, faint laughter. Lu Khen refused to listen. Panicky in his resolve, heart racing, he sprang forth in rapid, flying steps. Up the stairway he ran with leaping strides, watching the lowering door as it responded to his approach, shutting out the dim ruddiness of the flame dove's light.

Lu Khen was weeping and made a lamentful cry, a sound like a pheasant's. He flung himself on his belly with both hands thrust before him, risking the loss of both hands as the slab sped downward.

He put branch and stone beneath the falling seal, having no time to spare. The branch splintered and, had he not blinked in time, pieces might have blinded him. The rock in his other hand stopped the door's descent.

He withdrew his hands, gasping with the horrid picture in his mind of how his hands might have been reduced to bloody paste.

He pressed his cheek to the ground and tried to see through the slit. He saw Mai Su's bare feet in the ruddy light. He saw the hem of her skirt. And he saw something else: four odd-looking, furry legs in one corner of the corridor.

"Mai Su! A tiger! Mai Su!"

She was humming a mystic, dirgelike tune and gave no evidence that she was listening to Lu Khen. Her feet did not move, did not return to the cell or seek any hiding place. She was completely distracted by a mutual cooing with the heavenly bird.

For Lu Khen, the flame dove had symbolized the unity of his and Mai Su's spirits, for his world revolved around her, so too all things of beauty. This being so, it was love that distracted her, and not the bird *per se;* their love put her at peril. It was a terrible thought and Lu Khen withdrew from it. The flame dove might be something else altogether, or many things at once. It might be something else altogether for Mai Su. It might be *of* Mai Su, while in the greater scheme, Lu Khen was nothing.

He grabbed the feather from out of his clothing. It shone a brilliant red. If it were part of Mai Su alone and not himself, then she had given him a part of her being, and that was something. If it were the uniting thread of life that made them one, so much the better. In either case, he said, "By this we are united. She must listen to me through this." Then, as much to the feather as through the door, he shouted, "Mai Su! Hide in a chamber! Get away from the tiger!"

Still she stood there humming without concern, dashing his dream of their oneness, heightening his fear for her well-being.

He could not clearly make out the exact nature of the thing he took to be a tiger. He could not see that it was white and black, for the flame dove's light made the fur orange, increasing Lu Khen's impression of a tiger. But it was impossible to judge carefully when only the lower part of the legs were visible. There was something of an ape about the stance—a bizarre ape. Lu Khen did not like to weigh what the Garuda had suggested of a murdering were-tiger. But the thing was above all a threat to Mai Su who by nature would not respond to danger.

It growled. It ran down the corridor. It leapt upward, legs vanishing from Lu Khen's narrow sight as he lay helplessly observant. Mai Su's melodic voice gave a startled cry as her song was silenced.

Lu Khen had never before heard a startled sound, or seen a startled moment, from Mai Su.

The ruddy light was extinguished. Lu Khen could see no more.

In Lu Khen's hand was no longer a feather but an ash. He gave a painful sob and rolled away from the door. The weight of the thick slab of stone belatedly pulverized the rock Lu Khen had placed to hold the door open. The last little space slammed shut.

Lu Khen squeezed the ash until it was a dark stain in his palm. Tears streaming, he thought: "Our bond is broken and Yeung Mai Su is dead."

And was his sanity challenged? If so, madness was a reasoning thing, as he had never guessed. He flung himself at the unyielding door, beating it until the whole length of his arms from fists to elbows were bruised and raw. He shouted curses and pleas, though knowing all too well there would be no entry to that place. He knew a tiger was at that moment enjoying its last meal. And Ou Lu Khen conjured in his mind the most grotesque, morbid and excessive vision possible, torturing himself by this means.

He stepped backward from the temple, gazing upward past the carved faces to the hovering dark. As he stepped back, he allowed himself to tumble headlong down the stairs. It looked like clumsiness, but he really hoped he would die and had done it on purpose. But he was only battered a little and got up, his lungs bursting with bestial sounds of sorrow.

Arms thrashing, he danced wildly, as a bird throws itself around when its head is twisted off. He scurried through the nighted courtyard, grunting. He grabbed a dog statue, held its neck and begged comfort. Then he grew wrathful and insulted the dog. Then he tried to pull old, stunted bushes out of the ground, but he lacked the strength required.

It was in all a frightful exhibition of mannered insanity. It was silliness and pathos together, for he truly did not know anything more reasonable to do. Only the totality and obviousness of his sincere anguish made him other than a clown.

If he had been a better and wiser man, he reasoned, he might have known that for *him* there was no serenity in madness. There could be only pain. What else could bring his rationality, his constant thinking, thinking, thinking tumbling into pieces—other than the rending and destruction of the one he most loved? What beyond the horrific comprehension that *he* had slain Yeung Mai Su by means of selfishness and desire, by means of his idiot's quest! He should have guessed this answer from the beginning, and so not come so far.

If he had won his madness, then he had done so by means of utter fallibility. He had done so by all sorts of crimes that were so subtle he and he alone could ever see what crimes they were.

All his antics were by some degrees contrived and by other degrees perfectly honest. He knew the starless night, or the ghastly being that made the night seem starless, observed him and enjoyed his every act. Lu Khen felt as though he had to put on a show for the observing demon. For if the terrible japes of devils gain too small a response, then other japes must be devised and heaped upon others. For this reason it is always best to entertain those who are cruelest.

He frankly did not know if he was mad or just pretending. What he felt was more complicated than grief alone. And the most horrible things he ever felt about himself and about his life were all at once heightened and abnormal. Every minor sin came back to him as atrocity. All his embarrassing mistakes, no matter how trivial, were remembered as proof that everyone he ever knew laughed at him or regretted his existence. He was no longer just stupid and cowardly and sinful and weak, but all these things by phenomenal measure. The world would have been better had he died at birth. All his life was trouble. He was a terrible young man, truly terrible. Naïveté was no excuse. No matter how innocent he seemed, he could not deny his worthlessness, his repugnance, his errors.

And while he judged himself so harshly, he continued to caper through the darkness like a wild marionette in the hands of a spastic god. Yet the capering heralded from within and he could blame no greater power. It was his choice to respond thus, or thus, or thus. Nothing really compelled him to shout in just that manner, or to fling himself at absurd angles and postures. There was no reason to tear at weeds, scratch at the bark of twisted and deformed fruit-bearing trees, and roll upon the ground, gagging. He had to make each decision, whether or not to roll his eyes and grab his ears and jiggle his head back and forth and make himself a macabre toy for a giant's imbecilic children.

Oh, what a blithering madman was he! He absolutely had to do these things and nothing else! Why did he have to blather? Because madmen are like that, are they not? It was only reasonable that, having been driven mad by the death of his beloved, he should carry on in this manner. It was logical and correct.

And so it was carefully worked out, was it? Then he was not a bit mad after all. "I'm not mad," he realized, or imagined, or feared. "I'm sane. I'll never be mad in this life. Too bad for me."

But at what point can madness see itself and ponder? Might he be all the madder for thinking himself curiously rational? Are there not levels of madness and of grief that he had not yet guessed? Was he merely tasting from insanity's shallowest pool, as yet unaware of what depths remained?

It was assuredly the wrong moment for the aborigine to appear. He stood in the gate to the courtyard, resplendent with primitive weapons, tattoos, feathered and embroidered cloak. How long he had stood there Lu Khen could not guess, for darkness hides many things. The aboriginal hunter was absolutely quiet, so he may have observed Lu Khen's histrionics in their entirety. It may have been the shouting and cursing that brought the fellow to that gate, so that he only just arrived and had seen little. But it was the wrong moment, whether to see all or little, for Ou Lu Khen was either not yet finished with his imitation of lunacy, or was working his way to a keener madness that required further evidence or action to push him over the edge.

Lu Khen had never harmed anyone intentionally but now he meant to try. He picked up a rough square of masonry and started toward the gate meaning the tattooed stranger injury. Or, it is likely, he meant to pit himself against those primitive weapons and die, thus rejoining Mai Su in the next life or in heaven.

As he ran, as he shouted, his topknot came untied and his hair fell down around his shoulders. What a specter he appeared! The aborigine seemed reluctant to fight, but started his leather thong whirling, setting up a weird whistle as counter-melody to Lu Khen's menacing shout. Whether from reluctance to hurt Lu Khen, or because so spectral an appearance unsettled the hunter's aim, his shot went awry. The stone was slung into no dangerous spot, but grazed Lu Khen's thigh. It hardly slowed him down. He limped onward, ungainly but swift, and planted the chunk of masonry flat against the aborigine's temple.

The hunter went to his knees, jabbering words Lu Khen could not understand, except that they sounded like a plea. And a familiar name was repeated twice in the phrases: "Ou Po Lee . . . Ou Po Lee."

What could this wayward hunter possibly have to do with Lu Khen's great-grandfather? The sound of Po Lee's name stopped Lu Khen from further violence. He took the stunned hunter by the shoulders, holding him in balance, and said back at him: "Ou Po Lee?"

Dazed, the hunter repeated, "Ou Po Lee," and in spite of the blow Lu Khen had dealt him, the aborigine smiled as might a friend.

Strange to say, Lu Khen was able to see beyond the patterns of the facial tattoos something of his own visage, something of himself. It was the visage of a lonely quester, a man apart.

"I am mad after all," Lu Khen whispered, "to see myself upon my knees in the guise of a native hunter, crying for Great-grandfather Po Lee." He was almost joyful at the thought of actual insanity. His grief and self-horror fled, if only for the moment, and in that moment he appreciated the irony of the happy things in life that must always end the same—must always end.

"There is no reason to be mad now," he said to the uncomprehending aborigine. "What good is madness when Mai Su is dead?"

There would be no happy union of madwoman and madman if one alone was living. By some means Lu Khen must die also. Only in death is there happiness. That is what his madness or his crippled reason said. What greater truth was there? What other thing was there that every individual in every case was positively destined to achieve?

He took from the stunned hunter a bronze knife, then quietly strode away. He passed through the city and, well before dawn, was in the dripping jungle, wandering far from paths in search of an anthill or carnivore's den by the side of which to slit his throat and pass into another, perhaps better, world.

Not even when one's view is clear and wide are things observable in their completeness, in all their aspects from every side, below, above, within, with all that everything implies or symbolizes. Lu Khen had been unable to see but a fragment of the events involving the tiger, the dove, and Mai Su in the temple. His conclusions were as good as the evidence he had. That is to say, they were no good at all.

Mai Su had awakened to the greeting of the dove. She began to hum happily as it cooed. It flew away from her a moment, and Mai Su rose to follow. In the corridor, the flame dove came back to perch on the back of her hand and hear the song again.

The temple door was lowering bit by bit, but to Mai Su this did not matter. She had dreamed of omniscience and did not feel herself to be merely within the temple. Hence there was no belief in traps, cages, or limitations.

The corridor's right-hand wall bent away, so that the hall became an enormous chamber. In the chamber, near the one wall left of the corridor, there crouched a tiger. Mai Su knew at once that it had once been the she-tiger that had died in her lap. And by her queer perception, she also knew that it was now a weretiger. But the man within was sleepy and withdrawn, so truly it was still mostly a tiger.

The beast to some extent recognized Mai Su. It remembered her friendship and how she had sung it into peaceful rest. Mai Su had no fear of attack and, it is true, the tiger was slow to do so. But Mai Su's song upset the tiger, whose nerves were taut. The melody reminded it of a dark void, a waiting-place or an ending-place, where there was neither sorrow nor reward, no hunting and no danger; where there was only emptiness that went on and on and also went within. The tiger had returned from that place as, very likely, no tiger had before accomplished. Rejuvenation made life a joy once more. And it did not wish to return to that oblivion and so disdained Mai Su's celestial music.

Tigers are a solitary lot as well. Friendships are slight affairs. Debts are rarely paid. Surely Mai Su knew the world was like this, and tigers no improvement; for Mai Su's vision was of an unusual sort, and she had to know. At the same time, she had never believed in peril for herself. Thus it must have been a rude surprise that the tiger sprang, knocking her over so that her head struck the wall and blood oozed from her scalp.

The dove had flown into the tiger's face as though to do battle with the beast, to protect Mai Su. It was instantly crushed in those jaws. Mai Su felt the pain as though it had been her own ribcage shattered. The pain swiftly passed, except where she had struck her head, while the tiger found it had only a mouthful of ash and that its mouth was burnt and blistered.

Mai Su lay upon her side in the sudden darkness. She saw Lu Khen's worried face at the same level, peering underneath the door's remaining crack. But he could not penetrate the darkness with his sight, could not know she was still alive. In the next moment, the stone door crashed down the final handlength.

Was Mai Su upset or angry with the tiger that had slain the dove? Was Mai Su capable of anger or of grief? Did she fully comprehend the meaning of loss?

She felt new things, that much was certain. She felt pain at her head—a slight wound, but her first. She felt amazement that anything in the world could mean her harm. So when she sat up, she was grave and perturbed. She was annoyed in an indefinable manner incomprehensible to common individuals. She glowered at the tiger and her eyes were darker than its own. Her eyes gleamed a sort of malevolence that reminded the tiger of its unholy master.

The tiger backed away and nursed its muzzle with its paws, having thus acknowledged powers greater than itself, wildness more extreme, mysteries beyond calculation.

Mai Su felt for the feather kept always near her heart, but it too had become ash. Mai Su knew nothing of unhappiness as others knew it. At the same time, she knew all. Odd, alien emotions played across her visage, one after another, and quickly. But these flickering feelings were like experiments. No test was quite exact or exacting. Each one fell away. If she were sad, it did not show, though there was always something of her nature that was melancholy.

She reached into a secret fold of her gown and drew forth a porcelain bird that had been given to her by Lu Khen when he courted her at the smallhouse. How long ago it was, or how far away, Mai Su did not envision. Time and distance were nothing to Mai Su. Death was nothing to her. She rubbed the porcelain bird until it shone as bright as molten steel. It was an object of white fire nestled among her fingers. She blew upon the fire a single breath, and— lo!, one frail wing opened, turning amber and then red.

The other wing performed similarly; then the redness of the pair of wings spread inward. The flame dove was reborn. It blinked its living eyes at Mai Su's wisdom and her strength.

It flew upward and went around and around beneath the vaulted ceiling, its light reflecting on the carvings there. Where it found a crack, the bird escaped, and Mai Su stayed in darkness with the cat.

Away, away the flame dove traveled, but it could not pass upward into heaven. Over the city there had spread a shimmering darkness through which the bird could find no passage. How easily evil was spread, while the bright bird was so little!

It darted among the trees and ruins of the city. It dodged the tendrils of dark night that dripped downward, seeking the dove as its victim. It flew into the jungle between trunks of palms, through limbs of silk-cotton trees, among the hanging vines. It broke speed only when it came upon the statue of the three-headed elephant Kala.

Thrice it passed above the statue, once over each head. Then it darted into the central trunk of Kala.

The flame dove had been invested with Mai Su's breath of life, the eighth element of the cosmos. It was life, therefore, that went into the trunk and ascended to the cranium of the middle head.

At once, the two eyes of that head became shining garnets, though Kala remained stone. Then the eyes of the right-hand head, followed by those of the left, began to glow in kind.

Kala stood as immobile as ever, though its three heads were filled with thought.

The bird and thinking Kala had been observed by the presence above. The glinting, crinkling blackness that was the Garuda's exposed and vicious spirit knew the game had but begun. It felt a perverted delight at the inevitable battle, though the outcome was unknown. It could not take itself for granted, but laid plans.

Darkness drew into itself, but the Garuda would not congeal with dawn so near. Rather, the shimmering anti-light gathered about the head of the huge Naga, a black halo investigating the many-faced cobra's expansive hood and body of stone.

The darkness seeped inward through many fanged mouths, as though the Naga were sucking in its breaths. When the darkness had been swallowed and the stars restored to their places, the Naga did not spring instantly to life, but its fangs dripped a cold oily substance. Its numerous eyes became as sapphires shining faint and blue, beacons of tempting beauty and absolute menace eager to be observed.

For all his torment and grief and feigned or real madness, Lu Khen retained awareness of his gloomy environment. He noted when the stars returned; he saw where the sky was graying in the east. At promise of dawn, evil spirits had to flee, and many were the fears and imaginings of men that fled as well.

Lu Khen had found no anthill or carnivore's den by the side of which to kill himself and leave his corpse for use by lesser creatures. But he had not lost his pathetic resolve. He was sure he would have better luck finding what he sought when the first light of morning showed the way. For the time being, he stumbled almost as blindly as before the stars were restored. He toyed with the bronze knife with which he meant to open his throat. As knife and sky held his attention, he paid too little heed of his direction and, clumsy fellow that he often was, fell over something and lost the knife.

The tumble was nothing, but the knife he could not see. He felt around in the leaf-mold. He crawled about, wondering how far the blade might have been flung, how much ground he ought to cover on hands and knees.

Dawn was still too slight to help, so he searched without much aid of vision. He found the knife when his knee lit upon it. He grabbed it with a cry of glee. As he reared up on his knees, he saw by the faint new light the elephant Kala.

From his knees, as he looked upward at the three mighty heads, he wondered if the trunk had moved or if it was a shadow. He reached out to touch the giant, assuring himself it was only stone. Yet the eyes gleamed brightly, six gems the color of a redder dawn than present.

"I am beyond concern for miracles," said Lu Khen. "They interest me no longer."

But he sat reverentially, mouth agape, and in a moment mused, "If you would really come to life, if you were more than a tortured mind's illusion, I would ride upon your back into the ruins of the Lost Dynasty's capital. I would have you tear that evil place to pieces. We would open the sealed temple to reclaim whatever is uneaten of Yeung Mai Su, and stomp upon the murdering tiger. Afterward, I would build a pyre for Yeung Mai Su. Into the pyre I would throw my living flesh to die horribly, so that her ashes and mine would commingle."

Beneath Kala's belly was an anthill hundreds of years old, and the ants now were coming out to greet the day. Lu Khen spied it in the rising dawn and smiled at the irony of the earth-elephant offering only this. But, honoring Kala,

Lu Khen bowed and thanked it for the hive of ants, then raised the bronze dagger to his throat.

He closed his eyes, emboldening himself, fully prepared to sink the blade into vocal cords and arteries. He begged Buddha's forgiveness and pulled the knife toward himself. But someone held him back.

When Lu Khen opened his eyes, he saw his wrist in the grasp of Kala's middle trunk. Another trunk reached toward Lu Khen and took the knife away. The third trunk raised and trumpeted.

Lu Khen grew faint.

Po Lee awoke, leaning on a stone wall between his walking staff and a basket. Just by opening his eyes and otherwise not moving, he could see Koy across a tiny clearing industriously pulling tubers, a type as strong as onions.

She looked toward her great-grandfather, smiled, and called, "I found these!"

Po Lee made a face and put out his tongue. Koy laughed and smacked her lips.

"They're good!" she said, and toddled to a spring in which to clean the gathered roots. Po Lee leaned forward and unhooked from the side of his basket a bamboo tube that was packed with dirt and coals from their last fire. He opened the container, felt the warmth at the top of the dirt, and was glad the temperature indicated the coals had held up well.

From inside his cloak he removed long sections of crisp palm leaves, brittle as papyrus. As Koy came back with the cleaned vegetables she said, "We do not need a fire. We can eat these raw."

"I don't like them raw," said Great-grandfather Po Lee, somewhat petulant when it came to such a harvest.

"We should not waste time but must keep looking for Lu Khen. He is somewhere around here, I am sure."

Po Lee rubbed sleep from the corners of his eyes, scowled and grumbled something like "the boss of me," then put the dry leaves back in his shirt and sealed the tube of dirt and coals. Then he took one of Koy's proffered onions and bit into it with a crunch. Koy grinned impishly and bit her vegetable as soundly. Po Lee said, "If Lu Khen smells us coming, he may run away."

There was morning grooming to be done, but less dawdling than was their usual habit. Soon the oldster and youngster were ready to begin the search anew.

From a hillock they were able to observe a lot of the land about. Numerous smaller temples were strewn among the greenness of the invading jungle, while tombs lay hidden beneath the line of trees. A particularly large temple held their attention for a while. It was built in the form of a mountain, shaped of beasts and dancers and flowers, at the peak of which was a single head with many faces gazing at the world in all directions. Halfway up the magnificent structure were larger faces looking across the city.

"We should go there," said Koy.

"Why do you think so?" asked Po Lee, leaning on his staff and fingering his recent growth of white, downy whiskers.

"Because it is an obvious place, sticking up like that. Is there something else as interesting?"

She looked about as though trying to find any other building as intriguing or as tall. As she scanned the vicinity, she looked back across the river and saw the raised head of the Naga.

"Great-grandfather," she whispered in restrained alarm, "look at the Naga."

He looked. He said, "What of it?"

"Yesterday, its hood was turned away. This morning, it is twisted about in our direction. Its eyes are turned our way."

Po Lee scruffed Koy's hair and said, "We were far down that way yesterday. Of course we only saw the hood from behind. It is only a stone Naga, great-granddaughter."

She had not seen it face-on before. She was appalled by its appearance. All around the edge of the single, huge hood were numerous eyes and mouths. In the mouths were fangs bigger than Harada's saber.

"I stood upon its spine," said Koy. "I would not like to think it was alive the whole time."

"It is not alive."

"But it seems to be alive. It seems to be watching. Do you see that shining in those eyes?"

"It is the morning sun reflecting."

"The sun is behind the hood, great-grandfather. How can light reflect within those eyes?"

"It is doing so, great-granddaughter."

"If it is the reflection of the golden sun, or of the coral sky, how is it that the eyes are shining blue? They frighten me, great-grandfather."

"Then you should not look. We will go down the hillock in this other direction. Maybe next you will see the faces on that interesting temple grinning, or hear them talk."

His humor did not cheer her. They turned their backs upon the Naga, though neither took much comfort in Po Lee's unpersuasive logic.

"There it goes again, great-grandfather." They were in a new position to see far off. Koy had looked over her shoulder. She said, "It has moved again."

Po Lee refused to look. He said with feigned exasperation, "If it moved, great-granddaughter, would we not have heard so big a thing as that coming our way?"

"It has raised its head higher in the air. It is peering at us from high above the trees."

Po Lee turned to see, and had to admit the Naga looked taller than before. A greater part of its long body was reared up. The hood was bent to a sharper angle, the faces watching him and Koy.

"It is we who changed our line of sight," he said. "It looks different from different places."

"I think its mouths were not open quite so far," said Koy, her tone surprisingly devoid of fear despite her feelings. Darkness swirled within those open mouths. The sun was still at the Naga's back, its grim visages shadowed, the blue eyes gleaming.

"Nothing about it moved," insisted Great-grandfather Po Lee.

But as he said so, a ripple began around the hood and continued along the serpent's back. The maw furthest left on the hood's semicircle yawned wider, wider, then stopped as though the beast were once again of stone.

"Pardon me," said Great-grandfather Po Lee, "but I have been mistaken."

"What should we do?" asked Koy, taking Po Lee's fingers, her eyes riveted on the Naga.

"If it wants to get us, can we stop it?" asked Po Lee, a question that did not give assurance to the girl. "We should put our faith in Buddha," was the best that he could suggest. "Also, we should get out of here as fast as we can go, and hope the thing cannot leave the city."

"What about Lu Khen? We cannot forget about him." Koy was not ready to give up.

"Maybe we will see him on our way," said Po Lee. "Or he might have seen the Naga move and has already taken Yeung Mai Su away. It might even be that the Naga has already eaten both of them."

Koy squeezed the fingers and looked harshly at Po Lee. "There is no need to say that they were eaten. The Naga lives across the river, and Lu Khen is over here."

"That might be true," agreed Po Lee, more excited than Koy, his knees and belly shaking. "But something as big as that Naga can get across the river as though it were a ditch. We had better flee is all I have to say. Ah! Too late! It's coming!"

Po Lee tugged at Koy, but she pulled her hand away and stood with mouth agape, looking at the movement of the Naga. How slowly it progressed! How sinuous and silent! It wove between the temples and the trees with such care, harming nothing, as though it loved the city and would not allow the great bulk of its body to damage the least thing.

"It is not very quick, great-grandfather. All the same, I think I am ready to run."

Hand in hand, helping one another, Koy and Po Lee hurried.

In the isolation of the temple courtyard, the aboriginal hunter knew nothing of the Naga. He did know that someone had been locked inside the temple. Had it been one of the tombs, it might have made him worry; he might have gone away.

But of all the tales of malignity told among his people regarding the ancient ruins, the tombs and not the temples were the focus of blame.

He picked up a rock with which to strike the door, seeking either entry or reply. No one tapped back. No one was concerned that he was knocking. With ear pressed to the edge of the seal, he was able to hear a wonderful, unearthly music. When he tried to duplicate the melody, he found that it escaped him, though it was clear enough when he listened.

He imagined it was an angel trapped within. Who is to say his faith held nothing of the truth?

To aid a heavenly spirit that was walking on the Earth was universally praiseworthy. All the hunters of his tribe were men of adventure, so he was unafraid. To be able to boast of saving angels, or wrestling demons to the ground, was a mark of prestige. It may have been selfish that he hoped the grateful angel would help him find his grandfather, but he could not help wishing such reward. If the angel could also open up an old man's eyes to his grandson's filial passion, he would certainly not complain about such happy intervention. But how might the seal be broken? How could the angel be released?

He was still busying himself with this puzzle, investigating the door and wall around it for the hundredth time, when Po Lee and Koy came scurrying to the courtyard path, so out of breath they might have been pursued.

"I told you we should look here," said Koy, but the aborigine could not understand a word. "That's my cousin and your grandson."

They kept looking behind themselves as though expecting someone and approached the aborigine slowly, catching their breaths. He met them more than halfway. Although the tribe's oracle had tried to teach him the tongue of the coastal settlers, in preparation for just such a meeting as this, his mind had always resisted what his heart desired. He could not find a single word of greeting outside his own language.

"Po Lee!" he exclaimed with heavy accent, his face one big tattooed smile, his eyes filled with tears of joy. He added several salutations and honorifics, but the only thing Koy understood was the occasional "Po Lee! Po Lee!" When he looked at her, he made a face as to a baby, saying, "Koy! Koy!" How happy he behaved; how foolish.

"I think he is like me, great-grandfather," Koy suggested, "in that he loves his family. That means you. He came all this way to help us. Am I right?"

"I think you are," Po Lee allowed, but he was not well pleased. Koy was perceptive in seeing that her great-grandfather felt no familial connection with a tattooed savage. As for herself, it was exciting to have a strange relative. She thought her great-grandfather ought to greet the fellow with a nice warm hug.

Po Lee talked brokenly with Koy's quarter-breed cousin in the aboriginal tongue. She kept interrupting, "What's that he said? What's he saying?" But Po Lee would not answer until the conversation was complete.

With pale and worried brow, Po Lee turned to Koy. "You won't like it," he said. "Your cousin thinks an angel is trapped behind that door."

It did not escape her that he said "your cousin," but it was not the proper moment to remind him that the aborigine was their mutual relative. "What kind of angel?" she asked, intrigued.

"An angel that is singing a pretty song," Po Lee said flatly.

"It's Mai Su!" she said excitedly. "Then Lu Khen is in there too!"

Po Lee shook his head with dour expression, shattering Koy's moment of delight. "Lu Khen made that bruise on your cousin's forehead."

"I cannot see a bruise."

"Look closely. Not all of it is tattoo. Lu Khen smote him then ran off into the night, leaving Mai Su inside the temple."

"He abandoned her? He could not do it! Not unless he were mad!"

They were silent for a moment, pondering Koy's unintentional conclusion.

"But he will come back to get her," Koy said more quietly. "If we wait, we will see him."

"I was afraid you would suggest it," said Po Lee. "You may have a wishful feeling that the Naga cannot see us here. But surely it approaches and will find us. We should go at once."

"The Naga doesn't break things," Koy had observed. "If we hide in the temple, it cannot get us."

"Your cousin says it will not open. He has been trying the whole morning, desiring to let an angel out."

"We should try," Koy said obstinately. "If it really will not open, there are some other places. We can hide until the Naga goes away. But we should be near or we will miss Lu Khen."

The aborigine gave a wild cry and backed away. He pointed upward over the trees. Koy did not bother to look behind. She closed her eyes, reached over her shoulder to touch the sword's hilt, and said, "One-two-three; one-two-three," but there are limitations on childhood magic, and she knew it was the end. She forced herself to face her doom with eyes open.

Po Lee had raised his staff above his head, as though he were convinced that striking an incredible giant with a stick would send it flying. The Naga's pace had obviously quickened from sluggish to that of an ordinary cobra. How foolish Koy had been to disregard Great-grandfather Po Lee's insistence that they hurry from the city!

The Naga had reared from among the surrounding trees to peer into the courtyard. Po Lee shouted something Koy did not understand, but her cousin knew the words. He grabbed her by the waist and dashed toward the line of guardian dogs and crouched between a pair. The Naga struck downward at Po Lee, its central jaws eager to snatch him away. Po Lee wedged his staff in the open mouth and fell away from the dripping fangs. The Naga spread its hood wider, shadowing the courtyard, and shook its many faces from side to side trying to dislodge Po Lee's staff from the center.

Before it struck with another mouth in charge, Po Lee had hobbled to a different pair of stone dogs far away from Koy and the aborigine. He crouched just as the monster's head swept by, tipping the stone dog for a moment. It fell back with a thud; the Naga inspected the statue frantically, annoyed that it had been drawn into so much as scratching an object of the city.

The staff in the central mouth snapped and splinters rained upon the courtyard. The monster's body slid around the courtyard and the temple, penning everybody in. The hood raised higher, higher as though to present itself to full effect, as if striking terror were as important as the slaying of its prey. It looked from one place to another, first at Koy and her cousin, then at Po Lee, and back again.

At first, Koy buried her face in her cousin's neck, her nose pressed to the middle of a whorl of tattoo coloring. For the first time that she could remember, she sobbed like a frightened baby. It was only a few moments before she got the better of herself, remembered she was brave and afraid of nothing. Boldness may have been an act, but she would do a good one.

Insisting that her cousin put her down, she drew from her shirt a thong like his own. Her cousin grinned at it. She pointed to the Naga's fiery sapphire eyes that gazed one way then the other. She gathered small stones from around her feet. Her cousin had better ones in a fur pouch hooked to his belt.

Side by side, they whirled the leather thongs around and around. Koy concentrated for all she was worth, hoping her slingshot would make its target. But her stone missed its mark and vanished into one open maw. That mouth clamped down as with surprise. Her cousin's stone struck one eye roundly at its center, causing the cobra to flinch, but that was all.

"Get down!" shouted Po Lee, motioning with his hands. He was upset to be apart from Koy at such a moment. He was more upset to see her foolish bravery. The Naga struck, but Koy and the aborigine had leapt and hugged the ground between the guardian statues.

Koy had taken Harada's sword from her back, unsheathed it, and lay upon her belly with the weapon in her hand. It was absurdly long compared to her small body. As she stood from a crouch dusting herself off, she was in Po Lee's line of sight again, and he yelled at her, "Koy! Koy! You better not do anything with that! You're too little! Crazy to think you can fight a thing like that!"

Koy was forever a combination of obedience and obstinance. But the fact was, she had no intention of fighting the Naga with Harada's sword. Po Lee, however, was not privy to her feelings about the sword. It was natural that he should fear she was holding it in order to do something stupid. Certain that she had some plan impossible to accomplish, he ran out from cover and started toward her, scolding all the while, "Did I tell you you could take it from the scabbard?"

"It is only a good luck charm!" she shouted in defense, and stamped a foot as much from frustration as anything else. She was sad to see her great-grandfather angry with her.

The cobra's head was descending. Koy saw that her great-grandfather could not reach new cover with his hobbling gait so insufficient. Koy's cousin took the saber from her hand and, before she could think, he had run into the middle of the courtyard, as though believing polished steel might slay a gigantic snake and save Po Lee.

He struck a fang with such force that it snapped. The fang reeled through the air to land among stunted bushes. The wounded mouth clamped tight upon the sword. The serpent reared up before the aborigine could let go. He rose into the air, kicking. When he did let go, he had a good long way to fall. He struck the ground beside Po Lee and Harada's sword fell beside them.

As the serpent prepared another strike, the aborigine had gained his feet and, hugging Po Lee close, ran with him so fast that the old man's feet merely skimmed the ground.

Koy's cousin was panting with the excitement of his deed. His eyes shone with the pride of his success. His lips were a copper moon in the cloudy whorls and designs. As Po Lee collapsed in his grandson's arms he said, "Do you care for me so much as that?"

"Great-grandfather," said Koy, "look at the back of his shoulder!"

The aborigine recoiled at the attempted touch. He knew well enough what happened and would not let anyone get the dark, oily substance on them. As he fell from the Naga's grasp, he had scraped along a fang. A long wound filled with burning black poison striped his back.

Still grinning proudly, he fell against one of the stone dogs and sat there dazed from the poison coursing through his body. Po Lee covered his face with both hands and wept, "Poor fellow. What a fool I've been." And Koy was not sure which poor fellow he meant.

Horror was heaped upon horror, strangeness on strangeness, and all the world that Koy could see *was* madness and confusion. Louder and louder, drawing from the distance with alarming speed, she heard the terrible crashing of trees uprooted, buildings knocked awry . . . and she tried to see over and beyond the encircling Naga to solve the mystery of the noise, to fathom every twist and channel of this whole demented world.

Treetops beyond the Naga were falling away from each other, dropping from view. The ground was thumped by a frightful weight and power. She could feel the land vibrating through her knees.

Then she had her first glimpse of what at first she took to be three elephants. She saw three trunks rise, heard them trumpeting together. A moment more and she knew the heads shared a body in common. Six tusks struck the side of the Naga, pushing it forward. The long, thick trunks wrapped around the Naga's neck and pulled it back.

Koy was so surprised by the sight that she leapt up and was atop one of the stone dogs before she could be stopped by Po Lee or her own better sense. But the Naga was no longer able to strike at them, so she kept her perch, and shouted with a combination of abject and horror-stricken awe:

"Great-grandfather! It's Ou Lu Khen!"

Po Lee remained at his aboriginal grandson's side, trying to be of some belated comfort. But he could see Kala well enough without standing. He saw Lu Khen upon the middle

head, hands flailing and pointing and directing the three-headed elephant's attack.

The Naga tried to coil itself atop the elephant but whipped its tail too swiftly, smashing into the side of the mountainous temple. A wall was shattered, a veritable explosion of stone and mortar. The structure tilted and began to collapse upon itself. The Naga looked away from its enemy as though to witness and lament the accidental harm it had done to the building.

The elephant was not concerned with what damage was done and was advantaged by the Naga's distraction. Lu Khen drove Kala harder at the foe. Kala kicked at the courtyard's statues and fruit-bearing trees, dug into the ground with six huge feet, tearing at and wrecking everything in its effort to maintain its purchase on the Naga's coiling body.

As the temple toppled, Lu Khen squealed with a crazed delight at the fantastic destruction. He gazed from his high seat and could not help but see Po Lee and Koy and one other. But the only sound he made at them was, "Ai-eeee! Ai-eeee!" And he waved his fists above his head as though he were the victor of the fight.

The Naga's tail whipped back around and struck along a row of dog statues, flinging them on their sides or on their muzzles. Koy jumped from the back of one such guardian, afraid it might be next to go. Po Lee, seeing the danger of one monster or the other striking near, dragged his dying grandson in a direction away from the titans' battle. The tail of the Naga snapped forth once more and the very tip caught Po Lee in the ribs and elbow. He cried out once, then tumbled across his grandson.

"Great-grandfather!" cried Koy, hurrying to him. "Great-grandfather!" Ribs were crushed so badly she could see the indentation even through his shirt. A sack of blood welled around his shattered arm.

"I'm all right," said Po Lee, striving with one good arm to lift himself. He failed to rise.

"You're not! You're not!"

And it was true. The injury would have been severe even for a young man with a better chance of mending.

The Naga had gotten itself wrapped around Kala. The battle had become a stand-off. Neither titan held sway over the other. If not for the efforts of the grappling trunks, Lu Khen would have been snatched from his seat and vanished down the Naga's throat.

As far as Koy could judge, her brother lacked any semblance of concern for her and Great-grandfather Po Lee. Tears streaked her face, but it made her angry that Lu Khen could be heartless. She stood and faced the elephant and shouted at her errant brother, "Stop laughing, Lu Khen! Stop it at once! Great-grandfather is dying! This other man is our cousin and he is dying too! Have you no sympathy for your family?"

Lu Khen stopped the gleeful squealing the instant he was told to do so, for it had been for show all along.

In that moment of Lu Khen's calming down, the might of Kala's trunks pressing or pulling in different directions snapped the cobra's body in half. The Naga instantly lost its pliancy and once more was stone. The hood and forebody toppled like a felled tree. The rest of the body lay still. In the hollows of the broken parts dark vapors retracted from sunlight. The evil hid in the cavernous depths of the serpent's halves.

Yet evil had not yielded. There is always one more captain where infamy reigns. Crawling from the rubble of the ruined temple, coming out of the settling dust, was the weretiger. It was hunched and leery, blinking in the light, disoriented and desperate for its life, and ready to kill anything that threatened.

Sternly now, and by this new attitude appearing madder than when shouting like a fiend, Lu Khen rode Kala away from the Naga's halves, intent upon challenging the tiger. The great cat was a tiny thing before Kala's magnificence. Vengeance was in Lu Khen's heart as he directed the three-headed elephant.

Though the tiger spat and set its ears flat, the elephant's central trunk grabbed the wriggling beast by the scruff and raised it from the ground. Shaking the animal like a dusty rag, the man within fell out. He struck the ground face down, arms spread. The backs of his legs and arms and neck and all around his spine were raw and bloody as though indeed he were a skinned cat.

Harada lay moaning, awakening from a nightmare, yet comprehending more than he preferred.

Before Lu Khen could have the malefactor stomped into a smear, his eagerness for revenge was siphoned away. For he saw Mai Su standing alive and healthy at the top of a stairway before the ruined temple.

Lu Khen, astride his eerie mount and scarcely moving, observed the strange behavior of his true love.

Great-grandfather Po Lee, Koy, and her cousin huddled together in a sad state. The aborigine was incoherent. He made unintelligible prayers, smiling the while, as though nothing pleased him more than dying. The appearance of Mai Su may have struck his fevered delusions as an answer to his nonsensical prayers.

Koy was heartbroken that her cousin was dying. But as she hardly knew him, she had to admit it was the condition of Great-grandfather Po Lee that broke her heart the most. She knelt with them and felt that she was helpless to comfort either, for she needed comforting herself.

She saw Harada Fumiaka, his back shredded meat, crawling toward the sword that lay in the courtyard. He hugged it by the hilt and cried for his father, then his mother, then his mother once again. Everyone in the world merited pity. But Koy felt she was most pitiful of all, bereft as she would be of the old man who taught her of adventure. It was impossible that he could ever heal and travel after such injuries. But he was at least coherent, and sat with his great-granddaughter and his gently raving grandson, hearing the whispered lunacies, understanding some of what was said and half believing.

Po Lee raised a palsied hand and pointed to Mai Su. She had descended the staircase and crossed the courtyard to the Naga's breach, and stood between the pieces. In the caverns to each side, the Garuda's halved and twisted spirit churned like a pot of water on the fire.

Come night the dark mists might reunite. Come night the Garuda could repair itself. The deadly power could rise anew. The gross strengths and corruptions that had erased a mighty nation and its people from the memory of time could yet have its way! Except that Mai Su stood between the shattered parts, and raised her arms, and called the beast into herself.

Koy observed first Mai Su, then Lu Khen. It was unlikely he understood the situation any better than did she, but the situation was odd enough that Koy could not blame her brother's expression of fear for Mai Su's safety.

He tried to climb from the elephant's shoulders but Kala's trunks went up and held him fast, to keep him from stopping Mai Su from what she was doing. Struggle was to no avail.

The darkness was drawn from its two hiding places, out into the light. It began to coalesce around Mai Su. It was all about her. It looked as though she stood in smoke, her arms upraised, her expression calm as ever. Koy wondered how she breathed.

And the smokey shades of evil began to take a loose form—the shape of the Garuda, but bigger and translucent. The madwoman stood at the heart of a larger being, a being that despised the sun, and she was that being's heart. The beak of its half-human visage opened as though to give a hawk's cry. If it made a sound, it did so at a range none could hear unless Mai Su heard it.

The insubstantial Garuda dwindled into a smaller size and was absorbed into the madwoman. As it shrank, the darkness of its presence became light. Mai Su became light. It was a light that none could stand to gaze on at its brightest ... none but Ou Lu Khen, whose face did not once turn from her brilliance.

Koy could not look, nor could Po Lee. He reached with his good hand to touch Koy's arm. And he whispered hoarsely, saying things that only the near-to-dying know, incorporating things he heard in the aborigine's murmurs.

"The universe is One, great-granddaughter. Sweetness and sorrow, cruelty and love, good and evil ... nothing exists without its opposite. How Lu Khen must suffer! He sought madness to be Her equal. But as his thinking mind withdraws, as he peers within the revealing light, he must know that She becomes an even greater thing. She becomes a bodhisattva—so even Lu Khen's burgeoning madness leaves him waiting far from Her enlightenment. How sad it is that Ou Lu Khen cannot catch Her in a thousand lives! How lonely he will be, doomed to such a separation!"

Mai Su was truly changed after the Garuda was a part of her and the revealing light had faded to a mere diamond shade. She was no longer mortal and might have sat with Buddha had she not lingered, as bodhisattvas do, to help the unenlightened. But it is false to think enlightened beings capable only of goodwill. They are all things and not one thing or the other. They bring salvation or terror as befits the moment. They are darkness and light together, the whirling substance of this living cosmos.

When she came toward Harada Fumiaka, who still crawled upon his stomach and hugged a sword, he tried to escape. But she was beside him and he could not escape. Whichever way he turned, she was there. She leaned above him and the light of her body soothed the pain of his skinned back. She healed him by her vision but left the horrid scars as reminders of his sins.

As Koy witnessed the miracle, her heart swelled with hope. She was glad when Mai Su Who Was No Longer Mai Su came forth to touch the wound of the aborigine. Her touch drew the poison into herself with only a momentary look of shared agony. Then the wound was closed and the tattooed man's eyes became clear.

"Save great-grandfather, too," begged Koy, and took the hand of the bodhisattva. The feeling of warmth and tenderness was difficult to bear in its intensity. Koy pressed the bodhisattva's hand to Po Lee's face, and Po Lee gave a happy cry of "Fa Ling!" and was gone to meet his wife.

Koy pulled back in horror of what the bodhisattva had done. Tears of disbelief glistened in her reddened eyes. She struck the bodhisattva, cursing. But she was striking at a substance without density. She was striking at a breeze. And the goddess floated upward from Koy's small fists.

Kala lowered its three trunks, freeing its hold of the only one who watched when Mai Su was ablaze. As Kala grew rigid and was, as before, of stone, the bodhisattva began to shrink as though into the distance, although she was only a little way above the ground and viewed from either side.

As she became smaller and smaller within the halo, her diamond brightness became ruddier and ruddier. Her robes became feathers and the feathers became fire. Lastly, as might a falling star in reverse, she shot into the bright heaven and was gone.

The rest can be briefly stated; it will be plainly told. Koy's cousin helped her build a pyre. Po Lee, reduced to ashes, was put into one of the bowls he had nearly thrown away earlier in their journey. Her cousin made a lid from a piece of wood and it fit well. Then, tying the makeshift urn about her neck, Koy resolved to take her great-grandfather's ashes to the place he had often said he would like to see again, his native home. Difficult though it was to make her cousin understand this decision, somehow she made him know it, and it was his resolve to help. For both of them were ultimately of Po Lee's blood. Both were blessed or cursed with his adventurous spirit.

This was not one day's work, but several. The ancient ruins had lost their haunted feeling. No one felt that they must hurry or that anything must be escaped. During this time, Harada Fumiaka was reticent and not helpful. But it was his shame that made him keep himself apart, not a sour nature. He was a changed man though it was hard for him to show it, unpracticed as he was. When Koy and her cousin built Po Lee's pyre, Harada found a quiet glade and dug a little narrow grave. Into the grave he placed his father's sword, the symbol of Harada's pride and all the many errors of his life. In this place he buried his mistakes, intent upon a better road thereafter.

And what of Ou Lu Khen? It is strange to say that nothing was heard of him again. Koy searched for days, delaying her pending journey with Po Lee's ashes. Even her cousin's excellent hunting and tracking skills were insufficient to locate Ou Lu Khen. He had run away, and that was that. Over the years, however, as legends grew out of these events—and there were three who went into the world to tell it from their varied points of view—there was an unexpected alteration to the tale that some may credit.

It was the story of a wild man living in the cold, high mountains between the coastal forests and the inland jungles. It was told that whoever happened upon the hidden hermitage was invariably treated to the wild man's sentiments. He shared them gladly. These sentiments were never written down, since no one who claimed to have met him could remember a thing. They only knew his ideas were demented, though wonderful to hear.

❧ EPILOGUE ❧

The Wayfarer

THE MERCHANT SHIP, a big full-bellied junk with pleated sails, drew into the river's mouth, easing into small harbors along the way. It traded goods from Ho for spice and raw materials of the Lesser and Greater Peninsulas. It took days to cover a small distance due to heavy trading. Four identical junks, part of a fleet, scoured other villages along the coast and inland upon the major rivers and the ancient canals. The present junk's journey took it from the river to one of the canals called Mak-lai which cut through the young province of Lin. It came to a village called Ki that had lately grown to the size of a city in terms of population, the place being well situated for trade. Here a nun prepared to leave the merchant ship.

She had been the ship's only passenger. The trip from Ho had been slow and uncomfortable, inasmuch as merchants were rarely prepared for holiday travelers. But she had worked part of the way, never complaining, and the time had not seemed long to her. And she was patient, as were most women of her calling.

A plank was put from ship to dock. The nun stood ready
to disembark. The captain stood beside her, bidding her
farewell. They were not likely to meet again, and he looked
sad, for he had grown to like her very much, as an individual
and for spiritual advice that was rustic, wise, and pleasing.

She wore black and yellow and her robe was threadbare
though clean. Her head, probably shaven but one could not
be certain, was wrapped in a saffron scarf which hung about
her shoulders. She carried a pilgrim's staff. It was taller
than herself. Its top was a single brass ring with a goddess
within. The goddess stood on one foot with her several arms
in attitudes of dance. From the ring hung a small basket to
receive alms.

The nun offered the merchant a coin, minimal payment
for her passage, but he refused, bowing and waving both
hands frantically. She bowed with grace and gratitude, then
strode the plank to the dock, then to the bank of the canal.

The water was crowded with slipper-boats in which lived
families of fishers. Along the canal's edge were closely-
built shanties slimed by lapping water. It was a discouraging
part of town, very poor. The canal flooded once every three
or four years and no one of any standing would live here.
But the nun did not hasten into the heart of the village where
life was picturesque. Rather, she strode the claustrophobic
avenues between tumble-down shacks. Dirty faces of children peered out from the cracks of crooked, shuttered windows. No one hurried out with offerings for the nun, for
they could scarcely afford charity, and in any case, she
strode quickly, as though hating to give them time to consider giving her a crumb or coin they could not do without.

She came to the bank's edge here and there, scanning
the boats and the faces of poverty. Though a traveler, she
was fastidious. Ragged though she was, her cleanliness put
her apart from these folk who smelled of fish and foul water.
By the curious faces gazing back at her it was clear everyone
wondered what she wanted, whom she sought. Cleverly she
avoided eye contact, so no one addressed her with questions
of any sort. She spoke to no one.

She spent a good while on her quiet search. Whisperings

wendy wees

swept across the impoverished district as a ripple on the canal. Everyone knew of the lank, hard, yet good-looking pilgrim. Everyone wondered what her quest could be in such a place as this, where no holy landmarks could be found. A new temple had been built inland; why did she not go there? A sanctified garden, where a saint once lived, grew beyond the village. Many pilgrims went there. They never lingered along these piteous neighborhoods with so searching an expression.

At length it looked as though she were giving up. She started away from the canal. But she had not come out from the maze of horrible little walkways and streets when a big man appeared in her path. He was no older than she, but a hard life had made him homely. He had a scar cutting through his short beard. His smile was lecherous and unpleasing. The nun stopped quickly, her tiny basket swinging from the upright staff. The broad-shouldered, vile-looking man dared her, by his aspect, to try to pass.

A second man appeared, smaller but apparently a friend. He put a hand upon the bigger man's arm. The smaller man spoke in the local dialect, which was strongest and least comprehensible in the poor district. But the nun happened to know the dialect and understood their exchange.

"Don't bother a nun, my friend," said the little man.

"Do I respect Buddha?" the other laughed. "She's handsome."

"Look then at that long stick. A nun like her can fight. All of those who travel can fight."

The bigger ruffian shook off his friend. He felt into his tunic and removed a thin, square coin. He strode toward the nun with threatening posture and held out the coin in a dirty hand, still daring the nun, daring her to reach toward his hand and take his holy offering.

She let her staff lean forward slowly, slowly, until the hanging basket was beside the man's hand. He looked from the nun's calm face to the basket and back to her face. His smug, bold look wavered. Then he put the coin in the small basket. The nun bowed, blessed him in his own dialect, which surprised him, and brushed by unmolested.

There was a forest road, very narrow and dusty, but shaded and nice. She passed nobody. There were no houses. She avoided the heart of the village altogether and seemed to know her direction. She paused one time, listening to the sound of rowdy children laughing somewhere to the south. The sound came closer for a while. She could almost hear exactly what the children shouted, though mostly it was laughter. She expected them to burst onto the path at any moment, out of the woods like an army of goblins. But their laughter began to fade after the first swell, and she knew they had bent their path elsewhere.

A new road now, somewhat weed-grown, but more people used it. There were farmhouses with only the thatched roofs visible, for they were set far off the road with fields of grass between. The nun took long strides as though certain of where she was headed. When she stopped, it was at a narrow path leading through woods away from the road. She looked at the path for a long moment, her brow knit as though finally uncertain. Then she started through the quiet wood that opened upon a bright garden. The nun's lips and eyes smiled at the vision.

The garden surrounded a small pagoda. How different it all was from the dirty slums along the canal! The air was perfume. Birds nested everywhere.

Behind the pagoda was a sturdy, rustic building of recent vintage, doubtless the house of the shrine's caretaker. The vagrant nun did not bother whomever was caretaker but approached the tall drumtower with a look of reverence and bittersweetness. Many pilgrims came to just this place, for it was the shrine of a bodhisattva whose mortal flesh was remembered by many who still lived. It was a place to incite the soul's essential need to wonder.

Children are great wonderers but also great sinners in their innocent manner. Presently two boys came running through the garden, upsetting birds, tearing plants, tossing sticks at one another, shouting in the frenzy of their game of tag. They spoiled the quietude of the sanctuary but the nun could not hide her smile.

It was then that the caretaker came out from some corner

of the garden where he had been working unseen. He carried a spade but did not brandish it at the children. He merely said, "Hey there! You boys!" He had a foreign accent of a kind unusual even in a port town. "Be respectful of the beautiful bodhisattva! Your parents knew her when she lived upon the Earth! Say a prayer! Do not shout!"

One boy was bolder than the other. He yelled back, "But you're shouting!"

The caretaker said, "I don't do it to sin. Come over here and let me show you something."

The bold one went right up to the caretaker, cocky as could be. The other followed, figuring nothing bad could happen. The caretaker said, "I was a sinner like you boys. Oh, how bad! I sinned a lot of years, and I suffered. If you want to be rowdy, I think that is fine, but this is not the place. You should pray to the beautiful bodhisattva when you come here. She loved peace and quiet and the sound of birds. You should never scare a bird in her presence."

Then the gray-haired caretaker took off his jacket to show the boys his scars. They gasped at the horror of his back. He said, "My crimes were very bad. Even such scars as these do not balance my sins. You may wonder that I live at all. Indeed I would have died but for the beautiful bodhisattva. So I work for her in this garden, though I know it will be many lives before I work away my crimes. But maybe She will have mercy and shorten my sentence. As for you, remember my scars when you cause trouble."

The boys were petulant, but they quieted down. They went away from the garden but at the edge the rowdiest and boldest of the two turned to face the pagoda. He pressed his palms together and muttered something. Then he left and moments later, away from the shrine, the two rowdy voices rose in renewed crescendo.

The caretaker put on his shirt and approached the pilgrim. She declined an offer of tea but said to him,

"I have heard the legend of this place. It is taught in Buddhist temples far from here. There is mention of a man of scars who for a while was a tiger. What a tale that one was!"

The pilgrim's eyes sparkled with delight at having met

the legend in person. But the caretaker was deeply shamed by his past and lowered his eyes. He said, "I myself rarely tell that part of the story. It is unsettling that you know it. After all these years, I feel badly. I began my evil course to reclaim a worthless, decrepit boat. And the irony is that, by the end, I had my boat returned."

"Did you?" asked the nun. "I did not know that part."

The caretaker sighed. "I had a terrible time getting to the ruins of the Forgotten Dynasty, as you know since you have heard the story. You call it a legend, and frankly I don't mind if you discount the things about me. I only want people to believe in the beautiful bodhisattva. But as some-one seems to know a lot about me, I will tell you the rest. After the ascension of the bodhisattva, I was a changed man, but still no good at living in the wilderness. On my own, I tried to return to my adopted home. I had gotten as far as a waterfall haunted by the Makara, the spirit of high water. I was worn out and lamented my sad end. Though willing to accept the punishment of death, I regretted losing the chance to right a lot of things I had done to people. The Makara heard my lamentations and bent down to whisper with a voice as sweet as water: 'For every loss, many things are found.' And from the pool my dirty boat arose, but it was cleaner than the day it was made, miraculously repaired and nicely fitted. I was able to get home and became an honest fisher. It took a long time for people to believe that I was not the same. But I did not mind if they reviled me so long as people listened to the story of the bodhisattva. Later I gave my boat to a poor family and have taken care of these gardens ever since. It is pleasant penance, not that I can live as long as expiation would require."

The nun said, "In a monastery where I lived a while, the priestess said enlightenment may find us in an instant, and our sins will vanish in the wind and we will be free."

"Did she think so? Well, I am glad. And I have the excellent consolation of telling pilgrims the story of the beautiful bodhisattva. It is a tragic love story if told entirely. At the same time it is the story of humanity's salvation. Should I tell it to you from the start?"

He beamed at the opportunity to tell the tale. The nun

gazed at him with affection. But she said, "As I mentioned, I have heard the story before. But maybe I will come again to hear the way you tell it."

Then, with a whispered prayer to the drumtower, the nun withdrew along the path, back to the narrow road.

She walked slowly, the basket swinging from her staff. She observed everything: where trees were cut, where others were left standing, where fields were planted, where ditches brought water to the paddies. . . . She saw a duck, a lone water buffalo, and many children. She bowed cordially to a monk walking the other way. It was the time of day for a bit of traffic and the nun blessed anyone who smiled. Those who could not smile she blessed as well.

There was a farmstead by the road and in the yard children played: two girls the same small size who looked alike and a boy swift and tiny. In the fields beyond were the older members of the family, working to their knees in mud. They were by no means wealthy; a wealthy family would have replaced such clothing long before. But they appeared happy, industrious, and content.

An elderly woman came out of the house and chased after the tiny grandson. He laughed and evaded her. She noticed the mendicant lingering on the road, so she hurried into the house to fetch a handful of raw rice to give the wandering woman.

When the pleasant old woman came to the road with the grains of rice, the nun leaned her tall staff downward so the basket could be reached. Before the rice was placed within, the old woman stopped in mid-motion. She looked startled and confused. She gazed at the nun's round face, and the old woman's eyes were filled with memories and tears.

"Forgive me," said the old woman, sniffing and drying her eyes on a sleeve. "For a moment . . . I must admit, you reminded me of someone I have not seen since she was tiny and wandered from this home."

"Mother," said the nun, "as the story of the madwoman and the doomed boy who loved her is famous, I had hoped you would not worry about me. For I am indeed Koy that you remember. I took great-grandfather's ashes to Ho with the help of a cousin among the aborigines. My cousin lives in Ho today, a famous tattooed knight and an educated man. I think he may one day return to his people or even visit this farm. As for me, I traveled beyond Ho to the land of Buddha's birth. There, I studied hard. Once I was ill and nearly died. Realizing I came close to death without seeing my mother again, I came home."

A silence fell between them that was broken by the three children who came running. Then the nun said, "For every loss, many things are found," and she was led to the fields to meet her relatives.

Stories
~of~
Swords and Sorcery

BESTSELLING
Science Fiction
and
Fantasy